ONE IS THE DEADLIEST NUMBER

A PURRS & PERSONALITY TYPES MYSTERY
BOOK 1

HADLEY HARTWELL

ONE IS THE DEADLIEST NUMBER

DEDICATION

Dedicated to my beloved sister Rachel, without whom this series would not exist, and my wonderful parents, Earl and Ros, who engendered in me a love of mysteries with Sunday night pizza.

PART 1

"There are a number of good reasons to study personality types, the most important of which is that human beings are inherently interesting—and dangerous."

DON RICHARD RISO & RUSS HUDSON,
PERSONALITY TYPES

PROLOGUE

Type One: The Perfectionist
Type Two: The Helper
Type Three: The Achiever
Type Four: The Individualist
Type Five: The Observer
Type Six: The Loyal Skeptic
Type Seven: The Enthusiast
Type Eight: The Challenger
Type Nine: The Peacemaker

1

CONSTANCE

CONSTANCE KINCAID KNEW how risky anger could be, which was why she never allowed herself to feel it.

Not when she was a child and her parents refused to sign her up for dance lessons because they cut into homework time. Not when she attended law school in the 1980s and was ignored by her professors. And not when she was 67 and her husband of four decades, Arthur, was killed in the passenger seat of a Mini Cooper convertible driven by an inebriated woman not his wife, on the way back from a romantic B'n'B weekend upstate. He was supposed to have been at a Continuing Legal Education conference in D.C.

On autopilot, she researched the best way to write an obit. "Since obituaries are typically published only once, it's important to get the facts straight," advised one article.

Yes, she thought, *that's true. Obituaries are typically published only once. Unless it's a Paul McCartney "Rumors of my demise..." situation. Or if someone faked their death, and then died for real, you'd have to write it twice. But how would you know?* Her thoughts spiraled outward in this manner until she forced herself to read the next tip.

"As the writer of the obituary, you never want to offend a grieving family member," the article cautioned. Constance tried not to offend herself. Was she grieving? Tough to say. If you removed the manner and circumstance of Arthur's death, she'd be inconsolable.

She decided to write the obit as though she didn't know how Arthur had died.

"An accomplished attorney, treasured for his enthusiasm, spontaneity, and a gentle sense of humor that always assumed the best of people, Arthur specialized in contract litigation at Kincaid & Kincaid law firm in Manhattan. He is survived by his loving wife and law partner, Constance, his older sister, Evelyn, and a coterie of close friends and colleagues. The couple had no children. In lieu of flowers, donations in Arthur's name to the Southern Poverty Law Center are appreciated."

Still on autopilot, with no co-pilot for backup, because Arthur's sister was trapped behind a storm in Montreal and didn't want to risk her own life getting out, Constance shopped for a somber black dress, handbag, hat, and shawl. She stayed up past 3 a.m. preparing Arthur's eulogy and writing on color-coded index cards.

As the deluge of rain slammed against the stained-glass windows of Morningside Co-op Church that dreary January day, her heart thumped erratically in her chest. Despite the miserable weather, hundreds had shown up to pay their respects to Arthur.

At the appropriate time, she stood from her solo position in the front row and strode up the steps to the podium. She leaned on her cane—C.C., Arthur had engraved it—for support.

She surveyed the faces of the people who had once composed her and Arthur's social circle.

A single thought cut through her mental fog: *These aren't my friends.* If they had been, one of them would have alerted her to Arthur's clandestine activities.

That realization was followed by another. *I can't stay here.*

She didn't mean the church, or the service.

She meant the city.

She meant her life.

Heat flared throughout her body, making her go limp. Her fingers opened, and her cane clattered to the floor. As the room swung sideways, she gripped the podium with both hands to keep from falling.

Someone in the crowd sprang up to assist her. Constance shook her head and waved them off. She straightened her spine and opened her mouth to speak.

The crowd leaned forward, eager to hear words of healing and hope, perhaps illustrated with examples of Arthur's famed spontaneity—all of which she'd prepared in her speech, and all of which she could no longer fathom saying.

One by one, she ripped her notecards in half, and let the pieces fall.

"As John Le Carré once said: 'Love means having something left to betray.'"

She barely recognized the sound of her own voice echoing through the church, amplified by the microphone. People glanced awkwardly at each other.

"The day he died, Arthur Kincaid was allegedly earning a C.L.E. credit at a conference in D.C. One of the learning modules was 'How to Identify Liars.' Perhaps I should have attended instead." She picked up C.C. by the handle. "Goodbye."

Murmurs filled the room, but Constance ignored them.

The walk back took much longer, because she didn't return to her seat in the front row. She and C.C. continued down the long aisle. She tilted her chin up, and cut straight through the middle of the church, past the people she now considered strangers.

She pushed the doors open and walked outside into the cleansing rain.

She closed her eyes and let the drops wash her face.

When she opened them, she saw the cat.

Its ruddy-colored fur was flattened by the elements, its tail plastered against its body like a soaked plume. It looked even more bedraggled than Constance felt.

"Rao," it said.

FORTY-EIGHT HOURS LATER, Constance began the arduous process of dissolving her law firm, selling her apartment, and selecting a new place to live. She yearned for someplace cheerful, where nobody knew her, or the humiliation she'd suffered. Someplace sunny and warm, where she and her newly adopted cat could thrive.

She'd christened the cat Mr. Cinnamon because of his warm, reddish-brown fur and spicy demeanor. The duo had had an adventure together after Arthur's funeral, establishing the cat's origin and history, visiting the vet, and purchasing all manner of food and comfort items. The vet's best guess put Mr. Cinnamon at eighteen months old. He was apparently a Somali mix cat—a sort of cousin to the Abyssinian, with longer fur and a foxlike tail. His breed, or lack thereof, meant nothing to Constance. The important thing was that Mr. Cinnamon had needed her, and she'd heeded his call. He would never be forced to wander the cold, wet city again.

Neither would she, for that matter.

She opened a bottle of Sicilian wine that she and Arthur had been saving for a special occasion, hefted an old road atlas onto the table, and flicked through its dusty pages until she came to a map of California.

The town of Cherry Hill stuck out to her because she thought it read "Cheery Hill." (She was tipsy and had misplaced her bifocals. It turned out Mr. Cinnamon had been sitting on them. Had he known where she needed to go?)

Decision made, she raised her glass to Arthur, who'd been allergic to cats.

How's that for spontaneity?

2

―――――――

CONSTANCE

ONE YEAR LATER

SATURDAY, January 14th.

Spontaneity had its drawbacks.

For example, when Constance had thrown caution to the ice-cold wind and tossed out her winter clothes upon moving west, she couldn't have predicted that Cherry Hill, California (population 15,000, with an additional 8,000 when tourism swelled its ranks) might succumb to a freak snowstorm. Her weather alert insisted it was coming, despite clear skies and temperatures in the 60s. She wouldn't have believed it except for an unsettling premonition in her right knee. It always ached before a storm.

She had better ride the trolley into town and purchase a coat before class.

Another drawback to spontaneity: Her frantic, Arthur-induced escape resulted in the purchase of a home known as the Upside-Down House. Some famous underground artist—was that an oxymoron?—had turned his bedroom into a tourist attraction in which the furniture was attached to the ceiling as though the ceiling were the floor.

The carpet was upside down. The queen-size bed was upside down. The chair and footrest were upside down. The lamps were upside down. The bedside table was upside down. The paintings and photos were upside down.

It was vertigo-inducing. Every piece of furniture looked as though it might fall and crush her at any moment.

Tourists paid twenty dollars to pose for photos and then rotate the image 180-degrees on their phones, so it would look like they lived an upside-down life, sleeping on the ceiling or clinging to the walls like spider people.

She'd purchased the property based on photos, having assumed—as any sane person would—that a website error had flipped the bedroom images on their heads.

She didn't like to think about the fact that her realtor at Berkshire Hathaway had tried to warn her, and not only about the house.

"I don't understand why you would choose Cherry Hill. It's a liminal space between other cities." (Read: better cities.) The realtor lowered her voice. "People call it the 'Poor Man's Palm Springs.'"

Constance had insisted.

"Well, okay. This is the most expensive property there, and it's been on the market for ages. There are several interested bidders waiting for a price drop, so if you offer ten above asking, you'll probably get it."

"Offer twenty above and guarantee it," Constance replied.

Another sigh from her realtor.

"What?" Constance asked, feeling impatient.

"It's a bold move. You'd really be declaring your arrival."

"How so?"

"It's the only house on top of the hill. The Cherry Hill, for which the town is named. The closest neighbor is half a mile down."

"That's a bonus, as far as I'm concerned."

"There's something else, and it's big—"

"I've decided."

"Okay, but you need to hear this—"

"I've decided! Place the offer, please."

From the outside, the house was charming: a quintessential Spanish-style California home. She loved the burnt sienna terracotta tiles on the roof, the white stucco walls, arched windows and doorways, and the black ironwork and wooden beams. There were multiple entries to the courtyard patio, which held two palm trees and a lemon tree.

When she arrived and saw the Upside-Down Room, she almost fainted. She was told that the house constituted a historical place of interest. She would be forced to keep all structures in place and allow visitors to ogle the authentic mid-century modern décor, upside down or not.

The contract did not stipulate how *often* she needed to allow visitors. Once every five years should do it. She didn't want strangers frightening Mr. Cinnamon. It was bad enough tourists shouted questions to them over the courtyard wall, where she'd built Mr. Cinnamon a catio with climbing walls, perches, beds, and a reading nook. Constance and her cat spent many a pleasant evening together, Mr. C with his tunnels and toys, she with her Agatha Christie and Enneagram personality books.

From her vantage point atop the hill, Constance could

see the entire town in a grid below her. It was stunning at night. By decree, light pollution was kept to a minimum. At sundown, the streetlamps blinked out of existence to showcase the stars above. It was an entirely different sky to the one she'd left behind in New York.

But constellations, a cat, and Agatha Christie comfort-reads, while lovely, were no match for human connection. Since arriving in Cherry Hill six months ago, Constance had re-read half the Poirots and all the Miss Marples.

Six months in Cherry Hill, without a single friend to show for it.

What had started as a bonus—no neighbors—had become a detriment.

She was lonely.

That was why she'd decided to teach a free class on the Enneagram, aka the nine personality types. Today at eleven a.m. in the library's community room, she would meet her students for the first time.

Before that: Main Street for a winter coat. She poured her cat's daily dose of "dental crunchies" into his bowl, which resulted in Mr. Cinnamon darting over to snack on them. His fluffy, foxy tail was raised high and curled at the tip, in what Constance thought of as his "happy question mark." The sound of contented crunching filled the air. The vet said his teeth could use the assist, and Constance had obeyed without question. Mr. Cinnamon had given her a reason to live; the least she could do was give him healthy incisors.

"Rao?" Mr. Cinnamon asked, post-food.

"I'll be back in a few hours," she assured him. He bumped his head against her hand, then went and sat on her cane, as though to prevent her from leaving. It couldn't have been comfortable, but as he'd proven with the bifocal incident, that didn't seem to bother him.

"I know it doesn't look like a snowstorm is coming, but my right knee doesn't lie, and I can't be worried about slipping on my first day of class." She scooped Mr. Cinnamon off her cane and deposited him on his cat climbing post, then took a moment to admire him.

He was a beautiful fellow, with a ruddy, apricot coat and a stripe of chocolate brown along his spine, head, and tail. His chin and front fluff were white, morphing into a golden-brown undercoat. His paws had an unusual brown-and-white mottling that she adored; it was what denied him a purebred Somali lineage but made him more special to Constance. One of a kind, was Mr. Cinnamon. His warm, butter-yellow eyes, ringed with a slash of peridot green, never ceased to enchant her. Furthermore, it looked like he wore eyeliner.

They performed an elaborate goodbye ritual, perfected over their months of acquaintance, followed by a last treat and head scratch. "Be good, love."

Outside, Constance set her gate alarm and walked to the bench to wait for the Cherry Hill Jolly Trolley to pick her up.

It wasn't technically a trolley. It looked like one, and people called it that because it was meant to be old-timey for tourists, but it ran on regular gas and followed a simple, casual loop around town, making it ideal for Constance, who didn't drive.

Not only was hers the sole house atop Cherry Hill, but the sole house on the aptly titled Hill Street, which intersected with Cherry Hill Boulevard. The street names in Cherry Hill were descriptive, as though a child had written them in crayon on a homemade map. Lone Tree Lane contained a lone tree. Mountainview had exactly that, until construction of the Vitality Hotel & Spa blocked it from street view.

Since the Upside-Down House was part of the Jolly Trolley's tour, Constance rode free.

The downside was that the trolley only went one direction, so even though she lived close to Main Street, Constance had to travel the full loop to get to it, while facts about her surroundings filled the air, like a deranged, unstoppable Siri.

She had memorized the tourism recording at this point.

"Ninety minutes east of Los Angeles, Cherry Hill stands proudly in the San Gorgonio Pass, formed by the San Andreas fault," blared the voice on the loudspeaker. "Nestled between the San Bernardino Mountains to the north and San Jacinto Mountains to the south, Cherry Hill is a favorite stop-off on the way to the Morongo Casino, the Premium Outlets, and the Coachella Valley, providing a quiet contrast to its flashier neighbors.

"Fine dining, local artisans, and of course, the pride of Cherry Hill, the Jolly Trolley—owned and operated by the Caldecot family, and continuously running since 1927—are here for your pleasure. Why not sit and rest for a spell?"

After picking up Constance, the Jolly Trolley proceeded down Cherry Hill Boulevard at 15 m.p.h., past single-family homes on both sides of the street ("Cherry Hill boasts the largest collection of fully preserved, mid-century homes in California"—loaded pause—"outside of Palm Springs").

At Lone Tree Lane, the trolley passed the infamous lone tree: a tamarisk, and the subject of controversy. Angry signs staked into the ground surrounded the tree, written from the POV of the tree ("I'm an invasive species", "Axe Me", "I'm BAD").

Sometimes, sipping coffee in her courtyard with only Mr. Cinnamon and Miss Marple for company, Constance felt like the tamarisk tree. Invasive, unwanted. *Bad.*

By teaching a free class, she hoped to prove herself worthy of the hill, worthy of the house that stood atop it, and worthy of human connection.

A few blocks later, the trolley crossed Main Street, where it refused to stop at the intersection even though A) Constance was the only passenger and B) that was the only place she wanted to go.

She'd been reprimanded once by the elderly driver, Isaac Caldecot, for using the emergency pull cord outside Dune Buggies, U.S.A. on the corner of Main Street and Cherry Hill Boulevard. She'd been hoping to shorten her ride by two-thirds, but he wasn't having it.

Isaac had pulled over and approached her, conductor cap in hand. His spine was bent, and he wore orthopedic shoes beneath his wine-colored uniform of pants and blazer. "I've driven this route since I was knee high to a grasshopper. Do you think I don't know where I'm going?"

"No, it's not that—"

"Do you think I don't know where my stops are?"

"No, of course not, but—"

"The Jolly Trolley's route has been curated to provide the maximum value for your tourist dollars."

"That's just it, though, I'm not pay—"

"EXACTLY. *You're not paying.* So maybe you should be grateful for the free ride and all the information you're receiving on such destinations as *the Upside-Down House.*" His eyes bored into hers, and she shrank back.

"Commemorative map?" He didn't wait for an answer

and flung one at her. The map had a Caldecot family crest in the corner, with "Calico" written beneath in smaller font, apparently a derivation of Caldecot.

If she closed her eyes and listened to the tourist recording, Constance could imagine Cherry Hill in its heyday as a thriving, arts-centered enclave featuring mom-and-pop restaurants, theatres, and shops. Eyes open, however, and the fantasy ended.

The art deco theatre was undergoing a renovation, but the tourism recording refused to acknowledge this. "The art deco theatre showcases classic and modern films, and features cast and crew Q&As, right here in Cherry Hill, where L.A. comes to play."

At that moment, they passed a poster attached to the construction fence with the same tagline printed on it. Someone had crossed out "play" in Sharpie and written "die."

The next area of interest was a well-kept public playground, which suggested youth and exuberance, yet the prime attraction, a metal tower shaped like a robot, whose arms were twin slides, had been permanently fenced off "to protect our youngest citizens from burns" while still "preserving the original, beloved play structure from 1966." *Because there's nothing children love more than a "beloved play structure" they can never access.*

Beside that bit of cruelty stood the elementary school, a daycare, and a public swimming pool. Finally, the boulevard and thus the trolley swooped toward downtown again, along the backdrop of the mountain view-obscuring Vitality Hotel & Spa and its enormous parking garage.

The trolley slammed on its brakes, throwing Constance forward.

Could it be? A second passenger?

A young man with a beard and unkempt hair, wearing a windbreaker and baggy shorts, climbed inside the trolley.

Instead of paying with cash or card, the unkempt man reached inside his jacket pocket and extracted a business-size envelope. The driver shook his head. The two men spoke quietly for a moment before the unkempt man returned the envelope to his pocket and exited.

Perhaps the young man had been offering to pay a backlog of fares, and the driver had forgiven them? He allowed Constance to ride for free after all, despite her tourism attraction remaining closed.

Not for the first time, she lamented the lack of rideshare or taxi drivers in Cherry Hill. The one local Uber driver, a harried woman in a cluttered minivan, was so dangerously inept that Constance didn't think she'd survive a second ride with the woman. The trolley might be slow, but at least Constance would arrive in one piece.

Amid clogged traffic, the trolley trundled slowly along so its sole passenger could revel in the flavor of local businesses.

No one else was reveling in them, because there were few places to park along Main Street, and anyone who attempted to squeeze into a spot was thwarted by the trolley's stops and starts.

An angry driver behind them shouted, "Get out of the way, you stupid trolley." The driver didn't react.

Constance swallowed and focused on CHATeau Savannah, a Parisian-themed cat cafe on the corner where the newsstand once stood. How did a cat cafe work? Would Mr. Cinnamon be welcome there while she dined, or would the cats-in-residence hiss at freeloaders?

The tourism recording offered no answers. It still

believed Lupe's Newsstand held the spot, offering newspapers in twenty-seven languages. It was a shame there was no mention of the cat cafe, which, alongside its neighbor, the Cut & Dried salon, were the only storefronts doing brisk business.

The Hummingbird Art Gallery was "Closed Until Further Notice," yet the recording maintained that tourists could purchase original artwork of "the smallest known avian theropod dinosaurs, or even welcome actual Trochilidae into your life with custom bird feeders."

The cognitive dissonance between the recording and the reality of Main Street was borderline dystopian. If she re-opened the Upside-Down House, would that help? *No, no, no. It's not my fault the town is in decline, and it's not my responsibility to fix it.*

A few more businesses and she'd be free of the recording and the guilt. The sign on Texican Table's window read: "Open for Dinner Only." Constance averted her eyes, as though giving the restaurant privacy.

After Texican Table sat Kaftans 'n' More. "With a Mediterranean climate to the west and a desert climate to the east, you never know when you'll need a kaftan. Or more!" The "more" included furniture, décor, postcards, and groceries.

The owner, Martin Onder, always greeted Constance by name. She was relieved to see several customers inside.

"Our final destination is the Visitor Center," shouted the recording. "Stop in for a free calendar of events and a Cherry Hill visor. New customers only."

At this point in the tour, the song would start. It was a Golden Age, World War II-era, Fox Trot Americana-style jingle with alternating male and female vocals.

Constance braced herself for it.

> Cherry Hill, Cherry Hill
> A place to get your fill
> Cherry Hill, Cherry Hill
> Where time stands still

A group of protesters exploded out of Dune Buggies, U.S.A. on the corner, chanting, "Hey-hey, ho-ho, the Jolly Trolley's got to go. Hey-hey, ho-ho, the Jolly Trolley's got to go."

Led by a fierce, petite woman with a bullhorn, the group of twenty people marched back and forth outside the Visitor Center, thrusting signs in the air to the beat of their chant.

Constance had seen anti-trolley protests before, during the holiday shopping rush a month prior, but she had assumed it was something to keep the Cherry Hillians occupied between bouts of kicking the tamarisk tree.

When the trolley's song started again, the group was prepared. Instead of "A place to get your fill," they shouted, "Where small businesses are killed" and instead of "Where time stands still," they shouted, "Where traffic stands still," and, well, they weren't wrong.

Multiple cars idled behind the trolley, in a cacophony of honks and shouts, as it made its way slowly up Main. Constance was aware of being the only passenger during the standoff.

Embarrassed, she hunched down in her seat to hide.

Seconds later, the window behind her exploded in a shower of glass.

3

CONSTANCE

CONSTANCE SCREAMED and kept her body curled up tight. Time contracted and sped up, as though someone had hit a fast-forward button on the world.

The trolley lurched as the driver hit the brakes. All was strangely silent. No song, no chanting. The protesters outside seemed as stunned as Constance.

She couldn't think or move.

When she finally gasped for air, time returned to normal, and she could hear again.

"Who did that? Who broke the speakers?" a voice demanded. That explained the song's abrupt end.

Constance unfurled and checked her body for damage. No tears in her clothing, no blood on her face or hands. She patted her hair and felt a few shards of glass, but most of the shattered window had fallen onto the seat behind her. Her heart spasmed in her chest, and she gasped for more air. She didn't want to leave the trolley, but she couldn't stay.

As she struggled to decide what to do, a man in a suit and tie appeared at the front of the trolley, like an angel sent from corporate. His frame took up the doorway, and his eyes scanned for passengers.

"Are you okay? Don't move. I'll come to you."

The man strode up the aisle and checked her over, then offered her his arm. She used it to rise, and couldn't help comparing his suit and tie against the slovenly clothes of the other young man she'd encountered that morning. *At least not every member of Gen Z in Cherry Hill dresses like a slob.*

She almost laughed.

Wow. I must be in shock if I'm judging other people's clothing.

The angel from corporate lightly touched her shoulder. "Ma'am, did you hear me? Can you talk?"

"I'm okay," she told him, not sure if that were true. "Just stunned."

His troubled eyes reflected concern. "Yeah. I'm stunned, and I was only a witness."

"Was it a gun?"

"A rock, I think. I agreed they could use my office as a base for the protest as long as there was no violence," the man said. He tugged on his cuffs, agitated. "I'm so sorry this happened to you."

"It's not your fault," she said, because that's what she would have wanted to hear.

"Let me get you somewhere safe. The sheriff's on his way."

"Thank you."

"I'm Aidan Zachary, by the way. I own Dune Buggies, U.S.A. on the corner."

She nodded and looked outside. Most of the protesters had fled, and the remainder didn't know what to do with themselves. They stood awkwardly amid the palm tree-lined sidewalk, signs limp by their sides.

Constance exited on trembling legs, shielded by her protector. As a native New Yorker, she could conjure a death-stare to freeze a mobster in his tracks, but today she didn't have the energy and was grateful to lean on someone else.

"Ma'am, is this your cane?" Aidan had gone back to retrieve it.

"Oh, yes, thank you."

Constance was relieved to see that Isaac Caldecot, the elderly driver, appeared unhurt.

He stood on the sidewalk, arms crossed, and chastised those who remained of the crowd. "You think a broken speaker will stop me? Ha! I'll sing the song myself." He launched into a side-shuffle and belted, "Cherry Hill, Cherry Hill, a place to get your fill…"

"Boo," someone said through cupped hands.

Constance agreed. Why on earth would he taunt a mob already proven to be violent?

"Someone needs to shut him up. Permanently," muttered a woman in her 40s.

Constance recognized her as Ana Whitley, the proprietress of the Hummingbird Art Gallery. She wore a hummingbird pin and held a bullhorn; she must've led the chant earlier. Was her gallery "closed until further notice" because of today's protest, or because it had lost so much business due to the trolley blocking customers from her shop?

Isaac Caldecot puffed out his chest. "Stop being cheapskates and pay for parking, because I'm not going anywhere. You might think I'm to blame for your troubles, but if anything, you owe me."

There was a collective gasp of rage.

"Main Street was *built* around this trolley," Isaac insisted.

"And now Main Street will die around the trolley," Ana said. "Unless you die first."

"Ana, don't talk like that," Aidan cried. "Especially after what just happened."

"Fine, not *him* so much as that belching, diesel-spewing, noxious, riderless, gas-guzzling heap of junk."

Not riderless, Constance thought nervously. She knew the trolley drove its route regardless of her presence, but these people might not know that.

"May I quote you on that, Ms. Whitley?" chirped a young woman with a fancy camera. Without waiting for an answer, she snapped a few images. Around her neck was a press pass reading "Shawna Neuman, *Cherry Hill Gazette*."

"What? No, stop taking pictures of me." Ana lunged for the camera.

"Don't! You'll break it." Shawna tried to jerk free.

They tugged back and forth until the camera went flying. It landed with a crunch and skidded beneath the trolley.

Shawna swore.

Aidan sighed and bent down, seeking the best angle to retrieve the camera. He reluctantly thrust his suit-clad arm beneath the trolley before handing the camera back to Shawna.

"Great, the SD card is damaged," Shawna moaned. "There goes my work from the past two days."

"Ana, for goodness' sake," Aidan said. "She was only doing her job. It's bad enough someone threw that rock. Did you see who it was?"

"No, *I* was here peacefully, and—"

"You call that peaceful?" Shawna interrupted, holding her damaged camera.

Aidan brushed at his pants, trying to wipe off dirt from his ground-crawl. "Anger doesn't help. Ow." He shook out his hand, which had a cut on it. "I think a shard of glass cut me."

Ana's anger receded. "I've got Neosporin in my purse."

"Thanks." Aidan accepted the small bottle.

"You're right, by the way," Constance told him. "Anger solves nothing."

"I don't think *you* have anything to say, keeping the trolley in business," Ana spat.

"Enough," said Aidan. He turned to Constance. "I was supposed to take you somewhere safe. Why don't you wait inside with Jenna until the sheriff arrives?"

He guided Constance inside the Visitor Center and left her in the care of a woman with the name Jenna Evert stitched onto the pocket of her button-down employee shirt.

Jenna closed the door firmly to the outside world. She looked to be five or ten years younger than Constance, somewhere in her late fifties. Her eyebrows were painted on in a thin, mahogany arc, giving her a surprised, kindly expression, for which Constance was grateful.

"I saw what happened," Jenna said. "Are you okay? Do you need a doctor?"

Tears welled in Constance's eyes. The lump in her throat was so large she couldn't speak. Why had this happened today of all days—the day she'd been looking forward to for months?

Her watch read 10:15. Still time to gather her wits before class at eleven.

"Constance...?" Jenna prompted.

"No, no, I'm fine. A bit rattled. How did you know my name?"

Jenna smiled, but it looked forced. "Everyone knows your name. You bought the Upside-Down House."

"Ah."

"I know everything there is to know about that house." Jenna indicated the TV in the corner, which played an old episode of the PBS show "California's Gold." On-screen, a white-haired, cheerful gentleman stood outside Constance's house.

Constance gave a start. "Oh, my goodness."

The host ambled inside the gate of her property as it used to be, years ago. No catio, no Mr. Cinnamon, merely a tourist attraction drawing visitors to Cherry Hill. Constance felt uncomfortable but was saved from further comment when Jenna remarked, "It's not the trolley's fault businesses are hurting. It's the Vitality." She spat "Vitality" like it was a dirty chaw of tobacco.

Both women looked out the window, at the behemoth across the street. Their side of Main Street was composed of seven owner-operated businesses. The opposite side held precisely one building: The Vitality Hotel & Spa, blocking half of the San Bernardino mountains from view, like a spaceship sent to conquer the town.

"How so?" Constance asked.

"They have plenty of parking, but they won't release any of it to us unless we pay up. Way up. The trolley's not the problem. It's just an easier target."

"Doesn't the spa bring tourism? And the hotel guests surely do some shopping?"

"Some," Jenna conceded. "Not as much as we'd hoped. Mostly they're in their bubble, staying on site, 'convalescing.'"

Constance was pretty sure "convalescing" meant "rehab."

"Meanwhile, the locals have nowhere to park if they want to shop here. Traffic's congested because of the trolley, and what little parking there is out front is rarely available, so they head to the Wal-Mart supercenter in Redlands instead. The newsstand had to close, and the rest of us are scared we're next. When the folks who work here see the trolley blocking customers and turning Main Street into a logjam, it makes them feel helpless. Hence..." She gestured to the sidewalk protest.

The front door swung open, and Constance tensed at the renewed sounds of arguing from outside. But the mob wasn't storming the gate. It was only a tall, ungainly man with thin, reddish-brown hair. He wore a deputy uniform and an expression of concern.

Jenna smiled at the deputy, which went a long way toward helping Constance relax. Even before the man spoke, she could see the family resemblance in their hair and eyes.

"Mom, everything okay?"

"We're alright, Max. But Constance here was on the trolley when the protesters attacked."

Max's attention swept to Constance. He looked perplexed. "No one rides the trolley."

"I do." Embarrassment filled her. She wanted to be on the correct side of things, and that usually meant on the side of the little guy. But who was the little guy in this scenario? A mob heckling an octogenarian driver, smashing his window, and breaking his loudspeaker? That didn't seem right. Then again, she was biased; she needed the trolley.

Max remained confused. "But why? None of the tour stops are open. The art deco theatre won't be up and running for months, the botanical gardens are under new management, and the woman who bought the Upside-Down House has got to be the most selfish, uncompromising—"

Jenna shook her head and made a frantic "psst" noise. Her painted-on eyebrows danced in alarm.

Constance wanted to disappear.

Max's eyes narrowed. "Oh, it's you. When do you plan to re-open the house?"

"Hush, Max," Jenna said.

"Um," Constance said nervously. "I'm not sure." *How about never?* she thought.

"Wow! Would you look at that! Isn't that amazing?" On TV, the amiable host of "California's Gold" gaped in wonder at the upside-down bedroom.

Jenna clicked off the show. "Don't you need to get a witness statement, Max?"

"Right. Yes." He cleared his throat and produced a recording device. "Please state your full name."

"Constance Angela Kincaid."

"Age?"

"Sixty-seven."

"Place of employment?"

"I'm a lawyer by trade. Self-employed, semi-retired."

"Current place of residence?"

"I believe we've established that," she gritted out, then closed her eyes. "Sorry."

She described her trolley ride, including the bearded, unkempt young man who'd tried to give an envelope to the driver.

Max tapped a finger against his chin. "Interesting. And you have no idea who it was?"

"No."

"Yeah, why would you? When you live up on a hill, why circulate with us commoners?" he groused.

Desperate to prove her value to the town, Constance retrieved a home-printed flyer from her bag and offered it to Max and Jenna.

"I'm teaching my first class on the nine personality types, or 'Enneagram,' today. Would you like to join us? It starts in twenty minutes, and you'll learn things that could be useful in both your professions." Having a mother-and-son duo in the class would be illuminating.

Deputy Max took the paper from her and read aloud. "'Have you ever wondered why people do the things they do?' Yes. Right now, I'm wondering why someone would *move into the Upside-Down House and then keep it to themselves.*"

"Max..." said Jenna.

"What's this symbol?" Max demanded. He jabbed the Enneagram image on her flyer, with the nine personality numbers around a circle, arrows connecting them.

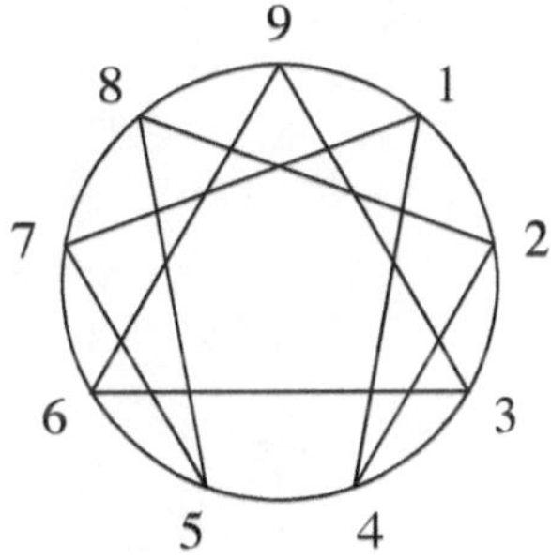

"Oh, that's—"

"Looks like some kind of pentagram," he said, popping the "p."

"Um, no, there are nine sides, you see? 'Ennea' means nine. 'Penta' means five."

"*Nine* sides?" He frowned. "Isn't that double worse?"

Constance struggled to respond. Besides the fact that "double worse" wasn't a phrase, she was suddenly aware that Deputy Max was still recording her.

"Mrs. Kincaid," he said ominously, "did you move here to start a cult?"

4

———————

CONSTANCE

OF ALL THE *conclusions to jump to!*

"No-no, my goodness, no," she stammered. She leaned closer to his recording device and spoke slowly. "It is not a cult."

"That's exactly what a cult leader would say, though, wouldn't they?"

"The Enneagram is not a religion, and it's not a cult. It's a toolkit for building self-awareness and empathy, based on the nine personality types and their dominant way of viewing the world, through thinking, feeling, or doing."

"I've heard of it," Jenna said. "Amy Poehler likes it. She's fine, Max."

Max glanced between his mother and Constance for a moment. Eventually, his shoulders relaxed. "Sounds pretty woo-woo to me," he muttered.

Constance was relieved he wouldn't be joining the class but saddened by his skepticism. "What about you, Jenna? Maybe you'd like to see how it works...?"

"Sorry, I can't leave the visitor center."

"I understand. Would you mind keeping my flyers with the other brochures?" Constance set five on the counter.

Jenna smiled, but didn't move to accept them. "Happy to."

"Thanks. And thanks again for the rescue."

To his credit, Deputy Max held the door open for her as she left.

Outside, grey clouds filled the sky, and rain fell—not snow, yet, but chilly. Police tape surrounded the trolley, and the protesters had dispersed, either due to law enforcement's presence or the onset of rain.

Constance ducked into Kaftans 'n' More for a coat, only to discover that several of the mob were inside. She didn't want to linger among folks who resented her, so she grabbed the first jacket she saw, along with six cans of cat food for Mr. Cinnamon.

The cashier was a twenty-something woman of Mexican descent who had a purple stripe in her hair and large, fake eyelashes that seemed more like an art project than a serious endeavor at fooling anyone. They worked for her, though, and Constance admired her nerve. The cashier changed her handwritten nametag every week. Today, apropos of the weather, it said, "Her Royal Highness, Duchess of Snow Globes." (Which were for sale in the discount bin.)

Once she'd rung up Constance, the cashier asked, "Did you open the Upside-Down House yet?"

"No, not yet," Constance replied vaguely.

"If you do, we'll host a grand re-opening for you at Texican Table," she said, referring to the Tex-Mex restaurant a few doors down. "My dad's the Tex, my mom's the Mex, and I'm the big old disappointment for not working there. What do you say?"

"That's kind," Constance said noncommittally.

Sensing this meant *no*, the cashier sighed. "It would really help Cherry Hill if at least *one* of our tourist attractions was open."

The man behind Constance called out, "Everyone ready for the snow? So fun, right?"

"As a native New Yorker, I can tell you it will be more like sleet," Constance said. "Or slush. Gray, wet, slush."

There was a tiny sob. Behind the man's legs, a little girl popped into view, gasping through tears.

"Way to ruin it for my kid," the man grumbled.

Constance shrank back, mortified.

She had thought it would be helpful to temper expectations, but she should've been more careful. There were a lot more children running around Cherry Hill than you'd expect, given its reputation as a retirement town.

She pulled on her new jacket and made a hasty exit.

"Wait," the cashier called. "My boss wants to talk to you." She yelled toward the back of the store, "Hey, Martin! The lawyer's here."

While they waited for Martin to emerge, the cashier said, "I wanted to come to your Enneagram class, FYI."

Constance felt a surge of hope. "You did?"

"Yeah, I thought it sounded cool. But it conflicts with my knitting class."

"Constance, *merhaba*," Martin Onder poked his head out from the storage room and greeted her with a rapid hello. His family hailed from Turkey and, besides owning Kaftans 'n' More, Martin led the Cherry Hill Chamber of Commerce.

He was in his mid-forties, with dark hair and a tidy mustache. His rolled-up shirtsleeves revealed tanned forearms that were no stranger to lifting heavy produce. Boxes were balanced precariously atop each other in the storage closet where he stood with a clipboard. Sweat dotted his forehead, and his hands fidgeted. "Can I tell you what is happening, please, Constance?"

Constance glanced at her watch—10:48, cutting it close—but Martin was the only person she interacted with in Cherry Hill who had never interrogated her about the Upside-Down House. The least she could do was lend an ear.

"Yes, of course, Martin."

Apparently, Martin and the other chamber of commerce members had launched several lawsuits against the Jolly Trolley for obstructing access to their businesses. To their astonishment, the trolley had deep pockets and deflected each one. Martin couldn't understand how such a small family company could afford to hire so many expensive lawyers from out of town. Who were they? Where had they come from?

"They keep sending more files." He indicated the boxes. "We'll never get through them."

A stockboy entered from outside, breathing hard. Martin nodded to him. To Constance, he whispered, "Always on a smoke break. What can you do?"

If he'd been on a smoke break, Constance didn't smell it on him, but then again, with the change in weather, her nose was congested.

"They're drowning you in discovery," Constance explained, regarding the boxes. "It's a common tactic to keep you from finding pertinent information to your case. It's unethical, and you should let the judge know."

She had assumed this would be welcome news, but Martin scoffed.

"Yeah, right. The judge is a friend of the mayor, and the

mayor is the niece of Mr. Caldecot, the trolley driver, so it's all the same family. You can't say she isn't pulling strings. Isn't that what they do, funnel money to their own?"

He ran a hand through his damp, messy hair and regarded Constance with a hopeless look. "Two days ago, we made a motion at the city council meeting. 'Retire the trolley, please!' Took us weeks to put together a presentation, and they shot it down before we even finished." Martin paused for breath and fixed Constance with puppy-dog eyes. "You want to join our team? I looked you up, you're a big shot."

"I specialize in intellectual property," she demurred. "I also have a conflict of interest because I rely on the trolley. I wish you well, though. I agree something should change."

Martin nodded, frowning. "If business doesn't pick up, I must let my staff go." He'd spoken quietly, as though talking to himself, but the stricken look on the cashier's face told Constance the young woman had heard. The cashier blinked in a flutter of enormous eyelashes, spun on her boot heel, and walked away.

Constance was eager to leave as well—it was 10:50 now—but Martin launched into a final lament.

"You know what's crazy?" he said. "Three times over the years, in my head I pick the winning Lotto numbers. Three times! But I'm not allowed to play, since I own the store. I could have retired many times. But no. This store is my life."

Feeling guilty that she couldn't help, and then frustrated for feeling guilty (*It's not my fault!*), Constance headed outside to brave the elements.

Shaking off her conversation with Martin as well as the frightening events of the morning, she felt invigorated as she strode. Maybe it was the wet and chilly air, but she imagined she was back at law school in New York, excited for the first day of class. Only this time, she'd be on the other side of the podium.

The library was a five-minute walk away, tucked into the civic center block that also housed the sheriff's department, the superior court, city hall, the regional planning office, and the public works and safety office. The fire station was a half-mile past, in its own building.

Huffing and puffing, she entered the library at 10:56. She'd have preferred to arrive ten minutes early, but this was okay. Despite multiple obstacles—violence! cult allegations! serving as Martin's sounding board!—she'd made it. She couldn't wait to meet her students.

Through the automatic doors, she spied a corkboard with an advertisement pinned to it: ENNEAGRAM FOR BEGINNERS: DISCOVER YOUR TYPE AND WHAT IT MEANS FOR YOUR LIFE IN THIS FREE CLASS TAUGHT BY CONSTANCE KINCAID, SATURDAYS FROM 11 TO 1 AND WEDNESDAYS FROM 4 TO 6.

The word **CANCELED** had been scrawled across it in red Sharpie.

5

CONSTANCE

LIKE MOST BUILDINGS in Cherry Hill, the library was mid-century modern with a long, diagonal roof and a garden of colored rocks and cacti outside. It was very pretty, very smart.

Inside, it was full of venom and spite, in the form of Roberto Guerrero, the head librarian. A Latino man in his 60s, the same age as Constance, he was broad shouldered and power hungry, with a resonant voice that was far too loud for a library if you asked Constance.

She had no clue what she'd done to annoy him. When she'd applied for a library card several months ago, he'd made her jump through hoops. She didn't drive, so she'd come with a utilities bill and her social security card, which should have been enough. Not for Roberto! He said she needed *three* forms of I.D. And then, when she came back later to offer a free Enneagram class in the library, he flat-out refused.

"No. I've lived here my whole life; I know the people of this town; they wouldn't be interested."

"They don't like mathematics?"

He squinted. "... Right."

"Good thing it's not mathematics, then," she said with a smile. "It's a study of the nine personality types."

"Still not interested." He looked behind her. "Next patron."

So, she did an end-run around him and booked it through the park district.

He had no choice but to allow her and her students access to the community room from eleven to one on Saturdays and four to six p.m. on Wednesdays, but he was not happy about it. He stamped the words, "Not endorsed by the Cherry Hill Library. Take at your own risk" onto the flyers she'd emailed for inclusion in the library newsletter.

It was galling. ("*Risk*"?) Still, he had included it in the newsletter and front glass display, so she'd assumed things were moving along fine.

Apparently not.

She tore the "canceled" flyer off the corkboard and marched to the back of the library, where she caught her saboteur taping another sign to the community room door. It read, "The Enneagram class has been canceled due to lack of interest."

"It most certainly has not been canceled, Roberto." Unlike Roberto, she used an inside voice: firm, but quiet.

"Ah, there you are." Roberto turned to face her, a gleam in his eye. "Five people are required to secure the room. You have four. They're inside if you'd like to explain to them why you failed to meet the quota."

Her stomach clenched. The word "failure" never ceased to ignite her, but she suppressed her anger and stuck to the facts. "Four students plus myself makes five."

"The instructor doesn't count," he said, his gravelly voice cranked up to eleven. "Chase, alert the Kings and

Queens Chess Club," he boomed. "They'll be happy to reclaim their time slot."

A lively blond man in his twenties leaped into view. "You rang?"

He was Roberto's opposite: young, bright-eyed, and charming. He didn't wait for Roberto to answer and pivoted to Constance.

"Hooray, you're here! Ennea-Gram, right? And you're the gram! So psyched you're doing this class. I'd come if I weren't working." He glanced at her hand clutching the flyer. "Did you like the poster? I added a few filters to your headshot to highlight your cheekbones and grey goddess chic. I was aiming for Anna Wintour meets Dame Judi, what do you think?"

Constance stepped back, startled. He was basically a can of Red Bull with the power of speech. She didn't know what to respond to first. Even Roberto couldn't get a word in edgewise with Chase around.

"What did you call me? 'Gram'?" she asked.

"Ennea-Gram. That's the name of your course, right? Because you're a grandma? Super cute."

"Oh! Not a grandmother, but thank you. There seems to be confusion about—"

"She's not teaching the class after all," Roberto interrupted. "One short of the quota. Too bad, so sad."

Chase folded his arms and narrowed his eyes at his boss. "Really."

Did Constance imagine it, or did Roberto look abashed? His cheek twitched, and he looked at the floor.

"BRB," said Chase, and disappeared down an aisle. Roberto and Constance stood in tense silence. Chase returned, pushing a library patron in a wheelchair. The patron was asleep.

"Zeke is taking a power nap, but he told me earlier he was interested in the class," Chase declared. To Constance, he added, "Kick his chair if he snores."

"You can't be serious," Roberto boomed. "He's not conscious."

"We both know he could wake at any moment, and when he does, he'll want to be in the right place. We can't deny him that opportunity." To Constance, Chase explained, "Zeke is our most loyal regular. He's here when we open, and he's here when we close."

"Is he... currently... unhoused?" Constance asked delicately.

"No, he just loves it here, as he should, because of the amazing programs we offer, *such as the Enneagram*." Chase patted Constance's shoulder. "You're good, Gram, I got your back."

"Not a gram, but thank you." She could have hugged him.

Chase preceded her inside the community room and got Zeke settled. Ignoring Roberto's scowl, Constance entered as well and surveyed her students. Including her unwitting savior, asleep in his wheelchair, two men and two women sat around the conference table.

The quota she hadn't known about until five minutes ago put a fire under her.

She locked the community room door (no need to risk hemorrhaging more students), set her cane against the wall, and handed out her syllabus.

Thank goodness she'd added a new element to her opening speech last night. The same website that had advised her how to write an obit one year ago suggested using an unexpected hook to garner interest.

"Hello and welcome to Enneagram Personality Types

for Beginners. My name is Constance Kincaid, and I'm delighted to see you. Who loves a good mystery?"

Every hand went up (well, minus Zeke's), and she allowed herself a moment of relief. The bait was set.

"The human mind is the ultimate mystery, don't you think? But don't take it from me, take it from Miss Marple." Constance cleared her throat and quoted from her handout: "'My hobby is—and always has been—Human Nature. You'd be surprised if you knew how very few distinct types there are in all.' That's from Agatha Christie's *Murder at the Vicarage*."

Rain cracked against the skylight above, giving the room an electric, ominous feel.

"For those who aren't familiar with her, Miss Marple is an elderly spinster. We have that in common," she joked, then paused.

Why did I say that? Why did I lie?

She thought of herself as an honest person. She hadn't shown up today intending to mislead her students. But really, there was no need for anyone in Cherry Hill to know about the humiliating tragedy that led her to move here.

"Anyway, Miss Marple solves murders by comparing the people involved in a crime with other people she's known or come across in St. Mary Mead. She uses this knowledge to predict what people might do, and why. The descriptions of the Nine Types range from highly integrated—that is, healthy—to average, unhealthy, excessive, and finally, disintegrated, or psychotic. That makes it useful as a predictor of behavior.

"What we think of as the personality is really a coping mechanism we created to protect ourselves. The word *person* comes from the Greek word *persona*, which means 'mask.'"

Her students hung on each word. Thrilled, Constance forced herself to slow down for the next part, her Enneagram origin story.

"I discovered the Enneagram in my twenties. As the only woman at my law firm—this was forty years ago—I felt invisible. I needed a way to stand out. Learning about the nine types—their drives, passions, fears and behavior—helped me tailor my interactions with clients, witnesses, opposing counsel, and even judges. Our personalities affect every aspect of our lives, from our worldview to our relationships. I started getting results the other lawyers could only dream of. They still dismissed it, made jokes about women's intuition and luck, but I knew the truth. As the years passed, I remembered less and less of it. Then, about a year ago..."

Her throat closed, and she saw herself outside Morningside Co-op Church in the rain. Defeated. Humiliated. Alone. *Don't cry. Don't cry.*

She bit the inside of her cheek and forced herself to picture the mischievous, fluffy red cat who'd saved her that day. She cleared her throat and began again.

"About a year ago, with help from my adopted cat, Mr. Cinnamon, I came across a revised and updated edition of Riso & Hudson's seminal text, *Personality Types*, and it renewed my interest. I earned my accreditation as a teacher, and here we are. It's my hope you'll find the Enneagram insights as useful as I do. So. All this to say: Welcome."

Constance pulled out a folder and dug through it. "I've got nametags here to pass around... somewhere... let me see..."

In her haste, she spilled the folder's contents. "Whoops, there they go."

A middle-aged woman with curly, ash-blonde hair,

wearing a faded jean jacket, dropped beneath the table to gather them.

"Oh," the woman yelped, and Constance looked down to see if she was okay, but the woman waved her off. "Sorry, hit my head. I'll pass these out for you if you like."

"Thank you. Did everyone take the online quiz I sent you when you signed up? Quizzes are not the best way to determine your Type, but they'll give us a jumping-off point to get to know one another. Also, what resonates with you at first may not indicate your Type but a surface-level under-standing, and that's okay. It still tells us something. Please write your name and your best guess for your number. I'll write them on the dry-erase board, too."

Type One: The Perfectionist
Type Two: The Helper
Type Three: The Achiever
Type Four: The Individualist
Type Five: The Observer
Type Six: The Loyal Skeptic
Type Seven: The Enthusiast
Type Eight: The Challenger
Type Nine: The Peacemaker

"Who'd like to start?"

The middle-aged, curly-haired woman who'd handed out the nametags raised her hand.

"Hi there! I'm Sam-the-SAHM. Samantha, really, but people call me Sam. Sam Orlaith." She smiled a golden smile, and it was impossible not to smile back. Constance felt herself relaxing in Sam's presence. Had they met before? Perhaps at the public pool?

"As for my Type, I keep going back and forth between

Type Nine and Type Seven. Peaceful but enthusiastic, that's me."

"Don't worry about being right at this stage. It's still valuable to see what caught your eye. What's a SAHM?" Constance asked.

"Stay-at-home-mom. Sam-the-SAHM is an easy way for people to remember my name. And to be honest, it's not *my* type I'm interested in, but my family members. I made my husband Will take it, and he's *one-hundred-percent* a Type Six, the Loyal Skeptic. I think I already understand him better."

"That's amazing, Sam, thank you. Who's next? How about the gentleman next to Sam?"

Constance nodded at a clean-shaven man in his twenties, with a crisp buzz cut and rimless glasses framing intelligent eyes. He'd written "Name: Trevor, Type: Five" in neat, small letters on his nametag.

Type Five was the Observer.

He looked stricken by her attention, so Constance backtracked. "Hello, Trevor, thanks for coming today. Do you feel like sharing, or would you prefer we get back to you?"

Trevor blinked. "Oh, um, it's okay. I can talk. I guess."

"What makes you think you might be a Type Five, the Observer?"

"I read Riso & Hudson's 'Personality Types' as well as 'The Wisdom of the Enneagram,' 'The Enneagram Made Easy,' and 'The Modern Enneagram.'" In his arms he held a stack of books like a shield. They'd been tabbed with colorcoded Post-its, Constance's favorite technique. "I'm still gathering information, but Five seemed to fit."

Constance beamed. She was ninety-nine-percent certain he was correct. The fact that he hadn't given any personal examples but relied on data all but confirmed it.

"That's tremendous. I look forward to learning more about you."

Trevor looked away and didn't say anything for the rest of the class.

"Well skip Zeke for now," said Constance, passing over the sleeping gentleman.

The next student was a stylish young woman in a tailored blazer. Where Sam-the-SAHM was quick to smile, with untamed hair, this younger woman was all business.

She embodied the Clean Girl aesthetic Constance had read about at the Cut & Dried salon: hair smoothed back in a bun, shiny gold hoop earrings, and perfectly manicured nails. She was half Sam's age, yet seemed to be the older of the two, not in her moisturized face but in her eyes, which were harder than Sam's. Hypervigilant.

"I'm Penelope Scott. What Type would you guess I am, based on first impressions?"

"Were you able to take the quiz, Penelope?"

"You mean the quiz that was, like, 600 questions? Some of us have jobs," she said pointedly.

"Or kids," Sam-the-SAHM chimed in, and laughed, which softened her words.

"I assume Ones are the best?" Penelope asked. She laughed, too, but her laugh was forced, and her designer pen hovered above a matching journal.

"There is no 'best' number," Constance said gently. "Each has strengths and challenges."

"You have to say that, so no one gets offended. Ones are the best and nines are the worst, right?"

"Ones are not the best! Far from it," Constance snapped, then covered her mouth, mortified. "I'm so sorry. But I want to be clear there isn't a hierarchy."

Penelope squinted. "Are you, like, mad?"

"No, not at all."

"You sound mad."

"Nope," Constance insisted.

"Great, then I'll be a One. The Perfectionist. Makes sense." Penelope wrote #1 in her journal.

"You don't choose your number; you *are* your number. It's a combination of nature and nurture and something essential within you, and they don't change throughout your life, either."

Penelope's determination didn't waver. "You said the personality is a construct—"

"Coping mechanism, I believe I said—"

"So, I'll construct the one I want."

"Is it *possible*," drawled a voice, "that the *Three* could cede the floor back to the *teacher*?"

Penelope whipped around. "What did you just call me?"

The long-suffering voice belonged to the final student, a man in a gray hoodie, cinched tight, who jotted notes in an old-fashioned steno pad with a stubby, well-worn pencil.

"'Some of us have jobs,'" he quoted acidly. "For instance, I'm writing an article for the *Cherry Hill Gazette* and it would be *helpful* if I could hear the *instructor*."

The man untied his hood and ran a hand through his thick, rumpled hair.

Constance stared.

He was the kind of person who made you realize you'd never seen true beauty, and now you had to reassess your life, because if someone this good-looking was possible, what else had you missed? And wasn't it wonderful and terrible to think about?

If only she could hit pause on the universe and take him in.

She'd put him at thirty, plus or minus a few years. His features shouldn't have worked. His Adams apple was too big for his throat. His hair was hopelessly mussed. His nose was well shaped but slightly asymmetrical, as though it knew his sculpted cheekbones and penetrating green eyes would be uncanny without a "flaw."

His nametag read, "Wesley, Type Four. Un(four)tunately."

Type Four, the Individualist, was sometimes known as the Romantic. Not chocolate-and-flowers romantic, but the literary kind, prone to melancholy and nostalgia.

Frowning, Penelope turned to Constance. "Why did he call me a Three?"

"I don't know." (She did know.) "But we don't Type other people, as it robs them of self-discovery."

Looked chagrined, Wesley ran artistic-looking fingers through his hair, mussing it further. "Sorry," he told Penelope. To Constance he added, "Do you happen to have duct tape in your bag?"

"WOW," said Penelope.

Constance held up her hands. "Let's take a beat, shall we?"

Sam-the-SAHM shifted in her seat and averted her eyes; Trevor opened one of his books; and Penelope shot daggers at Wesley, who kept his gaze fixed on Constance.

Zeke snored.

How to get the room back on track? What had they even been talking about?

The tension proved too much for Sam. "Maybe you can't say which one's the best, but can you say which one's the worst, so we can avoid those people, ha ha?" As before, Sam's laugh was so golden it invited others to join in.

When the chuckles died down, Wesley said, "Fours are

the worst." He pinned Constance with his green eyes. "Come on, you know I'm right. No one wants to be a Four. Or at least, they shouldn't want to be."

He looked miserable. Nothing said "snake-eating-its-own-tail" like an unhealthy Four. For good and ill, they were the most self-aware Type of the Enneagram.

Constance sat and placed her elbows on the table. "I promise all of you, there is no best and worst. There are only levels of development: healthy, average, unhealthy, in excess of their number, and psychotic, and what that means and how it manifests is different for each Type."

Penelope only worked harder. "But if you had to ratio the strengths to weaknesses, which Type would you *recommend?*"

"Read the descriptions, and the one that humiliates you the most is your number," Wesley snapped. "It's not that hard. And if you don't have 'time', there are plenty of Buzzfeed quizzes that'll tell you which Disney Princess you are."

"Funny story," Constance interrupted, unable to help herself. "I was once approached by a Disney executive at a party who demanded a way around the fair use exception to shut down what he saw as theft of I.P. He couldn't get it into his head that it's not actionable."

A small head popped up from under the table. "She said, 'I pee'!"

Constance nearly fainted. Another hidden child! The little boy looked about eight? Ten? She could never tell.

"I'm a copyright lawyer," she explained. "I.P. stands for intellectual property."

The child screamed with glee. "She said it again."

To Constance's surprise, the child turned not to Sam-the-SAHM but Penelope. "Sorry, Mom."

Penelope sighed. "It's okay, baby. I shouldn't have made you hide."

Penelope couldn't have been thirty and looked more like the boy's sister than his mother. Constance felt a rush of compassion as Penelope's impeccable, put-together façade melted away.

"This is my son, Henry. The sitter bailed on us at the last minute. I thought if I could get you to tell me my Enneagram number right away, I could make the most of things before I had to leave. I'm sorry, okay? I'm sorry."

"I tried to help you, Penelope," Sam blurted out. Penelope looked alarmed to be addressed by Sam. "I never hit my head. I saw him under the table, and I shouted, but I kept your secret."

Constance rubbed her eyes. "Did everyone besides me know he was here?"

"No," said Wesley. "Honestly."

"I'd love for you and your son to stay," said Constance. "Believe me, I would. But the librarian's already unhappy with me, and if he discovers anyone under the age of sixteen in the class, he'll use it as an excuse to report me to the park district and cancel it."

"I get it. Whatever." Penelope grabbed her son by the hand. "Come on, sweetie. We'll head out early on the Boy Scout trip to Big Bear."

Penelope and her Surprise Child left, apparently to ski. Four students remained, but only if you counted Zeke, who continued to snore.

"Want me to wheel him out?" asked Sam.

"No," Constance cried. "We need the headcount."

Not that it mattered, without Penelope. Constance had spent months preparing for this day. After all her preparation and hard work, how could the class just... be *over*?

Without this class, how would she fill her days?

Trevor the self-described Five—the Observer—raised his hand. If nothing else, *he'd* been prepared. *He'd* been interested. She could take solace in that.

Fighting tears, she smiled encouragingly. "Yes?"

"When does the class end?"

6

CONSTANCE

ALONE IN THE LIBRARY BATHROOM, Constance tried to compose herself, but the tears came anyway. She slumped onto the floor and sobbed into her hands.

It wasn't only the class, of course. It was the terrifying incident with the trolley.

The shattered glass, the attack... She'd done her best to push it aside until class was over, but without adrenaline protecting her anymore, her back, neck, and shoulders screamed in pain from the stress. She wiped at her eyes, and reached for a paper towel, only to find the dispenser empty. She crouched under the hand dryer, which made her hair blow back like a lunatic's.

Why on earth did I try to dry my tears that way? What a ridiculous thing to do.

They'd still had forty minutes to go, but... "It can end right now," she'd told Trevor, defeated.

He'd shrugged and gotten up, holding his stack of books to his chest like a tower of knowledge. She'd failed him.

She'd failed all of them, as Roberto predicted. Including herself.

The remaining students had gathered their items and shuffled out. Well, except for Zeke, oblivious to all that had occurred.

No one likes you, a voice in her head said.

It was Arthur's voice.

You irritate everyone you come across, from the library to the visitor center to the corner store. Did you think your students were going to become your <u>friends</u>? Please! The only friends you ever had were because of me. My friends took pity on you, and you tossed them aside, thinking it would be easy to start over someone place new.

But no one in Cherry Hill wants anything to do with you. Not even when you offer a free class.

The weird thing was, the real Arthur would never have spoken to her that way. She wasn't sure why he was doing so now. The real Arthur would have made her laugh. He'd have said something like, *Take comfort in the fact that it wasn't <u>your</u> lecture that turned Zeke somnolent.*

Above all, once they'd had a full accounting of her misadventure over a glass of red, he would've told her, "Chin up, Connie. You'll figure it out. Tomorrow is a new day."

But Arthur was dead, and there *was* no "real" Arthur. Their marriage had been a lie.

I guess that's why you scratched me out of the picture, the snide version of Arthur said. *A spinster, in Miss Marple jargon. Never married. Really, Connie?*

Because that's how it feels, she replied, and wiped away more tears.

Eventually, she stood on shaky legs and surveyed the damage in the mirror. She patted her hair, dabbed on a spot of under-eye makeup, and readjusted her bag. She wouldn't give Roberto the satisfaction of seeing her laid low as she made her way out of the library.

She barely registered the fact that snow was falling in a soft white blur, coating the library roof and surrounding desert plants. The cold air felt refreshing after the heated embarrassment of her class.

Her foot skidded on the sidewalk, and she almost fell. She must've left her cane in the community room. If Roberto saw her, so be it. It's not like she could feel any worse than she already did.

She trudged back inside and spotted the large, irritating head librarian in the community room, gathering her syllabi and tossing them in the recycle bin. To her surprise, he kept one and slid it inside his pocket.

She took a deep breath and walked over. "Have you seen my cane?"

"Yes," he replied gruffly. "I was about to put it in Lost & Found. Here."

"Thank you," she said, glad to have it back.

"I read your syllabus..." he began, and she braced herself for more insults.

But before Roberto could continue, Wesley, the handsome journalist, appeared. "Constance, I'm happy I caught up with you. May I interview you for the *Cherry Hill Gazette*?"

"Are you sure you want to?" she asked.

"Are you kidding? Most fun I've had all month. I'll promote the heck out of it. We'll double, nay, *triple* your head count."

She scanned his face and did not detect sarcasm.

"Well, okay," she said. "We have the room until one o'clock, after all."

Roberto frowned. "Technically I can say no since it's only two of you—"

"Step aside or I'll 'forget' to write about the Friends of the Library bag sale," Wesley said, and winked at Constance.

~

TWENTY MINUTES LATER, their interview complete, Constance felt hope stir in her chest. Maybe this was a sign, in the form of free publicity from a Byronic hero in ripped jeans, that there was life in the class yet. It wasn't over.

She and Wesley lingered inside the community room, chatting.

"Forgive me if this is blunt," Wesley said, "but most retirees of your stature would opt for Palm Springs. Like the song says, 'Cherry Hill, Cherry Hill, a place to get your fill…' *of gas*, so you can make it to Palm Springs from L.A."

"Main Street is looking a little shuttered," she admitted. *Where small businesses are killed.* She'd never be able to hear the trolley song again without remembering the protesters' version.

"Except for the cat cafe." He sounded bitter. "That's doing gangbusters. Who cares about the newsstand, right?"

Chase, the energetic assistant librarian, walked past, his straight blond hair pinned beneath a knit cap. He saw Constance and waved. "See you Wednesday, Gram."

She waved back. Chase gave the back of Wesley's head a significant look and pretended to fan himself from the searing heat of Wesley's existence. They grinned guiltily at each other.

"Who cares about news when you can have 'mews'?" Wesley ranted, oblivious.

Constance forced herself to frown in sympathy. No need to tell him she was excited about the cat cafe.

Perhaps a change of subject would help. "Between you and me, by which I mean it's off the record both professionally and personally—"

"Cone of silence," Wesley promised, and pantomimed zipping his lips. Then: "I don't know why I zipped my lips for the cone of silence." Face pink, he brought his hands up to his chin and splayed them out like a cone.

He'd gone from Byronic to awkward in a heartbeat, and she loved it. It made him more human.

"If I were forced to guess Penelope's Type, I would've said Three as well," Constance admitted. "The Achiever."

"Right? Thank you."

"To be clear, the world needs Threes. Riso calls them 'nature's movie stars.'"

"What does he call Fours? Nature's brat pack?" he joked. But there was pain in his eyes.

"The world also needs Fours, my dear," she said. "The Individualists are vital. How else would the rest of us access our emotions if we didn't have you paving the way so beautifully?"

He didn't look convinced. "Thanks for taking the time, Constance."

"It's me who should be thanking you."

"I'll run the article on Monday, and hopefully that'll draw new students for Wednesday."

Outside the library, they parted ways.

Constance lost herself in thought. How could she help Penelope attend the next class? She needed a reliable sitter. Maybe Constance could ask around. *Right. Because you know so many people here.*

Constance zipped up her new jacket, and strode across

Chaparral Street to the corner of Cherry Hill Boulevard and Main Street to wait for the trolley.

Oh. Wait. She couldn't possibly ride it after what happened this morning, could she? Assuming it was even running after the attack?

It was no longer parked outside Kaftans 'n' More with police tape circling it, so it must be trundling around somewhere. Unless it was getting serviced. The idea of boarding the trolley filled her with dread, but her cane was no match for the wet, icy hill that led home.

She looked around for Wesley, but he was long gone.

Okay, Connie. Think logically. Maybe it's better to ride it again as soon as possible, to normalize it. It was only a broken window. No one aimed at _you_. They were aiming at the loudspeaker.

As if in answer to her prayers, Sam-the-SAHM pulled over to the curb in a minivan and called out: "Are you waiting for the trolley? I wouldn't ride it if I were you. My husband, Will, rode it a few weeks ago for a holiday lights tour, and it broke down. He said the engine was a *disaster*." Sam flicked on her hazard lights. "Let me give you a ride. I won't charge you, ha ha."

Constance stared at Sam's minivan, her heart pounding. Something about it produced a visceral panic inside her. Flashes of memory tore through her brain. The clutter. The scratches on the side. The dented bumper. Sam's golden laugh, suddenly sinister.

She'd been inside that minivan. That's how she knew Sam. Sam was the terrifying Uber driver, the one Constance had employed once and never again.

"Oh! That's so kind of you, but I'll be fine. Not to worry."

As if in answer to a new, better prayer, the Jolly Trolley

turned the corner into view. Considering the cacophony that usually accompanied it, it was in stealth mode. No song, no tourism spiel blaring from the speaker.

It honked at Sam, who looked startled, but moved up so the trolley could park behind her.

Neither option was ideal, but the trolley was slower and therefore safer. It had to be. "I appreciate the offer, Sam, but I'm good. I'll see you Wednesday?"

"See you then." Sam looked oddly put out. "Don't say I didn't warn you."

Sam peeled away, and the noise of her screeching tires told Constance she'd made the right decision.

Isaac Caldecot, the elderly trolley driver, called to Constance. "What are you waiting for, young lady? Get out of the cold."

"I'm from New York," she quipped. "We eat snow-storms for breakfast." She strode inside, her insides twisting. *This is fine. This will be fine. Sit up front this time.*

"No functional damage from this morning, I hope?" she asked.

"Ha! This trolley has survived two wars. Takes more than a broken speaker to slow me down. My benefactor will have everything fixed by Monday," he said. "It'll be better than ever. You're going to love the changes."

Ah, yes. The mysterious benefactor, whose paperwork dump had reduced Martin to tears, and whose skills apparently included fixing broken windows and speakers 24/7.

Isaac hunched over the enormous steering wheel, gloved hands cradling it. "I'll be suing that unruly mob, of course."

They drove in silence toward her house, but it was companionable. The trolley creaked and groaned in the cold white air. Wind whistled through the missing windowpane several rows back. If the speaker hadn't been broken, the tourism recording would be bragging about the Upside-down House at this point.

She knew she couldn't accept free rides anymore, no matter what Isaac said.

Starting Monday, she'd buy a pass and pay full price. That should rid her of her guilt.

After depositing Constance outside her house on Hill Street, the trolley backed up and pointed itself in the right direction to head down the hill.

From the corner of her eye, Constance saw it lurch.

Something was wrong.

She could only gape as the trolley careened down the hill, crashed into the tamarisk tree at the intersection of Cherry Hill Boulevard and Lone Tree Lane, and exploded.

7

───────

CONSTANCE

SHE SCREAMED and dropped her bag. It opened, and the cat food cans rolled out, dented from the fall. She unlocked her phone with cold, wet fingers and called 911. She wanted to run down the hill and see if there was anything she could do to help, but she was afraid she would crack her head open, and she didn't want to get too close to the fire.

As explosions go, it was minor. There and gone, a burst of a fireball, but the fact that it happened so soon after Constance exited the trolley twisted her gut into knots.

Fire trucks arrived within minutes, sirens blaring. Numb, Constance stared as the firefighters doused the flames and extracted Isaac Caldecot from the vehicle, laying him on a stretcher and loading him into the back of the emergency truck. Everything happened in slow motion, just like it had that morning when the rock shattered the trolley window so close to her head.

How long ago that seemed now, and how comparatively harmless.

Haze filled the air. Her eyes watered and her nose

burned from the smell of burning metal and rubber. She could just make out the trolley's crumpled form through the smoke. It looked as dented as her cans of cat food.

The tamarisk tree was badly damaged, too. It was a fire hazard, she recalled from old protest signs. And here was the proof.

Three sheriff's vehicles pulled up and blocked off the scene, and various figures in protective gear took photos and collected samples.

She couldn't say how much time passed while she waited to be seen, observing it all at the top of the hill. She didn't want to distract anyone from their crucial activity. She sensed—she knew somehow—the driver was dead.

He'd called her young lady. He'd been prickly every other time she'd encountered him, but today he'd bantered with her. They'd been through an attack together, but he'd carried on as though it were nothing, and spoken optimistically about the future. *"You're going to love the changes."*

She couldn't move her legs. All she could do was stare into the distance.

"Rao?" came a voice from the catio. Constance came back to herself, blinked, and unlocked the courtyard gate. The cold hit her again with the force and weight of a snowplow. She scooped up Mr. Cinnamon, taking comfort in his purring warmth. Ever since that rainy Sunday morning a year earlier, he'd been her rock, and she felt a burst of gratitude to have him in her life. She cuddled him close and bustled them inside the house.

"Oh, my goodness." The cabinet beneath the kitchen sink was open, Mr. Cinnamon's bag of beloved crunchies torn open, the pebbles scattered across the floor and under the fridge.

Mr. Cinnamon struggled to be let down, then strolled

with great dignity through the mess, his feet flicking to dislodge the pieces stuck to his paws. He stopped and looked up at her, as if to say *Can you believe this? Who would do such a thing?*

"Rao?" he repeated.

"Yes, I saw. Those were meant to last you a month. If you're not too full, I have your wet food here. Don't mind the dents."

"Rao."

By the time the sheriff knocked on her door an hour later, she'd swept the kitchen and placed the crunchies in a higher cabinet. Mr. Cinnamon stretched out beside her on the couch, on the verge of dosing while she stroked his back. He rarely sat still for long, but perhaps he sensed she could use a friend.

Really, who else did she need?

Humans were overrated.

8

CONSTANCE

SHERIFF IAN PITTMAN was a man who seemed to embody the middle of things, any way you sliced him. He was middle aged (she put him at mid 50s), middle height (not much taller than Constance, who stood 5'8"), middle bellied (neither fit nor fat), and middle speed (he didn't plod, but he wasn't quick). His face was clean-shaven, and he wore a Stetson hat with a sheriff star affixed to it. Watching him made Constance feel as though she'd entered a 1960s TV show against her will.

He squinted at Mr. Cinnamon, flung around her neck now like a stole. "Is that a fox?"

"He's a Somali mix cat. Somalis are genetically identical to Abyssinians, but with fluffier fur from a recessive gene."

"Beautiful creature." He reached out a gentle hand to give Mr. Cinnamon a pat. Her cat didn't stir. Constance wished she could join Mr. Cinnamon in sleep, wake up again, and discover that today had been a horrible dream.

"My wife nursed one back to health when she was a child," said the sheriff. "A fox, that is, not a Somali mix. She said it was incredibly loud. Which I wouldn't have suspected. Of course, she had to let it go; they don't make good pets. Illegal, as well."

Constance recalled an article in the *Cherry Hill Gazette* last Thanksgiving, about an escaped turkey wandering Chaparral Street outside the civic center. It had taken Sheriff Pittman and two of his deputies six hours to catch it. Perhaps he should have deputized his wife to help, since she had luck with wild animals.

"May I offer you a coffee?"

He demurred, stating that caffeine gave him stomach cramps. He preferred to use sunshine to start his day rather than a cortisol-depriving substance.

"We've been short on sunshine lately," she pointed out. "Offer stands if you change your mind."

"I won't." His demeanor shifted. "I hate to disturb your fox-cat here when he looks so content, but I think it would be best if I took your statement down at the station."

She stiffened. "Why?"

"I thought you could sign your statement from this morning. Two birds, one stone."

❧

THEY TOOK a circuitous route that gave the crash site a wide berth.

As they pulled into the parking lot, sandwiched between the library and the courthouse, and traversed the outdoor walkway into the Sheriff's Station, Constance couldn't help picturing the turkey's glorious bid for freedom. Had it hidden in the succulents? Had it flapped at its pursuers, gobble-gobbling? She smiled at the absurd image, then berated herself. *Who would smile at a time like this? What is wrong with you?*

An acrid, chemical scent filled her nostrils. Was it her? Did she smell like the crash? Would it be part of her from this day on?

Sheriff Pittman saw her standing stock still beside the desert plants and came back to speak with her. "It's the creosote bushes," he explained gently. "They smell like petroleum after it rains."

"Oh."

Inside the station hallway, Sheriff Pittman was joined by two deputies: tall, gangly Max "Double Worse" Evert, son of Jenna Evert (the visitor center proprietor) and a shorter female deputy whose tidy box braids were pinned back from her round, pretty face. Her nametag read Regina Cole.

"Now it's my turn to ask: would you like a coffee?" the sheriff inquired.

"Yes, please."

It was one level above sludge, but the warmth of the mug felt good in her hands. She took a few sips and tried not to let her expression reveal how nasty it was. No wonder Sheriff Pittman didn't drink it if he thought *this* was coffee.

After being led into a private room, Constance was disturbed to learn Deputy Max would be taking her statement again, as he had that morning when he'd made his dislike of her clear. Would Deputy Regina Cole have been more sympathetic? Too late. She was gone.

Deputy Max positioned a video camera on a tripod, angled it toward Constance, and hit "record." Sheriff Pittman observed them from the corner of the room, as though overseeing a training exercise.

"We meet again," Max said. "State your full name."

"It's the same as it was this morning, as are my occupation and address."

"You were the last person to interact with the driver before his death, were you not?"

She didn't like how that sounded. "I suppose so."

"The only reason it was running at all, in fact, was for you. Is that safe to say?"

"Well, no, I wouldn't put it that way."

"I would."

"Max," Sheriff Pittman said. Not a warning, exactly. A re-set.

"Stricken," said Max loudly, and leaned into frame so the camera would see him nod in a business-like manner.

"You're not in court," said Constance. "It's not stricken. You said it, and it's being recorded. You can't edit these things. That's tampering with a witness statement."

"Please answer his question," Sheriff Pittman said from the corner.

"What was the question?"

"The only reason it was running was for you, is that accurate?" Max repeated.

Constance felt waves of guilt wash over her. "No," she bristled. "I mean, yes, at that moment, before the—before the crash. But it had another passenger earlier in the day, remember?"

"The so-called man with the envelope, whomst no one else saw, and whomst's identity remains a mystery to you? That one?"

"'Whomst's' isn't—never mind. Yes. He had a scruffy beard, and he wore shorts and sunglasses. I have no idea who he was."

Max's eyes were full of fire. "You said this morning that he exited right away. He didn't ride it. So that's not a passenger, is it? *You* were the only passenger *all day*, isn't that right?"

She took a calming breath. "It's my understanding that it drives the route regardless. Isn't that why there was a protest? It's always blocking traffic?"

"You don't need to speculate about why there was a protest," Sheriff Pittman said.

"Yeah," said Max. "Maybe it was because you won't open the Upside-Down House."

"Max," Pittman growled. This time it *was* a warning.

Constance cut to the chase. "The driver..." Her eyes filled with tears. "He... he called me young lady, and he kindly... picked me up in the bad weather, and dropped me off outside my house, and then... he... he..."

Sheriff Pittman brought her a handkerchief. The action fit with his old-school demeanor and snapped her out of her tears. "I saw it swerve down the hill, crash into the tree, and catch fire. I immediately called 911."

She remembered sputtering, "It went boom. It just went boom!" like a dumbfounded child. She hoped she would never be in a position to hear that call.

The door swung open, and Deputy Regina Cole walked in, carrying a tape deck.

Oh, no.

Deputy Cole addressed the camera. "This is a recording of Constance Kincaid's emergency call. It perplexed us, and we are seeking clarification."

"That's right," Sheriff Pittman said. He motioned for Max to get up so he could replace Max across from Constance.

The real interview had begun.

Pittman hit play on the recording. The Constance of two hours ago made an idiot of herself. "Boom," etc.

"What went boom?" the dispatcher asked.

"The Jolley Trolley!"

And then, to Constance's surprise, her voice continued: "It wasn't a philosophical exercise. No one was forced to choose from a spectrum of terrible outcomes. There weren't two tracks with five people versus one. It was just me and the driver. And it's real!"

Sheriff Pittman paused the recording. "What were you babbling about there?"

"Honestly, I don't remember saying it."

Sheriff Pittman waited, no expression on his face.

"The Trolley Problem," she said slowly, "is a theoretical conundrum whereupon you're asked to decide what would be worse, one death or multiple deaths."

"One death or multiple deaths?" His eyes were wide. "Who's deciding? You?"

"No! Not me. 'You.'"

"*Me?*"

"Not you-you; the people studying the trolley problem." She tried again. "There's a runaway trolley, and it's going to hit five people unless you divert it to a different track where there's only one person."

"I'll ask again. *Who decided* the Jolly Trolley would be involved in one or multiple deaths?"

"No one! It's — it's not real."

He rewound the recording and hit play. The Constance of two hours ago bleated, "And it's real!"

The Constance of now tried to explain. "I was pre-empting the 911 operator asking me if I was referring to the Trolley Problem, uppercase philosophical exercise."

"I can't follow a word of what you're saying." Sheriff Pittman turned to Max. "Are you following this?"

"I think she's guilty of something," Max said. "I just don't know what. Yet."

"I think she was, and continues to be, in shock," Deputy Cole said.

Sheriff Pittman turned back to Constance. "Is that what it is? Shock?"

"Yes." *At least this time I didn't quote John Le Carre during a funeral service and then skip town.*

Sheriff Pittman stood, hands on the table. "Don't make any plans to leave Cherry Hill."

"I can't." She teared up again. "I don't drive. The trolley was my only form of transportation."

PART 2

9
____

WESLEY

WESLEY HOLLOWAY KNEW THE TRUTH.

Constance could say whatever she wanted about none of the personality types being worse than the others, but that was a lie.

It had been excruciating to discover he was a Type Four. The Tortured Romantic. Sorry, *the Individualist.* Well, apparently not individual enough. Apparently, his worldview was so *commonplace* that it fit a *type.*

It was as though someone had opened his brain, looked inside, and concluded, "You're not special, even in a bad way. Did you really think you were?" Cue the sarcastic laughter.

Maybe it should have been comforting to discover he wasn't alone, but it wasn't. Because if he wasn't different, if he wasn't set apart in some way, what was the *point* of him?

Type Five, the Observer, *should* have fit him. He was an investigative journalist, or at least he used to be, back in Seattle. But that was three years ago. Now he was a hack managing editor and staff writer for the *Cherry Hill Gazette,* and the only things he observed were street closures, store openings, high school sporting events, and city council meetings. Oh, and once, last Thanksgiving, a slapstick comedy starring an escaped turkey.

But he knew in his mangled heart he wasn't a Type Five. The problem was his *feelings*. Fives could dissociate from those (lucky Fives), whereas feelings were all Wesley had.

So, yeah. He was a Type Four. The Individualist.

The Fool Who Thought He Was Different.

The Worst One.

He liked Constance, though. She was a high-functioning weirdo, like him. For example, she was pretending she'd never been married, but a basic search revealed she'd run a law firm with her late husband. Curious.

After interviewing her, he'd headed home to type up his notes and put the finishing touches on his other article: Thursday's surprisingly packed city council meeting. The topic? A petition to get rid of the Jolly Trolley. Good luck to them—it was the cockroach of Cherry Hill.

A knock on his apartment door nearly made him spill his coffee. The freak weather had inspired cozy-wear; upon arriving home he'd changed into pajama pants and a concert T-shirt. He pulled on a wrinkled button-down from his laundry basket before answering the door.

Sheriff Pittman stood in the hallway of Wesley's eight-unit apartment building, trailed by his deputies, Max Evert and Regina Cole. Wesley interacted occasionally with Sheriff Pittman during press conferences. He knew the sheriff as a slow-moving but meticulous man.

Max was neither of those things; all bluster, he was a regular on the pickleball court and questioned every call not in his favor. Deputy Cole was quieter, with a sometimes-impatient intelligence. Before its renovation, she organized an African diaspora film festival at the art deco theatre.

"May we come in?" the sheriff asked, hat in hand like a Turner Classic Movies lawman. His temples were gray, and his face looked more creased than Wesley remembered it being. To be fair, the lighting of Aunt Nora's apartment did nobody any favors.

"Of course, sorry. I wasn't expecting anyone." Wesley tried to kick his overflowing laundry basket to the side. He kicked too hard, and it toppled over, spilling boxer shorts on the carpet, which he then kicked individually under the couch. It took several lifetimes.

Dying inside, he backed up as the deputies walked around his dirty clothing to join him at the kitchen island.

"There's been an accident," the sheriff said.

Wesley's heart pounded, and he thought, "Please not Aunt Nora" until he remembered she was already gone, gone from cancer, not an accident, and he had inherited the very apartment everyone was crammed into.

"The Jolly Trolley crashed into the tamarisk tree," Pittman said matter-of-factly, "and shortly thereafter exploded."

Wesley's hand flew to his mouth.

He hadn't heard sirens earlier, but that wasn't surprising; he listened to loud music when he wrote.

"The driver, Isaac Caldecot, didn't survive," Sheriff Pittman told Wesley. "We're waiting for the medical examiner's report, as well as the arson investigator's. Could be as simple as icy road conditions, and wear and tear on the vehicle, but—"

"We have reason to suspect someone tampered with the engine," Max blurted out.

Deputy Cole blinked in irritation at her colleague's lack of discretion.

"Nothing's confirmed," Sheriff Pittman said, with a sideways glance at Max.

"But you think it was deliberate?" Wesley asked, shocked.

"You know those fabric scissors?" Max leaned in. "The ones that have zig-zag teeth?"

"Pinking shears?" Wesley asked. Aunt Nora had had a pair in her sewing kit.

"Yep. We think someone used those to cut a bunch of wires," Max added importantly.

"We don't think anything yet," Pittman reiterated.

Wesley stumbled backward and sat on the arm of his couch. What a horrible shock to the Caldecot family—including Mayor Trudy Caldecot, Aunt Nora's best friend.

After the driver's barnstorming taunts at Thursday night's city council meeting, not to mention the protest earlier today, Wesley knew anger had been mounting toward the driver, but... murder? In Cherry Hill?

Sheriff Pittman continued, "We understand things got heated at Thursday's city council meeting, and since you were there, we'd like your impressions as a reporter."

"I just finished my article. I'll print it for you."

"Any contemporaneous documentation?" Deputy Cole asked.

Wesley froze. "My notes, you mean?"

"Yes, they might show something that didn't make it into the article. Is that a problem?"

Wesley had given rude nicknames to the business owners of Main Street to save time (and stave off boredom) when he'd jotted notes during the meeting. "Oh. Well, I use my own, uh, shorthand that I developed, but I could give you a cleaned-up, typed version."

The sheriff ignored his squirming. "No, we'd prefer the original."

Wesley tore the sheets from his steno pad and handed them over. His stomach hurt.

"For now," said the sheriff, "can you give us a, whaddayacallit, overview? Anything that stood out at the meeting."

"Yeah. For one thing, it was packed, which was unusual. Everyone who got up to speak was furious at the trolley for blocking access to Main Street. The chamber of commerce wanted to file a motion forcing the trolley to retire, but were denied. The mayor gave a speech about how we needed to work together to save Main Street, instead of suing and protesting each other all the time. She stressed the historical importance of the trolley and urged everyone to be patient while the art deco theatre, botanical gardens, and Upsidedown House were fixed, renovated, or re-opened, and that the trolley's importance would become clear once the places it served were up and running again. She also urged the business owners to consider purchasing parking spaces at the Vitality Hotel and Spa and validating tickets for their customers, at which point multiple business owners accused the Vitality of price gauging. Apparently, for each week that they don't buy spaces, the price goes up."

"Did Mr. Caldecot, the Vitality Hotel, or representatives for either of them, respond to these assertions?" Sheriff Pittman asked.

"No one from the hotel attended, but Isaac Caldecot seemed to relish the fight. He said he had no intention of retiring, no intention of altering his route, and no intention of speeding up. He said, quote, 'Stop being cheapskates and pay for parking, because I'm not going anywhere, and I'll outlive you all.'" Wesley paused to let that sink in. "I almost believed him."

"Is there an heir to the Jolly Trolley?" Deputy Cole asked.

"Besides the mayor? She's his grandniece, but she has no interest in the trolley," Wesley said.

Sheriff Pittman nodded again. He placed Wesley's steno pages in a file folder. "We'll call if we have further questions. Thank you, Wesley."

"I'd better get to the crash site," Wesley said, his mind racing.

The Associated Press might want to purchase his story. It had quirky, sensational, small-town mystery written all over it. Everyone in town would buy a copy—it could boost *Gazette* sales and make up for the newsstand's closure, at least for a few weeks.

But then, the dreaded words came. The Scoop Killer.

"Go ahead and write about the crash, but don't mention suspicious circumstances," Sheriff Pittman said. "We've got a lot of people to talk to, and we don't want them tipped off beforehand about the nature of the investigation."

Seeing Wesley deflate, the sheriff added, "Hold off for a few days. After that, I'll give you a, whaddayacallit, exclusive."

Considering the *Cherry Hill Gazette* was the only paper in town, an exclusive wasn't the treat the sheriff seemed to think it was. Still, better to get the facts straight than race to print something inaccurate.

He could still tackle the mystery in the meantime. Deputy Max's loose lips had already proven useful. If sewing scissors were used, did that mean a woman had tampered with the engine, or did that mean a man had, hoping for gendered assumptions?

After everyone left, Wesley ditched his pajamas for real clothes and headed out the door.

10

———

WESLEY

WESLEY ARRIVED early to work on Monday.

The *Gazette* sat between a pawn shop and a private gym. As with most institutions in Cherry Hill, it was a family legacy. Editor-in-Chief Theodore Reilly III had spread his wings as a war correspondent for the *Washington Post* in the 2000s, but family loyalty pulled him home to take over after his father passed away. Reilly had overseen the *Cherry Hill Gazette* for two decades and had kept it solvent against all odds.

Despite his brusque demeanor, Reilly favored feel-good articles. He wasn't naïve—his years covering conflict zones dispelled that notion—but his view regarding the *Gazette* was that you could find any number of horrific stories online or in a large city paper; for a print edition on your porch, why not emphasize *good* things?

The *Gazette* consisted of three reporters (including Wesley), one managing editor (also Wesley), one editor-in-chief, one circulation manager, one business manager, and one sales manager. The sales manager had left a year ago, forcing Reilly to fulfill that role.

Wesley unlocked the back door and strode past the break room into the Town Square, as Reilly called it, an open floor plan without walls or cubicles, just three large tables housing laptops and printers. Everyone on staff sat together because according to Reilly, a lack of artificial boundaries encouraged communication between departments.

Reilly himself had a private office, but he often circulated to give advice or hop on a laptop to edit.

Considering it was barely seven, Wesley was surprised to see lights on in Reilly's office. He hadn't expected to see anyone until nine, but then again, murder changed everything.

He cracked his knuckles and logged onto the archives. Late last night, he'd remembered an angry letter to the editor that might be relevant. It was dated six months ago.

To Whom it May Concern:

As a local businessperson of Cherry Hill, I have requested multiple times that the tourist trolley ("The Jolly Trolley") retire. My reasons are fourfold:

1. It's needlessly large, the size of a city bus. It blocks customer traffic and street parking on Main Street.

2. It's an environmental menace, puffing out exhaust as it lurches around town, as well as a sound polluter with its incessant tourism recording and jingle.

3. It is both slow and cumbersome. Isaac Caldecot drives 15 mph so that nonexistent visitors can leisurely enjoy the sights. But what about those of us who live and work here year-round?

Are we to be at the trolley's mercy till the end of our days?

4. It's a financial black hole, and its devastating impact on local businesses cannot be overstated. Layoffs and store closings are imminent.

I submit that the Jolly Trolley commit to ALL the following upgrades and modernizations:

A. Alter its route to exclude Main Street during business hours.

B. Replace its current diesel engine with solar panels.

C. TURN OFF THE SONG or provide it strictly via headphones.

D. Speed up!!!

As you can see, I have provided concrete, actionable advice. Mr. Caldecot is fully aware of these issues yet has done nothing to address them. It's not right.

If my concerns cannot be resolved in a just manner, I will be forced to take action.

Sincerely,

A Concerned Business Owner of Main Street

Wesley copied the link and sent it to Sheriff Pittman, then left voice messages with Martin Onder of Kaftans 'n' More, Ana Whitley of the Hummingbird Art Gallery, Danny Flores of Texican Table, Krista Locke at the Cut & Dried Hair Salon, and Aidan Zachary of Dune Buggies, U.S.A. asking them to contact him.

Aidan was the first person to call back, via FaceTime.

"Hi, Wesley, what can I do for you?"

Aidan was younger than Wesley but twice as burly. He

had acres of muscles crammed into his suit and tie, but unlike the arrogant jocks Wesley had known in high school, Aidan's demeanor was that of a friendly, diligent quarterback who said hi to everyone.

"Sorry to bother you so early, but I found a letter in our archives, and I wondered if you knew who wrote it. I'll share my screen with you."

Aidan took a moment to read. "I haven't seen it before." He seemed to realize that meant he didn't subscribe to the paper and quickly added, "That is, I don't remember seeing it before. But I know the chamber of commerce filed a lawsuit, so you might start there. 'Forced to take action' could refer to that."

Wesley recalled something cub reporter Shawna had told him about the protest. "I hear you calmed things down on Saturday with the trolley?"

Aidan looked uncomfortable. "I wish I hadn't had to. If I'd known things would escalate, I wouldn't have let them use my office. Anyway, whoever wrote this letter didn't loop me in. Cut and Dried is the only place that hasn't taken a financial hit, so it could be anyone."

"Haircuts are the only thing you can't do virtually, or order online," said Wesley.

"Same with dune buggy rides, thankfully. My office on Main Street is strictly admin, so the trolley didn't affect my bottom line, but lots of people were hurting."

"Did you see who threw the rock?"

Aidan paused, as though struggling to remember. Wesley wasn't buying it. "No, I didn't. Did the other reporter get her camera fixed?"

"Not yet. She's working on it, though."

"Maybe she caught something, or someone, on film without realizing it."

"Could be. Thanks for your time, Aidan." *Liar*, he added silently.

"Oh! I just thought of something," said Aidan. "The cat cafe couldn't have written the letter, either. They weren't here six months ago, and they bought into the hotel's parking scheme, so the trolley hasn't prevented her customers from accessing the cafe. You can cross her off the list."

Wesley already had, thanks to the same reasoning, but as far as he was concerned, the cat cafe was guilty of its own crime: murder of a newsstand.

"You called it a parking 'scheme'," Wesley pointed out. "Why 'scheme'?"

Aidan laughed darkly. "The Vitality Hotel and Spa is shaking everyone down for spaces they can't afford."

Wesley thanked him again and printed the angry letter to study further. He liked tactile evidence, and reading a paper copy gave him a break from his screen.

As the noise from the printer stopped, raised voices erupted behind Reilly's door, right before the door flew open and slammed into the wall.

Martin Onder, the normally affable owner of Kaftans 'n' More, stormed out of Reilly's office and out of the building.

Wesley had never seen Martin so angry. He wasn't quick enough to chase Martin down and ask him about the letter, but maybe that was for the best. He should talk to Reilly first and find out why Martin was so upset.

He strode to Reilly's door. "Knock, knock."

"Come in," Reilly said. The older man looked tired. He was pushing sixty, and no longer smoked or drank, but both vices had taken a toll on him earlier in life.

On his desk sat an open takeout container from Texican Table, the Tex-Mex restaurant on Main Street. A mouthwatering aroma of fried corn tortillas, salsa, eggs, shredded chicken, and cheese tantalized Wesley's senses. The protein bar he'd inhaled earlier was a joke compared with this.

"You got chilaquiles?" he moaned. "How? That's so unfair."

Budget cuts at the restaurant meant they only served dinner, but apparently if you were old friends with the Flores family like Reilly was, breakfast still came your way.

Restauranteur Danny Flores, nee Smith, had taken his wife's last name when they married, which Wesley had admired until the cashier at Kaftans 'n' More, Olivia Flores, told Wesley it was a stone-cold business decision to underscore the authenticity of the Mex side of the establishment.

"Can I carve off a piece?" Wesley begged.

Reilly didn't answer. He looked shaken.

Wesley tried to ignore the fresh breakfast. "What did Martin want?"

"He's worried the lawsuit and your city council meeting write-up—nice job on that, by the way—makes him a prime suspect."

"*Should* he be worried?"

"He wanted to know if we could help him mount a defense. I told him we didn't know anything—"

"Or at least nothing we can talk about because of the Sheriff's moratorium—"

"—and he accused me of lying. I hate this. Like the town's not divided enough already."

"Maybe if we shine a light on everything," Wesley said earnestly, "people will learn to trust one another again."

Reilly took a bite of food. "I thought you didn't get up before nine. Don't you need your beauty sleep?"

"Ha. Guess we both got up early. Doesn't seem right

that *one* of us ate chemicals and *one* of us got the world's best chilaquiles for their trouble, though, does it?"

Wesley's phone buzzed. Seeing Mayor Trudy Caldecot's name on the caller ID brought a smile to his face. He had fond memories of hanging out with Trudy as a kid during those summers he spent in Cherry Hill visiting Aunt Nora.

"I should take this. It's the mayor returning my call."

"Let me guess," said Reilly. "She wants to put her own spin on the trolley killing. 'Freak accident, all is well, this certainly doesn't reflect badly on the mayor, even though I've kept the trolley shielded from consequences all these years.'"

Wesley's eyes widened. It wasn't like Reilly to be that cynical. Or at least not out loud.

"Everyone wants to control the press," Reilly lamented.

"Well, the trolley driver *is* her great uncle. I figured a personal angle to the death was warranted. And she's like family to me, so..."

Reilly rubbed his eyes. "Sorry. I shouldn't have bad-mouthed her."

"Hi, Trudy," Wesley said into his phone. "I'm in the newsroom, and you're on speaker. I'm so sorry for your loss."

"Thanks, kiddo."

Wesley cringed. It was another reason to dislike living in Cherry Hill: everyone knew him as a child.

Trudy asked to meet for coffee. "How about CHATeau Savannah, the new cat cafe? I'm here now for a photo op."

"I will *never* step foot in that newsstand-destroying *abomination*," Wesley swore.

"He'll be there in ten," said Reilly.

The world went cold. "Just a moment, please, Trudy."

Wesley muted his phone. "Weird time to crack a joke, but okay."

"No joke. You're profiling the cafe. That's your next assignment."

"You're asking me to celebrate our own demise?"

"I'm not thrilled about it taking over the newsstand either, but we need to highlight local businesses, so they'll subscribe in the hopes of being mentioned. It's the only way to survive."

Wesley raked a hand through his hair. "There's a murderer on the loose, and you assigned me a literal fluff piece."

"The purpose of this paper isn't in one big shocking event," Reilly told him. "It's in the day to day."

"I think you mean the Monday, Wednesday, Friday," Wesley snapped, referring to their print schedule.

Reilly chewed his food and stared at Wesley, who apologized, knowing he'd gone too far.

"Day-to-day stories make this paper, and this town, worth something," Reilly opined. "We're a community here, and the paper should reflect and reinforce that."

"But—"

Reilly snatched Wesley's phone and unmuted it. "Save him a seat."

11

WESLEY

WESLEY SKIDDED into an empty spot in front of CHATeau Savannah, sending a wave of water up the curb.

Mayor Trudy Caldecot waited for him at a window booth, two coffees in hand. She raised one to him in a "cheers" motion, and gifted him a genuine smile, not the political facsimile.

Getting to her proved cumbersome.

First, he had to hang out in a holding area that served as an extra protection for the cats. Before the second door could open, the first door had to be deadbolted, and Wesley had to convince the "bouncer" (fine, the host) that he was cat-worthy. No, he didn't have a reservation. Yes, he was here to meet with the mayor. No, he wasn't looking to adopt any cats, but if he were, he understood bonded pairs must stay together. Yes, he would sign an allergy waiver. No, he didn't want to purchase a bag of treats. Yes, he would treat the cats with respect and not move them around.

At last, he was granted entrance. To his annoyance, the place was clean, airy, and bright, with tall ceilings and exposed beams. Tables and chairs were scattered throughout the warehouse-like space, but most of the room was filled with cat beds, scratching posts/climbing apparatuses, blanketed banquettes for humans and felines to lounge upon, and couches covered in pillows and cat toys. T-shirts and tote bags for purchase hung on the interior brick wall, featuring the CHATeau Savannah logo: a cartoon image of an African wildcat wearing a French beret and sipping Italian espresso. There was a lot of cultural confusion going on, but he guessed French was the dominant theme, given the blue-and-white striped awning out front and the name of the establishment (*chat* meaning cat, *chateau* meaning house or castle).

Several tabbies, a black-and-white kitten, a large gray Ragdoll, and a few other sizes and breeds of feline took notice of Wesley's arrival. The black-and-white kitten tried to climb his leg, but he ignored it and focused on Trudy.

"Hey." He opened his arms, and she walked into his hug. He couldn't help thinking of his aunt and long-ago evenings sitting on the couch between Nora and Trudy as a kid, watching movies during his summer visits.

Wesley asked how she was doing.

"Not great, but I take comfort in the fact that Isaac died doing what he loved, and that he had a long, rich life."

"Yes. That's good to remember. Sorry I'm dressed like this."

Trudy wore her usual uniform of tailored pantsuit, and he felt self-conscious next to her, in his tattered baseball cap and equally worn jeans. He had never gotten around to doing his laundry after the sheriff's visit on Sunday.

"Whatever. You're gorgeous and you know it," Trudy teased him. "Although you're certainly trying to cover it up today."

People had been telling him that he was good-looking,

either with their words or their eyes, his entire life. Try complaining about it, though. No one wanted to hear it! And yet, it *was* a problem. He'd once had a woman on a blind date take out her phone, snap a picture of him, and text it to her friends with the drool emoji before they'd even said hello.

Maybe Trudy was on to something. Maybe he should dress poorly on purpose so people would notice *that* instead.

"Isn't this place darling?" Mayor Trudy gushed. But then, she would say that. She always wore a calico cat necklace, something to do with the Caldecot family crest. "Each ticket comes with a drink included." Trudy indicated a tortoiseshell cat on the window ledge. "Doesn't she remind you of Goldie?"

Wesley didn't like to think about Goldie.

Along with his aunt's apartment, he'd inherited his aunt's cat, Goldie, when Nora died. The cat was arthritic and elderly. He'd cried like a baby when Goldie passed away, six months after Nora. He'd cried like the world was ending.

"They opened early for me, so we have the place to ourselves," the mayor said.

"Amazing," he said dryly. "Do they sell dewormers with the coffee cream?"

"Our kitties are all dewormed, vaccinated, chipped, tested for feline leukemia, and sweet as can be," said a voice.

Wesley looked up. The voice belonged to a Korean American woman in her early thirties, with cat's eye glasses (har), and a sleek bobbed haircut that swished when she talked. She wore black cigarette pants, a striped t-shirt (underlying the French milieu), and an apron with the restaurant logo on the front. Her movements were quick, despite the medical boot on her foot.

"Hi, I'm Crystal Bae, and I'll be taking care of you today. What can I do to make your stay as purr-fect as possible?"

"They make you say that, don't they, Crystal?" he asked in a low voice. "Are you here against your will? Blink once for yes, twice for no."

Crystal's smile had a clenched, deadly edge. "I'm the owner of CHATeau Savannah, and I approve all cat-related puns."

"Oh. I'll cut to the chase, then. Do you think it's sanitary to have cats in a restaurant?"

"We don't have a kitchen on-site," Crystal replied in clipped tones. "We outsource our menu items from the Vitality Hotel and Spa across the street."

"Got it. Well, that was my main question. Enough for a paragraph on page twelve, don't you think?" he asked Trudy.

"What my friend's rude nephew is trying to say is that he'd love to interview you for the *Cherry Hill Gazette*," Trudy told Crystal.

Crystal stared at Wesley. "Is that right?"

"Yes," he mumbled.

Crystal folded her arms. "Well? Say it, then."

He glanced nervously at Trudy, then back at Crystal. "Say...?"

"*Say you'd love to.*" Crystal's voice was steel.

Wesley cleared his throat. "I'd, uh, love to interview you, if you could spare a few minutes after my meeting with the mayor."

Crystal's expression didn't waver. Wesley's heart pounded.

She made him wait.

And wait.

Dominance established, she shrugged. "Fine."

"Actually, why don't you do the interview now, so you don't cut into her business hours," Trude suggested. "You open in twenty minutes, right?"

"Yes," said Crystal. "I appreciate that because we're booked solid."

Wesley couldn't stand her gloating. "Do you know what this place used to be?"

"A failing newsstand in a perfect corner location that hadn't paid its rent for a year and a half?"

"Where are people supposed to buy the paper now?" he asked. "The newsstand made up sixty percent of our non-subscriber sales."

"That sounds like a you-problem."

"Are you aware the Vitality Hotel and Spa is pressuring every business on Main Street to buy parking spaces? Yet somehow you evaded that. Why is that?"

She looked perplexed. "They gave me free spaces because I'm providing another location to sell their coffee. Look, we're wasting time. There's someone you need to meet."

Crystal pulled out a whistle from her striped cotton T-shirt and blew twice.

"OH MY GOD." Wesley almost jumped out of his skin. An enormous, sleek cat with a harness and leash dragging on the floor behind it sauntered into sight. It was the wildcat from the store logo, in the flesh. Er, fur.

"Meet Savannah." Crystal unhooked the leash and cooed at the creature.

Wesley could scarcely hear her. His eyes were glued to the beast. It was as long and athletic-looking as a mini-cheetah, but instead of small round ears, it had large triangular ones that stood up tall from its body.

The "cat" approached Wesley, circling and sniffing him, and butted its head against his shin.

Crystal looked surprised. "Huh. She likes you. It usually takes her a while to warm up to people."

"Cats always love him," Trudy explained. "They can sense his indifference. His aunt, my best friend, had a cat named Goldie—"

"We don't need to talk about Goldie," Wesley said quickly.

The beast rubbing against his legs was long, lean, and deadly. He fought the urge to flail his legs and startle it away.

"She's stunning," said Mayor Trudy. "What is she?"

"A Savannah," said Crystal proudly. "They're a cross between a serval and a domestic. Our best guess is she's an F4, which means 'filial generation' or four generations removed from a serval."

"Wait, she's a Savannah named Savannah?" Wesley asked. "Kind of lazy, don't you think?"

"That was her name when I rescued her, and I didn't want to confuse her." Crystal rubbed the cat's cheeks. "She's a year old, she loves to play, and she loves to be walked on her leash."

"In other words, all the pain of owning a dog, but in a feral cat that could turn on you at any moment."

"She's not feral and she's not going to turn on me! Again, she's an F4 rescue, and she's a sweetheart. CHATeau Savannah partners with local shelters to save lives. Savannah's the star attraction of my cafe, but all the other cats are available for adoption. I'll never say goodbye to my sweetie, though. She's staying with me, forever and ever, aren't you, sweet girl?" Crystal blathered on.

She stroked Savannah's chin, and the cat's purr reverberated through the cafe. Wesley had never heard a more menacing sound. His breath caught in his throat when Savannah jumped onto his lap and began kneading his thighs.

It could go for his throat at any second.

And then—it did. The cat stretched its enormous neck upward to nibble and nuzzle his neck. It didn't hurt, but it felt weird, and Wesley froze in place.

"We think she was weaned too early by her abusive previous owner," Crystal explained, as though he cared *why* the cat was slurping him. "It comforts her to suckle."

Wesley's breath came out in anxious puffs. "You get how this is terrifying, right?"

Crystal took pity on him and threw a toy into a far corner of the cafe. The wildcat launched itself off Wesley in a spectacular leap. He dabbed at his neck with a branded napkin. "Do I have a hickey?"

"Savvy's attention would flatter most people," Crystal said. "Ask Trevor. He'll tell you."

She jerked her thumb toward the back, where another customer sat, holding the gray Ragdoll cat Wesley had clocked earlier.

"I thought you weren't open yet," Wesley said.

"Trevor bought a monthly membership, so he gets early-hour visits and all-day drop-ins without a reservation. His favorite cat is Purr-cy. Hey, Trevor," Crystal called. "Tell the reporter why you love CHATeau Savannah."

Wesley recognized Trevor as the self-described Type Five (the Observer) from the Enneagram class.

Oh, no. The Enneagram article! He'd forgotten all about it. Was there room to run the piece in Wednesday's edition? He liked Constance, and he'd let her down.

"Hello again." Wesley waved. "We met at the Enneagram class."

"Oh. Yes. Hi." The young man with the buzz cut and rimless glasses had clearly not expected to interact with anyone but the cats today. He needed a shave, and he looked depressed at having been roped into the conversation.

"Tell him how relaxing it is to hang out with the cats," Crystal prompted.

Trevor closed his eyes briefly, as if gathering strength. "When a cat's laryngeal muscles twitch at a rate of 25 to 150 hertz, we find it calming."

His statement hung in the air.

"Are you talking about purring?" Wesley clarified.

"The vibrations have been known to heal injured or broken bones, joints, or tendons. Cats are remarkably self-sufficient." Trevor blinked and returned to his book, and Purr-cy.

"There have been studies that prove interacting with animals lowers blood pressure, reduces stress levels, and increases oxytocin," Crystal told Wesley. "I'll forward them to you."

Trudy glanced at her smartwatch. "I've got to run—they'll be reading Isaac's will—so could I steal Wesley back for a minute?"

"Be my guest." Crystal thumped away in her medical boot.

"I'm disappointed in you, Wesley," Trudy admonished him. "You never asked her why she's wearing a medical boot. Anyway, I'll be blunt. I think someone sabotaged the trolley, and I don't trust the Sheriff's department to solve it. If a turkey could outsmart them for six hours, think what a human could do."

"Who do you think sabotaged it?" Wesley asked, pulse racing.

"I don't know, but a lot of people have been furious at Great-Uncle Isaac. Off the record, I think he was approaching senility. I'm ashamed I didn't do anything about it. I couldn't bear the idea of losing another person to hospitals and confinement."

The loss of Aunt Nora hung in the air. It had been Trudy who took Nora to her appointments, Trudy who kept Nora's spirits up. Trudy who watched her waste away.

"Years ago, tourists shopped on Main Street while they waited for the trolley," she added. "But lately, nobody rides it, and they blamed Isaac for idling in the street and blocking traffic. I know for a fact he ignored his parking tickets, and when he got a court summons, he claimed harassment and hired an expensive team of lawyers from out of town."

"Do you know the name of the firm?"

"No, and I don't know how he afforded them, either."

"There have been rumors *you're* the one funding them," he said quietly.

She frowned. "You know better than that."

"What if it's someone in your office, without your knowledge, thinking it's what you wanted?"

"My staff doesn't do anything without my knowledge," she said. "Honestly, he wouldn't tell me. Kept calling them his 'benefactor.' They were also defending him against the chamber of commerce lawsuit." She swallowed her last drop of coffee. "One more thing, and it's terrible. A friend of mine at Senior City told me there's a gambling ring there. Specifically..." she wrinkled her nose. "A dead pool, placing bets on when Isaac would die."

On that disturbing note, Trudy took off, and Wesley texted Reilly at the *Gazette* office. "Got a lead on Isaac. Permission to abandon cat cafe?"

Reilly texted back, "Denied. Finish the interview."

Wesley clenched his teeth as Crystal thumped back over in her medical boot.

Before she reached him, Savannah the wildcat wrapped herself around Crystal's non-injured ankle, twining quickly. Crystal gasped and pitched forward. Wesley jumped up and caught her in his arms.

They looked at each other. Wesley became aware of his own breathing, and the fact that Crystal smelled nice.

Really nice.

He made sure her feet were stable before letting go of her and sitting back down.

Neither of them spoke.

"I think she tripped you on purpose," he goaded. "And it's not the first time, is it? That's why you have the boot, isn't it? How many attempts has she made on your life?"

"None! Shut up! It wasn't her fault! It happened when the trolley exploded!"

His gaped at her. "You were there? What did you see?"

She narrowed her eyes at him. "That's not what we're here to talk about, though, is it?"

"Let's start over." He clasped his hands like a good boy and pretended to eat humble pie. "Hi, Crystal, nice to meet you. I'm Wesley Holloway of the *Cherry Hill Gazette*, here to interview you about your amazing cafe, which, I have to say, is shockingly clean. Well done, you. But before we get into that, I should ask about your ankle. I'm so sorry your hurt yourself. It looks painful. Would you mind telling me in nice, slow detail how it occurred?"

Thrown, she hesitated. "Well, okay. I didn't get hurt in the explosion, but I *was* nearby. I was walking Savannah on the opposite side of the street. She needs her exercise, rain or shine. The crash was loud, and it startled us, and before I could figure out what was happening, she took off, and I got yanked so hard by her leash that I twisted my ankle."

Crystal's eyes shifted as she spoke.

She's lying. She knows something, or she saw something. Aidan was quick to defend her on the phone with me earlier, too. Are they in cahoots?

"Please think back to what you saw. It's important."

She glared at him. "No. You're supposed to be profiling my cafe."

Incensed, Wesley flipped to the next page of his notepad. "Here's a question for you: What happens when Savannah dies?"

Even Trevor reacted to that. His eyes widened, and he turned his back as though he and Purr-cy could keep each other safe from Crystal's reaction.

"Did you just threaten my cat?" she asked in a low voice.

"No! I was merely pointing out that basing your entire *business model* on your cat's *image* could be construed as *naïve*, considering that she's *mortal*."

Crystal's eyes were black pools of rage. "I'm calling Deputy Max and telling him you threatened my cat's life."

"If you falsely accuse me to Deputy Max," Wesley said, "I'll call the board of health and tell them I found a hairball in my latte."

She had already dialed. "Hi, Deputy Max, it's Crystal Bae. I'm standing next to Wesley Holloway, who..."

Wesley frantically made a call of his own. She'd called his bluff, and now he had to act. "Yes, hello, I'd like to report a public health violation at CHATeau Savannah..."

12

WESLEY

"I'LL TELL you about the gambling ring," said a man in his seventies with a full head of paper-white hair and a sly, conspiratorial manner.

After fleeing the cat cafe in disgrace, Wesley had driven straight to Senior City to investigate Mayor Trudy's tip about the dead pool. Cherry Hill's raucous retirement community encompassed 150 condo/apartments and included on-site laundry, maid service, and a 24-hour diner, the Atrium Lounge—called "the Ate" by those in the know.

Wesley had been treated with suspicion when he asked the lobby receptionist if he could speak to some residents in the Ate for a story, and when he brought up the possibility of a dead pool centered on Isaac, every old-timer he approached had clammed up.

Until this man. With thick fingers, the guy motioned Wesley over to his table. "Pull up a chair, friend-o."

"Thank you."

"Yeah, you're welcome. I'm kind of a big deal around here; you're lucky I had a hankering for French toast sticks and cafe au lait this morning. Kidding, I drink decaf.

Anything stronger makes me feel like I'm on acid. But the French toast sticks... that's my death row meal, right there." He paused, dipped one of the sticks in a cup of syrup, and smacked his lips with relish as he chewed. "Anyhoo, I host bingo night and collect the..." he lowered his voice meaningfully, "'other' bets, if you catch my drift, but I don't participate. It's not good for me, you know what I mean? You picking up what I'm putting down?"

The man's eyes twinkled; he enjoyed playing the role of smarmy bombast, and there was something familiar about his voice and mannerisms.

Wesley pointed. "You're Kelly Arden."

The affectionate twinkle in the man's eyes vanished. "Says who?"

"Reverse Google image search."

"I've never been so insulted in my life. That has-been?"

Kelly Arden, living in Cherry Hill. Why had Aunt Nora never told him? Maybe she didn't know? It was surreal.

Wesley leaned in, excited. "Do you still watch the show?"

"The show" was *Saturday Night Live*, of which Kelly Arden had been a featured player in the late 1980s. He crashed and burned during a month of awkward fill-ins for the usual Weekend Update host, but prior to that he'd done good character work and impressions, some of which Wesley could still quote from YouTube. Kelly's exit from the show was followed by voice over gigs and small-venue comedy shows. He had a cult following (or at least, he used to).

"Do I get together with pals and turn it on?" Kelly asked incredulously. He smacked the table, making his French toast sticks jump. "No. No, I do not. Would *you* want to watch people doing your job? Would *you* enjoy that?"

Wesley's cheeks reddened.

"Just hearing the opening credits and theme song spikes my cortisol levels so high I might join the dead pool. The stress, it lives in you. Which brings us back to our topic. You need to steer this interview better, son."

Wesley laughed despite himself. "Fair enough. But could I come back another day and profile you for the *Gazette*?"

"I don't know; could you?"

"...Yes?"

"Wrong! You think I want people to know where I ended up? If I'm ever in the paper again, it's going to be for doing stand-up at Morongo Casino. Except not there. The temptation is too great. It's hard enough I'm surrounded by it here."

"Gambling, you mean?"

"Yes, gambling. Sorry, am I going too fast?" he quipped. Abruptly, Kelly lost his playfulness and fixed Wesley with shark eyes. "The dead pool wasn't on Isaac. It was on the trolley. 'When will that hunk of junk finally kick it', right? *No one had anything against Isaac.* We loved the guy. In fact, he sometimes played the odds, too. He won a decent pile of cash when the newsstand folded."

Wesley groaned. At least *someone* had benefited.

"Only time I ever lied to him was about this. He would've been insulted if he knew we talked about the trolley that way."

Wesley showed Kelly his phone, opened to one of the sidebars from his article on the crash. "Here's a list of every time the trolley broke down in the last few years. Do these dates mean anything to you?"

Kelly flicked through his ledger, swiping his thumb to his tongue to help separate the pages, until he found the page he was looking for. "Yep. It broke down, it got fixed. It broke down, it got back up. It died, it resurrected. And each time, the pool got larger as more people joined the fun. The catch was, it had to be kaput for good or no payout." Kelly raised his eyebrows. "I think that explosion qualifies, don't you?"

"So, someone definitely got the kitty?"

Kelly winced. "Let's leave the Depression-era lingo to the seniors, okay, pal? Besides, the term you want is jackpot."

"Who won the jackpot?"

Kelly looked at him. And looked at him. "Eh, who can say? Don't remember."

"Oh, come on—"

"Dementia is a cruel mistress."

"It's probably written down right there." Wesley lunged forward to look, but Kelly was quicker.

He tore a piece of paper from his ledger, stuffed it in his mouth, chewed and swallowed. "Delicious. Almost as good as my toasties."

"I can't believe you did that."

"Did what?" He took a deep breath and made his voice tearful. "Where am I? Is it dinner time? I want more toasties!"

"Can you at least give me a list of residents who participated?"

Kelly's shark eyes returned. "Residents? Hooo, it wasn't just residents. Walk-ins, visitors, family members, delivery guys... It was a free-for-all, and none of us will squeal."

"How high was the jackpot?" Wesley demanded quietly. "Was it worth killing over?"

"WHO ARE YOU? Young man, put down the knife!"

AFTER BEING ESCORTED out of Senior City for "upsetting a resident," Wesley arrived back at the *Gazette* office, his mind racing.

"How were the cats?" Reilly asked.

"I had to cut that short so I could track down my hot lead."

"I told you to follow the lead *after—*"

"Hear me out. The mayor told me about a gambling ring at Senior City, and I confirmed it with the guy who runs the numbers. Someone made a lot of money when the trolley exploded."

Reilly blinked, surprised. "Go on."

"Also, there's a letter from our archives last summer." He thrust the printout at Reilly. " 'Suffer the consequences.' 'Forced to take action.' If you compare it to my transcript from the city council meeting, you'll see there's consistency of phrasing. Lots of motivation floating around out there."

"Okay. Good work. Send everything you've got to Shawna."

Wesley froze. "Why?" He had nothing against the cub reporter—she was a great photographer, too—but this was his story.

"So she can follow up at the sheriff's press conference tomorrow."

"I'm doing the press conference. The sheriff promised me an exclusive, remember?"

"You had first crack, front page and all the glory. Now it's Shawna's turn."

"We could go together," Wesley offered desperately. "She could shadow me."

"Nope, sorry. As long as I'm in charge, everyone on staff gets a chance to cover every type of story, from ribbon-cuttings to social events to crime. Why would anyone work here if it's not a training ground?"

Wesley didn't like to think of the *Gazette* as a training ground. Because what did that say about Wesley?

Maybe he could check in with Shawna tomorrow and ask how the press conference had gone.

Reilly read his mind. "Don't insert yourself into her process or try to influence how she writes it. She'll learn by doing, and I will edit her if need be. Got it?"

He nodded, wilting. "Got it."

The words of Kelly Arden, *SNL* refugee, filled his head: "Would *you* want to watch someone do your job? Would *you* enjoy that?"

No, Kelly, as it turns out, I would not.

13

____

PENELOPE

PENELOPE SCOTT always carried a copy of the *Cherry Hill Gazette* with her to avoid talking to the other parents at school pickup. Normally it was a prop, but today the front-page story grabbed her by the throat.

The hometown Jolly Trolley had crashed into a tree on Saturday and—could this be right? —exploded. Exploded!

Thank God she and Henry had been skiing at Big Bear with his scout troop and hadn't arrived home until Sunday night. He'd been asleep when they drove past what she now understood to be the crash site at the bottom of Cherry Hill Boulevard. The trolley had been cleared away by then, so she'd assumed the taped-off area indicated the imminent removal of the weird tamarisk tree.

The driver, Isaac Caldecot, had been pronounced dead on the scene.

According to his obit, he had lived his entire life in Cherry Hill and had only taken an accumulated six months off work over an 80-year span. As a relentlessly hustling career woman and single mother, Penelope had to admire his work ethic.

She would have chosen a different image for his photo, though. Just like she would've chosen different words for the trolley's tourism recording. She would never forgive it for referring to hummingbirds as "avian theropod dinosaurs" and getting Henry excited about what turned out to be a turgid art gallery where he wasn't allowed to touch anything.

The trolley was prohibitively expensive, so she and Henry had only ridden it a few times, but Henry liked to pretend it was the trolley from *Daniel Tiger's Neighborhood*. She prayed he hadn't heard about the explosion at school. Who knew what he might picture in his head? The Tiger family's limbs scattered for miles?

She'd moved to Cherry Hill to start over after her divorce. It basically *was* Daniel Tiger's neighborhood here, not just because of the Jolly Trolley, but the mom-and-pop stores and small-town, clean-cut vibes. You could walk everywhere, and the real estate was insane. When a stunning two-bedroom, one-story bungalow with a recording studio in the detached garage came up for sale, she wrote an impassioned letter to the seller that shot her to the top of the list. The house was owned by an obscure comedy actor, Kelly Arden, who had downsized to a retirement community nearby.

She figured she'd never hear from him once the house sale went through, but he'd proven to be a helpful mentor. Once a month they ate lunch at "the Ate" in Senior City, which sounded like the subject of a Dr. Suess book. ("Want to eat at the Ate? Food's great at the Ate.") Kelly always brought a friend from L.A. to join them and offer industry advice. She suspected Mr. Arden was bored; he wanted to launch a career comeback but didn't know how. A marketing and branding expert herself, Penelope yearned to help him.

Someday. When she had time.

The bell rang, signaling the end of the school day, but Penelope was so engrossed in the trolley article, she didn't see Sam the SAHM until it was too late.

The curly haired woman pushed down on Penelope's newspaper and peeked her head over the top.

"Hi, hello, sorry! Didn't mean to scare you. Dale and Henry are wondering if they could play at the park for ten minutes," Sam said, a hopeful gleam in her eye.

Sam the SAHM was the cringingly eager second-grade room parent who kept trying to exchange numbers so their boys could play. It wasn't that Penelope didn't want Henry to have friends; she just didn't want him to befriend that specific family. She knew in her bones Sam would attempt to recruit her into the P.T.A., aka free labor, and then judge her when she declined. As if Penelope had time for such antics.

When Sam showed up at the Enneagram class on Saturday, Penelope had nearly fled. It was just as well her babysitter had flaked.

"Well?" Sam prompted. "Can they play?"

The playground next to the school offered less than the playground *at* the school, but the kids didn't care. They didn't even care that the playground's best feature, a cool robot tower whose arms were twin slides, was permanently caged off, taunting them.

"Unfortunately, we don't have time." Penelope scanned the playground for Henry and called his name.

"They're by the robot slide." Sam pointed. "They're trying to breach the fence."

Perhaps they *did* care.

"Henry, we need to get our coats from storage." Penelope made an impatient "Let's go" gesture. When your garage was a studio, there wasn't room to store bulky, little-worn clothing. They'd borrowed winter gear from another boy scout for skiing, which had been embarrassing, and since the cold weather didn't appear to be letting up, it was time to visit U-Stor-It & Car Park to retrieve their own clothes. She couldn't keep mummifying Henry in layers; he could barely move. On the plus side, it provided padding as he hurled himself against the robot slide's fence.

"Why on earth don't they knock down the slide if it's such a 'safety hazard'? It's taunting them," Sam remarked. This was so like Penelope's own thinking that she almost reconsidered her anti-Sam stance.

"When I was growing up," Sam added, "every slide was a metal slide. Did we get third-degree burns? All the time! But it was fine."

"Ew, it smells," Dale shouted, waving a hand in front of his nose. "Henry, smell it," he ordered Henry, and to Penelope's chagrin, Henry obeyed. The boys sniffed at the fence and made disgusted faces.

Penelope called her son's name again. Henry flinched but pretended he hadn't heard.

He'd had been doing that a lot lately; ever since he'd started second grade.

Sam fidgeted. "The thing is, I need to use the bathroom. Could you keep an eye on the boys? I'll be right back, I promise."

"Uh…" Penelope scanned for Henry again, who'd vanished.

"They're playing zombie tag now, by the swings. Give me two minutes?"

"Okay."

Henry's mummification made him an effective zombie, lurching about. At least he'd stopped braining himself against the robot slide fence. Keeping her child and Sam's child in sight, Penelope sat on a bench at the edge of the playground.

On the next bench over, two men and one woman were talking about the trolley crash in low voices. She recognized the owner of Kaftans 'n' More and the earth-mother-goddess woman from that ridiculous Hummingbird Art Gallery; the one who'd snapped at Henry and told him not to touch the "theropod dinosaurs." Ana Someone. The third person, whom she didn't know, wore a large, knitted scarf and hat that obscured his face.

"They're calling it an accident, but I know for a fact they're bringing people in for questioning," said the man she didn't know, the one in the amateur-looking knitwear. "Everyone who spoke at the city council meeting and everyone who was at the protest."

Wait, what? Penelope's body stilled. Bringing people in for questioning? Was the explosion...*caused* by someone?

The article hadn't said anything about that. Cherry Hill was safe. Cherry Hill was not dangerous. Because she wouldn't have moved her son to a dangerous place.

Shielding herself with the paper, Penelope listened.

"So, what, now we're being punished for expressing our views?" Ana snarled. "No one is sad it's gone. Let's be real. It was ruining the town."

Wow. The trolley was irksome, but to claim it had ruined the town was unhinged.

"No one's sad it's gone," Ana repeated, as though she'd heard Penelope's skepticism.

"Well, the mayor probably is," the owner of Kaftans 'n' More said. Martin was his name. She liked him; he always set aside things from the dollar bin for Henry that he thought Henry might enjoy. "Not that I'm a fan of hers," Martin added.

"Why does it have to be someone's fault?" asked the scarf-and-hat man. "The weather has been crazy. A crash was bound to happen. And sometimes things work out the way they're supposed to, for the collective good."

"Exactly. Whatever happened to a good old-fashioned act of God?" Ana agreed.

Penelope frowned. An act of God generally didn't include bumping off old people in trolley crashes, though, did it?

They were speaking quietly now. Penelope strained to listen.

"You know we gave him so many options... and none of them worked," the mystery man pointed out.

"You don't think it was...? Was it... planner?" Martin asked.

Penelope's brow furrowed. Was *what* planner? Had someone *planned* it? Her heart pounded, and she felt sick. Was she really hearing this?

"No," the unknown man insisted loudly, and then lowered his voice. "No. That was a joke. I wouldn't even talk about it. No."

"That's right," Ana, the art gallerist, said vehemently. "I got what I wanted, I'm not going to look too closely at the hows or whys. You both got what you wanted too. I think we should thank our lucky stars and be done with it."

Penelope was jolted out of her surveillance when Sam sat beside her, the boys in tow. Shaken, Penelope folded the newspaper before Henry could see the front page.

"Hi baby," she stammered. "Good day at school?"

Henry bit his lip. Uh-oh. She knew that look.

"Sorry," Sam said, "I got caught up in a conversation with their teacher. I guess the boys were hiding in the hallway under a table after recess."

"Me and Dale were sneaking," Henry admitted. He looked down. "Like I did at the library."

Penelope swallowed. "That was a one-off, remember? Not to be repeated, and especially not at school."

"Dale did it first! He hid in the filing cabinet."

Sam looked embarrassed. "Dale's been trying to find the smallest space he can fit inside. Let's hope it's a phase, ha ha." She changed the subject. "What did you think of the Enneagram class?"

That it was a disaster. Everyone probably thought Penelope was an idiot who hadn't taken the quiz. Of course she'd taken the quiz! She just hadn't liked the result. Type Three (The Achiever) was shallow, nakedly ambitious, always *using* other people. She was nothing like that.

The quiz was wrong, and so was that stupid reporter. (Why had he called her a Three? What had he seen in her, to conclude that?)

Penelope forced her face to remain blank. "Eh. Not my thing."

"Dale's sitter would be happy to watch the boys on Wednesday, and Saturday too," Sam offered. "When it's raining, she can keep them in the kids' section of the library, and when it's nice out they can play on the baseball field."

"Please, Mom?" Henry squeezed her hand and violently swung their arms.

Penelope pretended to consider it. "Oh wow, that's so nice of you. I'll think about it. We need to get our cold-weather clothes out of U-Stor-It and our Uber's almost here, so..." It was a blatant lie. Her driver was still forty minutes away.

There were no rideshares in Cherry Hill, or at least, no Uber Black ones, the luxury tier that Penelope preferred. She'd sold her own car to make the down payment on her house, and she didn't miss it. Well, except on days like today when a speedy getaway would've been nice.

Sam gasped with excitement. "I'm an Uber driver. We'll take you." Before Penelope could react, Sam leaned over and canceled Penelope's ride. "Free of charge. Mom-to-mom."

TRAPPED in the front passenger seat of Samantha's 2005-era minivan, it took Penelope about ten seconds to realize Sam shouldn't have a license. They hit the curb exiting the school parking lot, swerved wildly into the far-right lane, got honked at twice, and "California rolled" a stop sign.

The kids bounced, made vroom noises, and pretended to drive dune buggies.

"Are you one of those people who gets carsick if they're not in the driver's seat?" Sam asked, her eyes full of concern as she looked at Penelope. Which meant her eyes weren't on the road.

No, I'm one of those people who get sick when the driver is a maniac.

"All good," Penelope gasped.

"I want to go to Dale's house after," Henry announced from the back seat. "His dad's a magician. Can I, Mom? Can I?" Henry grabbed Dale's arm. "Do you have rabbits?"

"Yes," Dale shouted.

Sam gave Penelope a baffled look. "No, we don't. Will isn't that kind of magician. No animals. He does mentalism, mind-reading, that sort of thing."

Did he brainwash you into staying home with Dale? Penelope thought.

Henry and Dale continued their inaccurate back and forth about Sam's husband, and an awkward silence fell between the moms.

"Can I ask how old you are?" Sam blurted out.

"Twenty-seven," Penelope replied stiffly. *Go ahead, do the math, subtract eight, and frown.*

But all Sam said was, "Boy, am I jealous of your energy levels. What I wouldn't give to have that again."

Surprised, Penelope laughed. "Don't be. It's not my youth. It's a caffeine IV."

Penelope had been one month shy of nineteen when Henry came along. When she didn't lose the baby weight quickly enough, her modeling agent dumped her, and so did her husband, whose struggling band promptly sold a theme song to a hit TV show. Penelope had written half the lyrics, but her ex fought her tooth and nail on residuals. The divorce went through in a single afternoon, uncontested, for $750, but the copyright fight was ongoing and consumed half her waking thoughts.

"It's interesting to me how the newer generations don't want to drive. I'm Gen X, and we couldn't wait to get our licenses. Soon as I got my permit, I went to the corner store to use the payphone to call a horoscope hotline, ha ha ha," Sam prattled on.

"Wild," Penelope deadpanned.

If Penelope were inclined to be equally stereotypical, she would've shot back with: "Whatever, Gen X, you don't care about anything. How's that working out for you?"

Except Sam seemed to care an awful lot about getting their kids, and themselves, together. Why? Was she lonely?

Her minivan was excessive for an only child, not to mention the fact that it was from twenty years ago, but the gear stuffed in the third row explained why: magic equipment. Contraptions, boxed items, and posters for a venue called the Magic Mirror.

"So, you're one-and-done, too?" Penelope asked. "One kiddo?"

Samantha glanced in the rearview mirror before answering. "One at home, and one in the field."

"In the field?"

"My husband," she joked. "It's like having two sons sometimes. Not really, but... you know."

Penelope did know, but she'd never admit her ex was a man-child.

Ten minutes later, the group arrived at U-Stor-It & Car Park, the storage facility and private garage on the edge of town. A small, faded tent of some sort had been erected in the parking lot near the main building.

"Is it the circus?" Henry trembled with excitement. "Is there a bounce house?"

Penelope wrinkled her nose. It looked like a fumigation tent. A man with a bizarre contraption reminiscent of a thinner leaf blower strapped to his back emerged from the tent.

"We'll wait for you here," said Sam, and Penelope tensed at the prospect of a P.T.A. pitch on the drive home, not to mention the threat to her and Henry's lives from Sam's driving.

Just then, a sheriff's patrol car parked between Sam's minivan and the faded tent. Thinking fast, Penelope unbuckled Henry and said to Sam, "You know what? I need to talk to the sheriff, and I'm sure he can give us a lift home, so you two go on ahead."

"Oh! Okay. Well, let's exchange numbers, and you can let me know about the sitter—"

"Another time, thanks for the ride, see you." She hustled her son away. "Stay close to me, Henry. Don't go near the tent. We'll grab our coats and get out."

But the row housing their storage unit was roped off, so she dragged Henry inside the lobby to find out what was going on.

"Can we scoot past the pest control guy real quick?" she asked, brandishing her key.

"I'm sorry, you'll have to come back," the employee told her.

"What kind of pests?" *Don't let it be bedbugs. They may as well firebomb the town and be done with it.*

"Only an annual precaution," the employee said.

The sheriff, a bland older man in a uniform complete with hat and star, argued with a different clerk. The sheriff didn't raise his voice but persisted in making his point.

"You knew we needed to get in here. We called first thing this morning. This will, whaddayacallit, compromise our search."

The clerk shrugged. "Sorry, but our annual pest control visit was already on the books."

"I'm going to need a list of the chemicals used..."

"It's a cedar oil fogging machine. He'll be done in a few hours."

"...and security footage from the last two weeks where the trolley was parked."

While the sheriff waited for the employee to return with the requested footage, Penelope strode forward, hand extended. "Hi, I'm Penelope Scott, and this is my son Henry."

They shook hands. The sheriff's grip was warm and dry. "Sheriff Ian Pittman, pleasure to make your acquaintance."

"I'm glad I caught you, because I heard something strange at school pickup, about the trolley, um, *incident.*" She gave him a significant look that attempted to convey, "Don't call it an explosion in front of my kid, please."

Henry wasn't listening to them, anyway, thank goodness.

Sheriff Pittman gave her his full attention. She relayed who was there (minus the identity of the scarf-and-hat man), how they resented any investigation, how no one felt bad about the explosion, and how they'd talked about someone, or something, called "planner" in regard to it.

To her relief, the sheriff didn't mock her. He listened, jotted notes, and thanked her for bringing it to his attention.

She hadn't realized how much it was weighing on her until she'd handed it off to someone else.

One more hard part to go. She hated asking for favors. "Sorry. Could we trouble you for a ride back to town?"

"No trouble at all. Would your son like a deputy sticker?" He held out a roll of them, and Henry selected one. The stickers were large, and surprisingly realistic looking, customized for Riverside County with a raised logo and shadowed edges.

On the drive, Henry wore his new deputy sticker and said he couldn't wait to tell Dale he'd ridden in a "prison car."

Penelope felt warm and cared for, sitting in the front of the sheriff's car as dark clouds gathered and rain began to fall. The car radio played softly, tuned to a 1980s station. The streetlamps came on, glowing in the fog, even though it was barely past four, and the combination of the sheriff's thoughtfulness and the feeling of someone making sure they got home safely made her want to cry. It all served to remind her why she'd moved here. You couldn't get big city amenities, and she was a young mom in a retirement community, but people looked out for you.

When they arrived home, Sheriff Pittman wrote the number for the senior center on the back of his card. "Uber and Lyft are touch-and-go out here, but the senior center van can sometimes pick you up if you're stuck. You just have to be willing to hear about the latest kerfuffle at bridge."

She laughed, accepted his card, and thanked him for the ride. She enjoyed having his direct number. *It's safe here,* she repeated to herself. *It's safe here.*

In the time it took for her and Henry to unlock the front door to their bungalow, shed some of Henry's layers, turn on the heat, and prepare an after-school snack, endless texts arrived on Penelope's phone from an unrecognized number:

> Funny story, I already had your number from the class list! (I'm the room parent) (someone's gotta do it LOL)

> It's Sam, by the way (Dale's mom)

> (You can put that under occupation)

> Not that I'm not other things!

> Let me know about the sitter when you get a chance. No pressure!

> Hope you got your warm clothes out of storage okay.

> If you need anything, we have extras. LMK

> (attached)

As threatened, Sam had attached several images of

warm-weather outfits laid out on her bed and carpet. Kid-size ones for Henry, and adult-size ones for Penelope.

Penelope zoomed in to check the label on one of the adult sizes. It wasn't a brand she wore, but it would fit her, which was surprising. She and Sam were different sizes. Whatever. Maybe Sam was one of those people who fluctuated, and these no longer fit.

Penelope might have tolerated the onslaught of messages and misuse of room parent privileges if not for what followed: a flurry of cold weather emojis. Rain, umbrellas, clouds, snowflakes, laughing/crying faces.

Free clothes aside, Penelope did not have the bandwidth for this level of neediness.

When Henry looked away to focus on his snack, she hit "block."

14

SAM

SAM KNEW Penelope hadn't wanted to swap numbers. But Dale talked endlessly about Henry Scott this and Henry Scott that, and Dale was so behaviorally challenged (as one teacher put it) that he sometimes had trouble making friends, so she'd tried on multiple occasions to engage the younger woman.

It was like talking to a statue.

When they crossed paths at the Enneagram class, she saw her chance. Penelope had a need—a babysitter—and Sam was happy to fill it, no payment expected. Where was the downside?

Oh.

Maybe Penelope was proud and wouldn't accept charity. And there Sam was, offering a free ride, free babysitting, and free clothes. Ugh. How could she have misread Penelope so badly? And then doubled down on it? Tripled down, even.

Shame heated her all the way through. It was a familiar feeling from dealing with Farren, her adult daughter, who had recently gone "no contact" with her and Will, and shattered Sam's heart into a million pieces.

That was the other reason—beside Dale liking Henry—that Sam wanted to befriend Penelope. She hoped Penelope might offer insight into winning back Farren's trust, since the two women were the same age.

She'd almost told her about Farren in the car, when Penelope asked if Dale was her only child. But it was too soon, and the embarrassment of her own daughter cutting her off over the holidays had silenced Sam. She'd covered with a lame joke about her husband being a second child.

Nothing was further from the truth. Will was the best man she'd ever known: a considerate, hardworking, and loving presence who would be home early tonight for Boys' Time.

Boys' Time meant Sam didn't have to cook dinner, help with homework, corral Dale into the bath, wash his hair while he thrashed, get him to brush his teeth, read another chapter in the *Goosebumps* horror series starring Slappy the ventriloquist's dummy, tuck Dale in, and re-tuck him in when he came out of his room three times.

While her son watched TV in the den next to the kitchen, Sam folded the laundry. She could have left it for Will, but she found the repetitive motion soothing.

At 3:15, Will called to say he'd be late; the lighting fixtures in the theatre needed an upgrade, and the guy could only come today. Sam took a deep breath.

"Good luck. See you when you get here."

Mondays, Tuesdays, and Wednesdays were dark at the Magic Mirror, the cocktail lounge and magic theatre Will had opened six months ago. Prior to that, Will had traveled constantly, performing his mentalism show on cruise ships or across the country at high-end corporate dinners. No two months were the same.

The Magic Mirror was supposed to stabilize their lives, create a set schedule, and allow Will to spend time with Dale. But they underestimated how time consuming it would be to run the place, not to mention the pressure of luring guest magicians to a small town 90 minutes from L.A. that was neither San Diego nor Palm Springs.

4:00 turned to 5:00.

5:00 turned to 6:00. Whither Boys' Time? This was extremely unlike Will.

Climbing up and down the stairs of their three-story townhome over and over, Sam completed her Dale-related care and feeding and thought about what she'd expected to be doing right now: binge-watching *Tiny House Hunting* after a long hot shower. She'd have turned her phone to airplane mode because her phone was the biggest stressor in her life.

Take now. It was after 7:30 and Dale was in bed (allegedly), so the usual cacophony of bleeps and blurps, notifications and requests, poured in on her phone. Could she bring bakery items to the P.T.A. meeting tomorrow morning? Sure. Did she know Dale's book report had never been turned in? No, she didn't. As room parent, could she volunteer for a double-shift at the class Valentine party since no one else had signed up? Yep, okay. Could she pick up a potted plant for the Green Team's garden before Friday? Uh-huh.

Frustrating how the only people she *wanted* to hear from (Will, Penelope, and Farren, always Farren) remained silent.

Sam forced herself to focus on dinner. Will loved salmon, and although Sam didn't care for fish, she sliced lemons and coated the filets with garlic and Dijon as per his preference and set them in the oven.

While it baked, she opened a beer and glanced at the *Cherry Hill Gazette.*

Today's front page was devoted to the Jolly Trolley's fiery demise. She winced, thinking of the driver's last moments. What a horrible way to go. She rarely rode it because it was both expensive and unreliable, and the loop it drove was limited—would it have killed the driver to include the Magic Mirror in its tourism stops?

As she'd told Constance, the trolley had broken down the day Will and Dale rode it for a holiday light tour. Will had boarded straight from work, so he'd still had his toolbelt with him and saved the day by tightening the oil filter in the engine.

She didn't like thinking about that day, which coincided with Farren's announcement of the No Contact Rule. To Sam's agony, the day was commemorated in a sidebar that listed the dates and times of the trolley's mishaps.

Where on earth was Will?

She called the Magic Mirror. "Hi, it's Sam. Is he there?"

"No," the manager replied. "I thought he was with you. He took off a few hours ago."

Her blood chilled. "Oh. That's—odd. Um, how are ticket sales looking?"

"Thursday's at thirty percent, and we're at half seats for Friday and Saturday," the manager replied wearily.

If sales remained sluggish, they'd have to hike the ticket prices. And if they hiked the ticket prices, people might not come at all.

She said goodbye and slumped at the kitchen table, staring into space.

The garage door didn't open until eight p.m.

Will saw her sitting at the table, and his face fell. He strode over and pulled her up and into his arms. She closed her eyes and curled into his body, inhaling the familiar, welcome scent of his Creed Aventus cologne. She'd splurged on it for his Christmas present years ago and it was still going strong. Sandalwood, a hint of fresh citrus, and something she could only describe as home.

They'd met as teenagers, and she'd read somewhere that when you fell in love, your image of your significant other remained fixed in that moment, no matter how you changed over the years. She was pleased to remember him as he'd been—lanky, thick-haired, sweet-faced, and dimple-cheeked—while also seeing, and loving, the person he was now: weathered but handsome, equal holder of their shared life together, and all the highs and lows it had entailed.

"I brought you tamales from Texican Table." He set the bag down.

That was their marriage: he'd known she would make him salmon, so he'd brought her something *she* loved.

"Thanks, honey. Where have you been? Are you okay?"

That's when she noticed how pale he was. He raked his hands through his greying hair. "On the phone earlier, when I said I'd be late, it wasn't for the reason I mentioned."

Her heart pounded. "Okay..."

He cupped her face in his hands and looked tenderly into her eyes. "You're the love of my life, Samantha Orlaith. Which is why we need to get divorced."

15

———

SAM

SAM LAUGHED. "What are you talking about?"

Will heaved his briefcase onto the old Ikea dining table, flicked it open and yanked out a thick, stapled packet. "The paperwork's all ready. If you sign here, here, and here—" he stopped. "Or, no, maybe it's better if you contest it first. That's more realistic. Yes, you should drag it out, act shocked and horrified—"

"I *am* shocked and horrified."

Well, that wasn't entirely true.

Will got like this sometimes.

She knew from her Enneagram research (making Will take the quiz) that he was a Type Six, the Loyal Skeptic. A Type Six's loyalty was a treasure never to be squandered. If you were lucky enough to have it, you could count on a Six to give you the world and travel through hell for you. Sixes scanned the horizon for threats and didn't trust easily. When stressed, they spiraled, imagining unlikely scenarios.

For example, a month before Will's annual physical, he'd become convinced he had all manner of rare-and-incurable diseases that would become known with the blood panel. When the blood panel came back fine, that didn't dissuade him. "What do doctors even know, really? What does *anyone* even know? We're all just dirt that learned to think."

Then there was tax season. "This is the year we get audited," he'd predict direly at 3 a.m. on April 14th. "All because of that dinner I wrote off as a business expense when really all I talked about was hockey." ("But how would they know?" had no place in the conversation.)

Oddly enough, Sixes were strong and bold in a crisis. They were so used to imagining terrible things happening that when something did, they snapped into action. It was their moment.

"If we play this right," Will said, "it won't look like fraud, so you and the kids will be protected. I know I catastrophize, but Sam, this is happening, and if we don't get ahead of it, it's going to ruin us."

"What's going to ruin us? The Magic Mirror?"

He looked offended. "No! The trolley! I'm the reason the old man is dead! That's why we need to shield our assets so you can survive when I'm in prison. Oh God, I'll be forced to join a prison gang."

"Hold on. Slow down. Go back."

Will yanked the day's newspaper out of the recycling bin, unfolded it, and stabbed the article sidebar with his finger. "The most recent time the trolley broke down was when Dale and I rode it for the light tour. Someone remembered me looking at the engine."

"To fix it," she said. "Obviously."

"Or sabotage it, according to the sheriff. He made me go over it again and again, what I did that day. One of the deputies, the woman, goes, 'Isn't it true you asked the deceased to include your magic theatre on its route, and he turned you down?' And then she asked if that had made me mad, maybe even vengeful. And I said, 'Of course not. Even if I had been mad, why would my tampering with the engine solve that? It wouldn't benefit me.' And then the other deputy, that Max guy, said, 'But you admitted you haven't ridden it since then. Because you did something to it, and you knew it wasn't safe.' I tried to explain I hadn't given it any thought. It was just the trolley being the trolley. And I never ride it normally, so the fact that I haven't ridden it since isn't proof of anything."

"Mommy?" came Dale's voice from upstairs.

"Go back to bed, please, Dale," she answered.

"Best-case scenario, they charge me with involuntary manslaughter; worst-case scenario, murder," Will said in a low voice, mindful of small ears. "Which is why we need to shield our assets... transfer everything to your name... no, not everything... it's suspicious if you do that... needs to look 'fair and equitable,' the lawyer said..."

"What lawyer? When?"

"That's what I was doing all afternoon." He gave her a look as though that should have been clear.

"Will. Sit. Please."

He did, reluctantly. His body vibrated with nervous energy. "I can't help thinking if I'd been out of town like normal, none of this would be happening," he said.

And Farren would still be in our lives, Sam thought miserably.

"Forget the..." she couldn't say *divorce* with a straight face. "'Shielding of assets' for the moment. Let's focus on one thing you can do right now to clear your name."

"Okay. They want me to bring in the toolbelt, specifically the wrench I used to tighten the oil filter, so they can see if it was the right type, or if I made the situation worse.

If I didn't crank it properly for that final half turn, for example, it might have spilled oil everywhere."

"If it were going to catch fire, why did it take so long?" Sam asked.

"I don't know! I only know they're determined to blame me."

She pulled him into a fierce hug.

"What are we going to do, Sam?" he asked, muffled, into her shoulder.

They held each other, seeking comfort and support in the only way they could. And then it came to her.

The Enneagram would save them.

16

CONSTANCE

CONSTANCE WOKE on Wednesday with renewed determination to make her class succeed.

It was true no one new had signed up to replace Penelope yet. It was also true that the promised article in the *Cherry Hill Gazette* had only materialized in *today's* paper instead of Monday's, but the short notice might appeal to those of a spontaneous nature. Wouldn't it be nice to have a class full of spontaneous, enthusiastic Arthurs?

She'd been thinking about her late husband with less than flowery language lately, so it felt good to focus on his better qualities. His joie de vivre. So long as she excised his betrayal from her mind, all was gravy. It helped that no one in Cherry Hill knew about him.

She played with Mr. Cinnamon all morning, admiring his athletic leaps and daring, hairpin turns as he chased his favorite string-and-catnip toy around the house.

"Who's a good hunter? Who's the best hunter in the whole wide world?" she cooed.

Sheriff Pittman interrupted their happy pastime, calling to ask if she was home and available for more questions.

"Yes, but can we make it quick? My class starts in an hour," she said anxiously.

"I'm coming up the hill."

What else could he possibly want to ask her? She'd read about Tuesday's press conference in the *Gazette*, and learned that he was treating the crash as suspicious, which was distressing—but what did that have to do with her?

When she heard his patrol car outside, she pulled on her shoes and went into the courtyard to unlock the gate. Sheriff Pittman nodded at her, and they returned to the kitchen without speaking and sat across from each other at the table.

He seemed less friendly toward her than he had during their first interview. Sensing the tension, Mr. Cinnamon hid beneath the couch.

"Why on earth did you move into the Upside-Down house if you had no intention of showing it?" the sheriff asked.

"It's my home, not a ticketed venue."

"When you move to a town as small and close-knit as Cherry Hill, it's my opinion that you should contribute to its success. It's a major attraction in our town. Surely you knew that when you moved in."

She hadn't, but she was too embarrassed to explain the context of her impulse buy or the fact that her realtor had tried to warn her and she hadn't listened.

"Why should I let strangers—"

"I'll get to the point. Your decision may be related to the trolley crash."

Her gut clenched. "What do you mean?"

"Since no one is allowed inside the house, and since your house is the only property on the hill, it's common knowledge you're the only passenger at that point in the tour. When it exploded."

"You think *I* was the target? And the driver was collateral damage?" She felt woozy.

Why would anyone have such powerful feelings about her? She barely talked to anyone in the course of a day. No friends. No neighbors. The Enneagram class was supposed to change that.

"During the protest and the crash, you were the only passenger," the sheriff said. "The common denominator in both incidents on Saturday was you, Ms. Kincaid. Perhaps you can help us make sense of that. We can't seem to square it."

His honesty moved her. He didn't sound as antagonistic as before.

"But I *wasn't* the only passenger," she reminded him.

"That's right, the young man who offered Isaac an envelope. The problem is, no one else can, whaddayacallit, corroborate that, and you don't know who it was, so it's a dead end."

"I could speak to a sketch artist, if that helps."

"Do you think we have the budget for a sketch artist?"

She shook her head, chastened.

"Look, we've asked around," he said, "and a lot of people are unhappy with you for not opening the Upside-down House. From a killer's perspective, if you're out of the way, maybe it gets re-opened. Do you have any enemies?"

"No, of course not," she sputtered.

"Take a moment and think about it."

The sheriff sat there, waiting, while her wall clock ticked closer to four p.m. If she were late to class, would everyone leave? How much of a grace period would Roberto give her? (None, probably.) Would Chase, the assistant librarian, try to keep people there until she arrived?

"Rao?" Mr. Cinnamon emerged from beneath the couch.

Her heart leaped at his reappearance. "Hello, my darling."

He jumped onto her lap, and she reveled in his soft, ruddy fur under her hand. "Rao," he said again, and butted her hand with his head.

Even the sheriff smiled. "Hello again, fox-cat."

Mr. Cinnamon jumped off and moved to his food dish. Constance felt calmer with him nearby, until Sheriff Pittman flipped open his notebook and referenced it. "Since you can't think of anyone, I'll go. A person who wishes to stay anonymous said you locked the door during your personality types meeting, thus preventing people from leaving, then demanded everyone's blood types and displayed a pentagram on the dry-erase board. This person said they feared for their safety and thought you were intending to keep people there for days or weeks while you indoctrinated them into a cult."

Constance threw her hands up. "What are you talking about? I can't even respond to such stupidity!"

"Well, I'm afraid you're going to have to. My own deputy said you approached him to join what he, too, described as a cult, so I'd like to know more."

"Why do people think it's a pentagram? These are basic geometric shapes, here! Why can't people just be grateful I'm teaching the class, and for *free*? That I'm giving of my time to better their lives?"

The sheriff waited.

She took a deep breath. "Okay. In terms of Deputy Max, I ducked into the visitor center to get away from the sidewalk protest. He was there checking on his mother, and to take my statement about the broken window and speaker. I offered him a flyer for my class. No recruitment attempt was made. I never asked for anyone's blood types. I was doing a 'get to know you' around the table and asked for their best guesses of their *personality types*. As for locking people in the community room, it was a reflex, not born of ill intent. I was simply trying to retain a quota of students, which I had only just learned was a requirement—"

She snapped her fingers. Of course. She did have an enemy.

At the sound of her snap, Mr. Cinnamon darted away. "Sorry, precious," she called to him. To the sheriff, she said, "The head librarian, Roberto Guerrero." She gasped. "He was your anonymous source, wasn't he?"

"Anonymous means anonymous."

"He hates me, and I have no idea why. He's determined to thwart me from teaching my class. *What is his problem?*"

"I'd be angry, too, if someone tried to stop me from doing something I cared about," the sheriff said.

Her heart pounded in her ears. She closed her eyes and counted to five in her head. "I'm not angry; I'm frustrated. There's a difference."

"Like I said, I'd be angry, too."

"I'm not angry!"

"Why not? You don't get angry?"

"No, I don't."

"And you can just... decide that?"

"Yes."

"I don't know how that would work. I suppose I could think about what my wife would do and try to do that. She's very peaceful, my wife, and that spreads to everyone around her. So, I understand aspiring to that state. I just don't think it's always possible."

The sheriff's description of his wife reminded Constance of Type Nine, the Peacemaker. Healthy Type Nines were relaxing to be around. He probably wished he was home with her instead of facing off with a belligerent Constance.

"Anyway," he finished, "I don't think it's a conscious choice."

"Agree to disagree," Constance said in a clipped tone.

Good people didn't get angry. And Constance was good.

Though if she'd *actually* been good—a good wife, a good partner, a good woman—Arthur wouldn't have left her for someone else, would he?

She shook her head out. "The point is, if I have an enemy, it's Roberto."

"Huh. Roberto's the one who told us people were unhappy with you. He volunteered the information unasked."

AT THE LIBRARY, she took a moment to peruse the New Fiction section, hoping to calm down while she waited for her nemesis to appear. It was well past time for Roberto to explain his irrational behavior.

At the end of her interview with Sheriff Pittman, she'd asked him for a ride to the library. Without the trolley, she was at loose ends, and it was the sheriff's fault she wouldn't make it to class on time on foot.

Sheriff Pittman agreed but lamented that no one drove anymore; the other day he'd given a ride to a mom and her young son who were stranded at U-Stor-It & Car Park. He would help Constance, considering the sheriff's station was next door to the library, but he urged her to figure out alternative transport or take driving lessons. She lived in California, for goodness' sake.

"To be on the safe side," he told her before dropping her outside the library, "Deputies Regina Cole and Max Evert will keep eyes on your property until we resolve this. You met them on Saturday."

She'd struggled to exit his car, shifting her shoulder bag to balance her weight. It felt heavier than usual, but then again, she'd eaten little that day, and still felt woozy from their conversation.

"Oh, and one last thing, Ms. Kincaid," the sheriff said.

"Yes?"

"Getting angry doesn't make you bad," he told her. "It makes you human."

She didn't respond, just thanked him for the lift and headed inside the library. It was only 3:50, though the darkened sky seemed closer to six p.m.

If getting angry made her human, she was feeling very human indeed when she located Roberto, lurking behind the reference desk. She marched over and set her bag on the table. He didn't look up from repairing the spine of a much-loved book, so she dropped the hardcover mystery she'd selected from the New Fiction shelf onto the table.

That got his attention. Barely. He pointed away from them. "Check out is over there."

"You told the sheriff no one likes me. Why?"

Roberto rolled his eyes. "Because it's true. The more information they have, the better. And as much as I... am not impressed with you, I don't want to be responsible for anything happening to you."

This response was so unexpected she took a moment to regroup. "No, I don't think that's it. I think you like telling tales out of school." He had to have been the anonymous source who told the sheriff about the locked door and "pentagram." Hadn't she caught him in the community room, looking at her syllabus when she'd returned for her cane on Saturday?

Roberto's voice was a deep rumble. "I haven't been in school for a long time."

"That's not the clever comeback you envision it to be."

"Why, because it means I'm old? So what? I am old. You're no spring chicken yourself."

Before she could reply, Chase, the assistant librarian, bounded over. "Ennea-Gram! Good news, I'm coming to your class today! It's my afternoon off."

He sent her a sly grin and Constance grinned back, her anger at Roberto forgotten.

"You're going to waste your afternoon off at her class?" Roberto boomed. *Ugh, why was he so loud? Did the rules of the library mean nothing to him?* "He won't be able to save you on Saturdays," Roberto reminded her.

And just like that, her anger—*no, frustration*—came roaring back. "What is your problem with me?"

He ignored her and picked up the hardback she'd selected. "This title is reserved for our mystery book club. You can't borrow it unless you join." He looked smug. "I knew it was only a matter of time before you came knocking."

"Excuse me?"

Roberto pulled open a filing drawer and extracted her class syllabus, creased from having been folded in his pocket. He smoothed it out with his large hands. "You think of yourself as a modern-day Miss Marple."

"No, I don't."

"'My interest is—and always has been—human nature,'" he quoted from the sheet. "Don't deny it." He jerked his thumb toward the community room. "You're Marpling in there. But Book 'Em is already on the case, so back off."

She stifled a laugh. "What, pray tell, is 'Book 'Em'?"

"The mystery book club, of course," he said, as though it should have been obvious. "We occasionally solve mysteries around town."

"Since when does Book 'Em solve mysteries?" Chase sputtered.

"Since crime landed on our doorstep."

"So, since Saturday," Chase clarified. "An entire four days."

"We're uniquely equipped to help law enforcement, based on our decades of reading and analyzing mysteries. And the fact that we know Cherry Hills and its people." That last part was directed at Constance, eternal newcomer. "No Marpling for you," he reiterated, eyes hard.

Was that why he hated her? He thought she was horning in on his territory? No, he'd treated her badly long before reading her syllabus.

"I assure you no Marpling will be taking pl—ouch!"

Chase had gripped her arm, his voice clenched. "May I escort you to class?"

"I'm not finished."

"It's not that," he whispered urgently. "You have a stowaway."

A movement in her bag was followed by a soft but distinct sound.

"Rao?"

17

CONSTANCE

TRYING TO ACT NATURAL, Constance swept up her bag with the wriggling Mr. Cinnamon inside and turned her back on Roberto. She lunge-walked to a quiet stack, Chase at her heels.

"What are we going to do?" she hissed. "Class is about to start."

Chase looked flushed and excited. "I assume this is your cat, and not a random cat? This cat is known to you, yes?"

"Yes, it's Mr. Cinnamon. He must have crawled inside and fallen asleep," she moaned.

"What a little sassy pants." Chase clearly approved.

"You have no idea. We can't let Roberto see!"

"Okay. It's okay. I'll take the hit for you."

"I don't want you putting your job in jeopardy."

"What's he going to do, fire me? Please. Come to my office, Sassy Pants. I'll find you a nice little box."

Constance was pretty sure Mr. Cinnamon wouldn't go quietly into a box, but seeing no other choice, she handed over her bag. Mr. Cinnamon's head poked out, eyes wide, and Chase used part of his blazer to cover the cat from view as he took off in a new direction.

Head down and heart pounding, Constance strode to the community room and almost collided with Wesley.

He wore tattered jeans, and a fuzzy, stained cardigan lopsidedly buttoned over a holey T-shirt. It was bizarre. He looked like an avant-garde runway model. He clutched the latest issue of the *Cherry Hill Gazette*.

"Extra, extra, read all about it," he said despondently. "Or don't, since all Shawna got at the press conference was a generic statement about a criminal investigation. Who have they talked to? Why are they treating it as suspicious? Is there a killer at large? Shrug. Who knows! If *I'd* been there, we'd have answers to those questions."

"I'm sorry. That must be difficult."

"Thank you. After you." He opened the community room door.

Trevor and Zeke sat next to each other. Zeke was awake!

Constance leaped into action, hand outstretched. "Hello, I'm Constance Kincaid, I don't think we've officially met. I'm so glad you—"

SNOOOORE. She jumped back, startled.

"He's been doing that," said Trevor, the Type Five (The Observer). "He sleeps with his eyes open."

Constance peered at Zeke, comfortably attired in his wheelchair with a quilt over his legs. His eyes were fixed on a far-off point.

"Here." Wesley placed a pair of sunglasses on Zeke, who didn't stir.

"We didn't meet the quota," Trevor said. As an afterthought, he added, "Sorry, Constance," and began packing up.

"Wait. Please. It's barely four o'clock. Chase is on the way, and I want to give Sam-the-SAHM a chance to arrive. Please stay."

Trevor looked at his smartwatch. "Mine says three minutes *after* four."

A crash sounded from the adjoining room. Chase emerged, holding a box, Mr. Cinnamon hanging off the side.

"He broke three picture frames and a coffee mug by tipping them off my desk, all while maintaining eye contact with me, so I think Sassy Pants is not a fan of offices and should probably stay with you."

"Mr. Cinnamon, no," Constance cried. "I'm sorry, Chase. I'll pay for the items he broke."

"It's okay." Chase grinned. "He is who he is."

Trevor raised his hand. "Is the cat's name Sassy Pants or Mr. Cinnamon?"

Before Constance could answer, the main door flew open, and Sam burst through.

"Sorry I'm late. I haven't slept since Monday, ha ha ha." Her laugh wasn't infectious this time. It was manic. "Why? Oh, I'll tell you why: because my husband Will, the kindest, most loyal, most hard-working man in the universe, is about to be falsely accused of the trolley murder. But everything's going to be okay because we're going to use the Enneagram to prove he didn't do it."

18
———

SAM

SAM'S BODY shook from the multiple Monster energy drinks she'd consumed starting at seven a.m. when Target opened. The Target parking lot was near and dear to her heart as a safe place to sob in her car. It had seen her though many of life's trials, but none so dire as today's.

Constance looked perplexed. "I'm terribly sorry to hear about your husband. But that's not how the Enneagram works."

Sam was ready for her. "You said human nature was the ultimate mystery, and the Enneagram would unlock it."

"I didn't *quite* say that—"

"You said Miss Marple solves murders by comparing one set of people with another set of people. 'You'd be surprised how few Types there are in the world.' I went through my collection of Agatha Christies that my mom left me. Here's what else I found." She flipped open her miniature notebook, where she'd scribbled notes at three a.m. "Ahem: 'Types are alike everywhere and that is such a valuable guide.' A valuable guide! That's from *4:50 From Paddington*, also known as *What Mrs. Magillucutty Saw*.

She basically used the Enneagram to predict motivation and behavior without knowing she used the Enneagram. So can we!" She gripped Constance by the shoulders. "With your guidance, we've got this. Think about it. Trevor's read every Enneagram book already, Wesley is a freaking reporter, Chase is a librarian, and you're an expert on human nature. *And a lawyer*. You said you used the Enneagram in your career. We all heard you."

"To tailor my communication methods. Not to solve crimes."

Sam addressed the room at large. "Come on, people. If we work together, we can prove Will's innocence by finding the real killer. Who's in?"

"I'm in," said Wesley. He raised the sleeping Zeke's hand. "'Me too,'" Wesley said in a low voice from the side of his mouth.

"Me three. Let's Marple," said Chase, who lived up to his name—he was like Dale after a Nerds gummy cluster. He'd once helped Dale find a Pokémon book in the graphic novel section and, if Sam remembered correctly, he ran the banned book club. Chase gave a wicked laugh. "Roberto will lose his mind."

Sam didn't know what that meant, but whatever. "Trevor?"

"I don't know..." said Trevor, eyes averted.

"Hold on, I had a lesson planned for today," Constance said.

"Trevor?" Sam repeated.

"Don't pressure him. You're not in charge here."

"TREVOR?"

"I want to help but I'm not sure we should apply our knowledge this way," said Trevor. "Not to mention I'd need a lot more books and podcasts before I'd feel comfortable participating."

"You can read and listen as you go," Sam announced, then faced off with Constance. "It's unanimous. We're Marpling."

Constance's face was red, and steam practically poured out of her ears. Sam almost backed down, but Will was counting on her, whether he knew it or not.

"You are mistaken," Constance said through clenched teeth. "While I empathize with your plight, Sam, it is *not* unanimous. Trevor's on the fence, and I'm not anywhere near the fence." She took a deep breath and muttered, "Why does everyone think I aspire to Marple-dom? Because I'm old?"

"Living in a small village," Wesley said.

"And a spinster," Sam finished.

Constance swallowed and looked away.

Sam felt ashamed. Had she been rude? "Nothing wrong with being a spinster. Trust me, I *wish* I were a spinster right about now, ha ha ha."

In the charged silence that followed, Sam thought she heard a cat meow. A chill went up her spine. Had lack of sleep caught up with her, in the form of auditory hallucinations? "Is there a cat in here?" she asked in a small, scared voice.

"It's Mr. Cinnamon—" Constance began.

"—Sassy Pants," said Chase at the same time.

"Where is he, by the way?" asked Constance.

Wesley rolled back in his chair to reveal a fluffy, reddish-brown cat sitting on his lap, kneading his thighs.

"I don't even like cats," said Wesley.

"They like *you*," said Chase.

"That's *why* they like you," said Trevor. "Want me to take him?"

"Yes, please."

Trevor held out his fingers for the cat to sniff. The cat rubbed against his palm and then darted to a reshelving cart in the corner.

"Sam, I'm afraid it would be unethical for me to use my expertise in this way," Constance said, calmer but no less firm.

Tears blurred her vision, but Sam wiped them away. Enough of them had fallen in the Target parking lot; right now, she needed a spine of steel.

"If you don't help me," Sam said, straightening her shoulders, "then I'm leaving. Goodbye quota and goodbye class."

She didn't like hurting Constance, but if she had to choose between hurting Constance and condemning Will to a life behind bars, the answer was obvious. "Unless the *cat* counts," she added sarcastically, to show she wasn't messing around.

Constance blinked. "Blackmail, is it?"

Sam almost poofed out of existence at the force of Constance's glare.

"Very well, Sam the SAHM," Constance spat, "I'll use my knowledge of the nine types for this exercise, but it's theoretical, for learning purposes only, and we will do it *my* way. Got it?"

"Got it." Sam crossed her fingers behind her back. She couldn't believe she'd staged a coup. "I'm sorry it had to be this way," she cried. "I'll never do it again."

Constance narrowed her eyes but didn't reply.

Well, you can't please everyone.

Penelope had never answered Sam about sharing the

babysitter, so Dale was stuck in the kids' section of the library with only his sitter for company, but for the next ninety minutes, Sam could focus on clearing Will's name.

"Sit, please," Constance said, her eyes hot.

"I'd rather stand. Sorry. Too much nervous energy."

"Fine." Constance ripped the cap off her dry-erase marker. "Tell us about Will."

"He's a Type Six, the Loyal Skeptic, whose core motivation is the need to be secure. So, right off the bat, it's ridiculous. Committing a crime is the *opposite* of security—he'd fear being caught every second of every day. Never mind that he doesn't have a motive! I mean, the sheriff thinks he does, but he doesn't."

"What's his motive?" asked Wesley. "Allegedly?"

"Revenge for not putting the Magic Mirror—his magic theatre—on the trolley's tourism route."

"Method? Means?"

She explained about the holiday light tour, and Will's use of his wrench to tighten the oil filter. "They wanted to know if his tool belt included sewing scissors. I thought that was weird."

"They think someone used pinking shears to cut a wire in the engine," Wesley explained.

"I liked what you said about Type Six, and their desire to be secure, Sam," Constance admitted. "Let's look at each Type's core desire." On the dry-erase board, she wrote:

Type One: The Perfectionist. Wants to be good.

Type Two: The Helper. Wants to be needed.

Type Three: The Achiever. Wants to be valuable.

Type Four: The Individualist. Wants to be known.

Type Five: The Observer. Wants to be self-sufficient.

Type Six: The Loyal Skeptic. Wants to be secure.

Type Seven: The Enthusiast. Wants to be free.

Type Eight: The Challenger. Wants to be independent.

Type Nine: The Peacemaker. Wants to be in harmony.

"Too bad none of them are nicknamed the Killer," said Trevor. "Wants to kill."

Chase laughed. "You're hilarious."

Trevor blushed and looked away.

"None of them seem like killers." Sam was disappointed. "I'd hoped a few of the Types would stand out as more likely."

"Well, exactly," said Constance. "It's not the Type, it's the level of health. Every Type is capable of a horrible crime if they've deteriorated to the point of psychosis. It's their *reason* for committing the crime that differentiates them." She looked at her notes, and clapped her hands twice. "To gain more insight into each Type's core needs, let's go around the room and discuss our own Types and how they manifest. Trevor, would you mind starting us off? Remind us of your Type, or suspected Type, and why you're here."

Trevor looked like he minded quite a bit.

The young man wore rimless glasses and had a mild, intelligent-looking face. His original nametag sticker from the first day remained affixed to his shirt, albeit wrinkled and worn. Samantha suspected he had forgotten it was there, laundered it, and then had no choice but to wear the same shirt today since the sticker was basically ironed on. Her heart went out to him; he was more boy than man. His buzz cut was so close to his scalp she could see a small birthmark on his skin.

As a baby, Farren had had a birthmark at the base of her skull. Sam had called it a target for kisses. How sweet she'd smelled...

"I'm a Type Five, the Observer," said Trevor. "I'm here because I like libraries."

Sam thought Constance might be insulted by his answer, but Constance looked delighted. "That's the best reason there is."

Chase's eyes twinkled. "Right on, Trev."

"The other day, when I asked what time class would end, I didn't mean it in a pejorative way, only factual. I like knowing what to expect, so I can relax," Trevor added.

"Enneagram Fives, the Observers, often feel as though they have an inner battery life that starts draining from the moment they wake up," Constance explained to the group. She seemed determined to walk a knife's edge between keeping Sam from leaving and continuing to teach her planned lesson. Sam would allow it. For now. "Knowing how long things are expected to take reassures you that you won't run out of energy. Does that gel with your experience, Trevor?"

He nodded, stunned. "Exactly. I—thanks."

"I don't think an Observer would sabotage the trolley," said Sam. If most Type Fives were like Trevor, she couldn't picture them harming anyone. The point, as she understood it, was that Type Fives preferred to stay safe behind research—not get their hands dirty in the real world.

She plucked Constance's dry-erase marker out of Constance's grip and drew a line through "Type Five: The Observer. Wants to be self-sufficient" on the board.

Constance frowned and held out her hand. Sam refused to relinquish the marker.

"I liked the trolley driver," Trevor said. "He was sort of a funny old guy."

"Oh, did you know him?" Constance asked.

"Not well." He looked uncomfortable.

"I'll go next," said Chase. "I'm a sexy Seven, the life of the party, the legend of the 'gram." Chase made an ironic raise-the-roof motion.

"Type Seven, the Enthusiast," Constance said. "I can see that."

"My problem is, I'm *too* enthusiastic. I can't make up my mind about what I want to do. Not just in life, but like, next week. I work here at the library, and I like it, but I also teach tae kwon do part time, and do event planning, mostly at the convention center, and I want to get my massage therapy license, and there's a pilot training program an hour away, which would be amazing... can you imagine getting to buzz these mountains? So, yeah, hot mess, major FOMO, cleanup in aisle Seven."

"Thank you for your honesty," said Constance. "That's a beautiful illustration of a Type Seven's need to be free. You don't want to choose *one* path because you're afraid it'll cut off all the *other* paths."

"Ohhhh nooooo. I just thought of something." Chase's eyes were wide. "What if the killer's a Type Seven because he wanted to know what it's like to take a life?"

"Um..." said Constance.

"A new experience. The thrill of the kill!"

"Do you *want* it to be a Type Seven?"

"No! Yes! If it's a Type Seven, who better to hunt them down than another Type Seven? I'll have insight into their twisted mind that no one else can match. Put me in, coach!"

"The Enthusiast seems too happy to kill." Sam crossed out Type Seven on the board.

"Their happiness is often a cover to outrun more complex and less desirable emotions," Constance explained.

"No, it's not," said Chase.

Constance and Sam glanced at each other but refrained from commenting. A snore erupted from Zeke, who wore sunglasses for some reason.

"Maybe Zeke is a Type Nine, and it's nap time all day every day," said Wesley.

Constance frowned. "Let's not disparage any number, please. Type Nine, the Peacemaker, is stereotyped as passive and slow moving, which isn't fair. They do seek harmony, though, and will do anything to avoid conflict, for fear it will disturb their internal or external peace."

"Not a killer," said Sam. She felt energized, crossing off Types left and right. They must be getting closer.

"I'm not finished," said Constance, and snatched the marker back from Sam. "The Type Nine Peacemaker is trusting, supportive, and optimistic. People love to be around them because they're adaptable, nonjudgmental, and openminded. They're also stubborn and hate being pressured into action. They might agree with others to keep the peace but secretly do what they wanted in the first place. This is off topic, but the way the sheriff spoke of his wife reminded me of a Type Nine."

Zeke gave a particularly loud snore and startled himself awake. Everyone watched, to see if... nope. Still sleeping.

"Can I disparage Fours? Given that I am one?" Wesley asked. Despite his mismatched, ill-fitting clothes, Wesley looked like the love interest in one of those vampire romance novels mothers and daughters read together. Farren had never asked, but Sam would've happily taken part in a buddy read with her.

"I'm Wesley, the Individualist, the Romantic, the Emo Brat, however you want to look at it, and I'm here because I think it will help me as a journalist to understand why people do what they do."

"Would you like insight into yourself, as well?" asked Constance.

He shuddered. "If anything, I'd like a break from that."

"Type Fours, the Individualist, are the most self-aware of the numbers. They're introspective and in tune with every thought and emotion that crosses their mind, however fleeting," Constance explained.

"Ask me if that's fun," said Wesley.

Self-absorbed, in other words, Sam thought. That seemed at odds with killing, in her opinion, because getting angry about what others were doing would mean being *aware* of what others were doing.

She clamped her hand onto the dry-erase marker, and she and Constance engaged in a tug-of-war over it. Sam won and crossed out "Type Four, the Individualist: Wants to be known" on the board. She also drew a line through "Type Nine, the Peacemaker: Wants to be in harmony."

"At their best, Type Fours are authentic and genuine, and expect the same from others," Constance droned on. Sam tapped her foot. "They have the gift of empathy and feel things deeply, using artistic expression to help the rest of us access *our* emotions. Above all, they want to be known, but because they overidentify with their feelings, which fluctuate wildly, that sense of self they crave feels out of reach."

Wesley had pulled his ratty cardigan over his head like a turtle.

"When upset, they withdraw, because they're in the withdrawing stance alongside Nines and Fives. However, that's a lot of information this early in the game," Constance said.

"Yes, yes, let's not get sidetracked," Sam said. "My turn. I'll make it quick. Still not sure if I'm an Enthusiastic Seven or a Peacemaking Nine—"

Had Constance huffed?

"Okay, maybe I'm not peaceful *today*, but—"

Constance huffed again.

"What?"

"Oh, nothing. Just that you were very *helpful* during my *first* class."

Unlike this one, when you became a power-hungry monster, went unspoken.

"And you're clearly *helpful* to your husband, even if I disagree with your method."

"I don't get what you're—Oh." Sam felt confused. "You think I'm Type Two, the Helper?"

"I would never normally suggest your Type, but since you broke the rules first by hijacking my class..."

The Helper. Huh. Maybe Constance was right.

Yes, dammit, I <u>am</u> helpful! Could someone please tell that to Penelope and Farren?

"The Helper is good at extending comfort to others," Constance said. "They're selfless, warm, and loving, the kind of parent we all wish we had. But they struggle with 'giving to get.' In other words, they give to get something in return."

"That doesn't sound like me," Sam said quietly.

Except... it did, didn't it? *I tried to manipulate Penelope into feeling beholden to me by offering her free stuff she never asked for. I pretended it was out of the kindness of my heart when really, I wanted her to allow playdates with our kids and help me with Farren in exchange.*

She shook off her shame. There was no time for it. "Here goes. I'm Sam the SAHM, and my family and I have lived in Cherry Hill for a decade. My son Dale is in second grade at the elementary school, my d—..." Her throat tightened. Constance had said Type Two Helpers embodied the ideal parent. It was so far from the truth in her situation that she couldn't bear to mention her daughter. "And, um, my husband Will—who, I want to stress, is not a murderer—runs the Magic Mirror theatre off the freeway. Which reminds me, I have coupons and drink specials. Bring your friends. We could use the business, ha ha ha."

She flung the items onto the table, and a few people reached for them, including Wesley.

"I'll pitch an article," he said. "My boss is eager to promote local businesses."

Sam smiled, imagining the look on her husband's face when he learned she had arranged free publicity. Then she felt sick, picturing a future issue of the *Gazette* sitting like a bomb on her porch. LOCAL MENTALIST CAUSED DEADLY CRASH. WIFE TO BLAME FOR MAKING HIM WORK IN ONE PLACE.

"I figured all your time would be going towards the murder," she told Wesley.

"You and me both," Wesley said bitterly.

"And what about *you*, Sam?" Constance asked.

"What about me?"

"You've told us about your son and husband, but what do *you* do, what are *your* interests?"

The question threw her. *Interests? Besides getting through the day?*

"I used to work at a non-profit. B.C. Before Child. Oh! I'm here at the class, or at least I was originally here, because I'd love insight into my d—Dale," (she'd almost said daughter again) "and my other *people*, so I can figure out what they need." Proving Will's innocence was the priority, of course, but she couldn't resist asking, "What number do you think Penelope is?"

"Three," Wesley said beneath a fake cough.

"Who's Penelope?" asked Chase.

"A young mom I know, who came last time," Sam explained. "I offered her my sitter so she could come, but she never answered. I'm curious what her Type is because she seems—closed off."

"Her unwillingness to share a sitter may have nothing to do with you," Constance told Sam. "But let's talk Threes, the Achiever, in *general* terms, unrelated to Penelope. At their healthiest, they bring out the best in others. They see potential and inspire those around them to reach greater heights. They're extremely ambitious, and charming."

"They're also fake," Wesley said. "What? It's true! That's why She Who Must Not Be Named wanted to know which number was the best, so she could fake it."

"What Wesley means, *unrelated to Penelope*, is that Type Three Achievers sometimes adopt a false front depending on who they're around," said Constance. "They reflect what they believe others value, so *they* can be perceived as valuable. Type Four, the Individualist, finds that maddening, as demonstrated by Wesley, because they revere authenticity. I happen to adore Threes. Now. Have we covered everyone?" Constance asked. "Wait, we're missing Eights and Ones."

"I'm looking at a One right now," Wesley said. Trevor nodded.

Constance's cheeks reddened. "That obvious?"

"You were adamant on Saturday that Type One was not the best."

"I said none of them were the best," Constance corrected him.

"Yes, but you *guffawed* when Penelope—look, she exists, okay?—suggested Type Ones were number one. And I thought to myself, 'There's something going on there.'"

Constance smiled timidly. "Guilty as charged. Want to take a swipe at it?"

Wesley cracked his knuckles. "Your inner critic says you're never good enough, which makes you try harder, which ironically *does* make you better than most people. Accept it, Mrs. Kincaid: you are the best one."

The group laughed, Sam included, though it annoyed her that Wesley called Constance "Mrs." Kincaid; how like a man to disregard a women's unmarried status. Constance had made it clear on multiple occasions that she was a spinster.

"Rao," added Mr. Cinnamon, trotting over. Constance picked up her cat and snuggled him before setting him back down.

"Very well. I'm a Type One, the Perfectionist, also known as the Reformer. We advocate for reform. We like to improve things." Constance thought for a moment. "We can be overly critical, inflexible, condescending, and judgmental. We tend to have black-and-white, binary thinking: something's right or it's wrong, it's good or it's bad, and we alone are the arbiters of such. We see what needs to be better, instead of what's already good. We can't resist correcting people." Constance swallowed, then gave a short laugh. "For example, the other day I was at Kaftans 'n' More, and a person in line was excited about the snow. I corrected him, because I knew he was wrong—"

"He was wrong to be excited?" Chase asked.

"Well, yes! He was wrong to think it would be *snow*. It would be more like sleet, or slush, and I told him that. I'm from New York, I know from slush. But what I didn't know was his little girl was there too, and she was excited, and I'd made her cry, which made me feel terrible. Unhealthy Type Ones view themselves as infallible—which is a ruse to cover up our fear, deep down, that we're the most corrupt. To deflect, we fixate on everyone else's faults. We want to be blameless."

"Our challenges are also our gifts, though, right?" Wesley said. "Tell us the good parts of Ones."

Sam was glad he'd said that. She didn't like seeing Constance put herself down in such a raw manner in public. Sam might have staged a coup, but it wasn't personal.

"Ones are diligent and responsible, self-disciplined, and objective. You can count on us." Constance shrugged. "We're moral. We really, really want to be good."

"So not a killer?" Sam asked. "Again?" This was getting annoying. If they didn't come up with something to help Will soon, she would burst. She moved to cross off "Type One, the Perfectionist: Wants to be good" from the dry-erase board. To her surprise, Constance stopped her with a gentle hand on her arm.

"You're forgetting that to a severely unhealthy Type One, killing might be the 'right' thing to do. It's a personal affront to a Perfectionist when others behave in a manner the One thinks is unjust."

Wesley stood. "'Let justice roll on like a river, righteousness like a never-failing stream.' Ana Whitley of the Hummingbird Art Gallery said that at the city council meeting last Thursday. Everyone was there to complain about the trolley, and she gave a fire-and-brimstone speech fixated on justice."

"It's her. She's the killer," Sam exploded. "Call the Sheriff!"

"Already dialing," yelled Chase.

"Wait, no, stop," said Constance. "Oh, my goodness. Phones down. We are not accusing Ana Whitley of the Hummingbird Art Gallery of murder based on a single line in a single speech—"

"It's more than that." Wesley dragged a hand through his award-winning hair, looking agitated. He rifled through his bag and yanked out a sheet of paper. "We printed this letter in the *Gazette* six months ago. See who it reminds you of. 'As a local businessperson of Cherry Hill, I have requested multiple times that the tourist trolley retire. My reasons are fourfold:'"

Chase laughed. "There's a word you don't hear every day."

Wesley continued, "Listen to the whole thing. '1. It's needlessly large, the size of a city bus. It blocks customer traffic and street parking on Main Street.

"2. It's an environmental menace, puffing out exhaust as it lurches around town, as well as a sound polluter with its incessant tourism recording and jingle.

"3. It is both slow and cumbersome. Isaac Caldecot drives 15 mph so that nonexistent visitors can leisurely enjoy the sights. But what about those of us who live and work here year-round? Are we to be at the trolley's mercy till the end of our days?

"4. It's a financial black hole and its devastating impact

on local businesses cannot be overstated. Layoffs and store closings are imminent.

"I submit that the Jolly Trolley commit to ALL the following upgrades and modernizations:

"A. Alter its route to exclude Main Street during business hours.

"B. Replace its current diesel engine with solar panels.

"C. TURN OFF THE SONG or provide it strictly via headphones.

"D. Speed up!!!

"As you can see, I have provided concrete, actionable advice. Mr. Caldecot is fully aware of these issues yet has done nothing to address them. It's not right.

"If my concerns cannot be resolved in a just manner, I will be forced to take action.

"Sincerely, A Concerned Business Owner of Main Street.'"

Sam kept her eyes glued to Constance while Wesley read.

"Wow. Okay." Constance placed a hand on her chest. She looked staggered. "That is textbook, classic One. The moralizing, the obsession with justice and doing what's 'right,' thinking they know better than the trolley driver."

"So, you agree? The person who wrote this murdered Isaac Caldecot, and if we find the One, we'll find the killer?" Sam begged.

19

WESLEY

"THAT'S A BIG LEAP," said Constance. "I mean, come on. It's one letter."

And there it is, Wesley thought. *The condescension Type One Perfectionists are known for. Meanwhile, Constance is still pretending she was never married. What's that about?*

"You literally called it 'textbook One,'" Wesley reminded her. He was eager to play along, not only as a reporter, but to help Sam.

He felt guilty about the sidebar he'd written that put Sam's husband under suspicion. He didn't think her husband was guilty; Will Orlaith wouldn't have tampered with the trolley's engine with his own kid onboard. He was being punished for a good deed and bad timing.

"It appeared to hit some of the points I mentioned, but anyone can talk about justice. It doesn't mean they're a Type One unless we know the internal logic that led to their way of thinking; the motivation *behind* the letter," said Constance.

Wesley disagreed. "'The trolley is a blight. The trolley is

an environmental menace. The trolley blocks traffic. The trolley is causing devastating economic impact.' *That's* the motivation. *That's* the internal logic. And the suggestions laid out in detail sound like a reformer's all-or-nothing thinking to me. They threatened him outright. They said they'd be 'forced to act.'"

"For all we know, the author of the letter meant he or she would be forced to sue, which they did. The chamber of commerce did," Constance said.

"If you're talking about Martin Onder at Kaftans 'n' More and his doomed lawsuit," Wesley replied, "that makes me suspect him *more*. Because the lawsuit wasn't getting results."

"I'm going next door to tell the sheriff about this," Sam announced. "How they need to be looking for a Type One Perfectionist, not a Type Six Loyal Skeptic."

"He will laugh you out of town," Constance said. "And make a mockery of my class."

"It's better than nothing! I can't just do nothing!"

"Like you said, between the six of us—" Constance glanced at Zeke. "Between the *five* of us, surely we can come up with something more actionable for you to tell him."

Sam squinted. "Are you helping for real now?"

In response, Constance raised her eyebrows and held out her hand for the dry-erase marker. Sam handed it to her.

"Sit down, Sam," Constance said with her whole chest.

Sam obeyed.

Constance uncapped the pen. "Wesley, who else spoke at the city council meeting?"

Wesley pulled up a Word doc on his laptop to share with the group.

"I'll get the projector," said Chase. He dashed into his

office, rolled a projector into the room, and attached Wesley's laptop to it.

"Thanks, man. Okay. Here's my transcript from the meeting."

Everyone looked at the large screen. Wesley realized too late he'd never changed the shorthand nicknames he'd used for the Main Street business owners. It was bad enough the sheriff's department had a copy.

"Who's T.D.?" asked Trevor.

Wesley's face felt hot. "Um, that stands for Turkish Delight. Which is what I called Martin Onder, who happens... to be... Turkish. As well as a... delight."

"You call the owner of Kaftans 'n' More and the head of the Cherry Hill Chamber of Commerce 'Turkish Delight'?" Constance clarified slowly.

Wesley thought he might puke. "Never before, and never since! It was for this one piece of shorthand, so I could write quickly. No one was supposed to see this."

"You could have used 'M.O.' for Martin Onder," Constance said.

But then it would look like modus operandi, he thought. "That's true," he said. He wanted to die.

"Let's move on."

"As you can see, Martin said the trolley had become so notorious for blocking traffic and blasting its 'bleeping' song —well, not 'bleeping,' he used a word we don't print in the *Cherry Hill Gazette*—that the townspeople no longer came to Main Street, preferring the relative ease of the big box stores. After that, B.B., uh, I mean, Ana Whitley—"

"Why do you call her 'B.B.'?" asked Trevor.

"I don't! I don't call *anyone* these things. It was just—"

"Shorthand, we know. Everyone stop judging Wesley or we'll never get through this," Constance said.

"Thank you, Constance. B.B. stands for, uh, Birdbrain for, you know, the Hummingbird Art Gallery. Ana Whitley backed up Martin's statement. Actually, her microphone malfunctioned at first, so I didn't hear the beginning of her speech, but the gist of it was that line from the Bible that I told you about, 'Let justice roll on like a river, righteousness like a never-failing stream.'"

"It's interesting she used religion," Constance said. "At their worst, Ones believe they're a punitive avenger. A god-like punisher, eradicating evil—evil they've projected onto others, mind you."

"Yikes." Chase winced.

"Eights, Nines, and Ones struggle with anger. Not me, though," Constance said, beneath a rictus grin. "I have that under control."

Wesley bit his lip. *Suuuuure you do.* Mr. Cinnamon leaped onto the table, scattering papers and pens. Wesley thought fast, crumpled up a sheet of paper, and threw it to the far corner. Mr. Cinnamon bounded after it.

"I was surprised she quoted the Bible," said Wesley, "because Ana Whitley looks very patchouli and granola, like she follows Goddess Gaia, not traditional Christianity. Anyway, after that, Sandworm—uhhh Aidan Zachary, took the mic."

"'Sandworm'?" Now Chase looked perplexed.

Wesley rubbed his eyes. "The manager of Dune Buggies, U.S.A. It was a reference to *Dune*. Anyway, Aidan Zachary called for cooler heads to prevail and offered his place of business for a peaceful rally that Saturday. He stressed peaceful, but we all know how that turned out."

"With a rock, a broken window, and a broken speaker," Constance reminded the others. "I was inside the trolley when it happened. Aidan rescued me, and he looked upset. How did people respond to his suggestion of cooler heads?"

"There were a few claps, but he was overshadowed by the next speaker, Danny Flores, who runs Texican Table. Danny claims his takeout business has cratered from lack of parking out front, because the trolley is always taking up the space of three cars. They only serve dinner now."

"Was Isaac there?" asked Constance. "Mr. Caldecot? Did he speak?"

"Yes." Wesley clicked to his last page of notes. "He was gleeful. 'My daddy and his daddy and his daddy before him all drove this trolley. We're not part of this town; we made this town. We were here when Cherry Hill was just an unpaved dirt road with a water well and a saloon. We've been here for a hundred years, and we'll be here for a hundred more. You have no idea what's coming, and soon, too.'"

"Oh, Isaac." Constance sounded sad. "He taunted them, like he did at the protest. I didn't know him well, but that last day—I felt like we had finally gotten used to each other."

"What was he talking about?" asked Trevor. "When he said something was coming?"

"I have no idea," Wesley said. Was it Wesley's imagination, or did Trevor look nervous?

"Also, how did it explode?" asked Chase.

"Last I heard, they thought someone used zig-zag scissors to cut wires in the engine. I was sidelined from the press conference," Wesley said, "so I don't have more recent details. But let's take a closer look at the likely suspects. I have images and bios here."

The door flung open, and Roberto appeared, taking up the doorway.

"What do *you* want?" Chase demanded. His tone shocked Wesley. Wasn't Roberto his boss?

"Quota check," Roberto boomed. He glanced around the room, frowning. "Looks like you managed it. What are you all talking about?"

"We're Marpling, isn't it obvious?" Constance said sarcastically. "Quick, Wesley, hide the frisky murder board."

By *frisky murder board*, she meant *cat*, he realized as he felt a movement brush his legs. Wesley dropped his pencil, pretended to duck under the table for it, and secured the reddish fluffball. He may as well use his cat whispering skills for good.

"Scram," said Chase.

Roberto frowned but retreated. The door slammed shut behind him. It was the loudest library Wesley had ever been in.

"How has he not fired you?" he asked Chase.

"Please, like he's going to find someone else to DJ the dance party fundraiser, which doubles our budget for the year? He needs me. There have been complaints to the board about him offending patrons when he runs his mouth. I'm the one who smooths things over."

"I suspected he was a Type Eight," crowed Constance. "The Challenger. That's the number we were missing before. At their best, they're tireless leaders, unafraid to tackle huge problems. When I say tireless, I mean tireless. They have the most energy of the Types. Word of warning, Chase. He might not fire you—he probably respects you for standing up to him—but he *will* outlast you. If you have an Eight in your life who loves you, consider yourself blessed. They're passionate, resourceful, caring, and will do whatever it takes to protect their people."

"At their worst?" Trevor asked.

"At their worst, they're domineering, paranoid about being betrayed or controlled, and aggressive and confrontational."

"Classic Roberto," Chase said with a chuckle.

"In their view, they're straightforward. It's particularly difficult to be a Type Eight Challenger as a woman, because society punishes those qualities in women."

Mr. Cinnamon brought Wesley the crumpled piece of paper and dropped it on his lap, eager to play more.

"Huh," he muttered.

Was Crystal Bae from the cat cafe a Type Eight? She was certainly protective of her cats. Maybe cats were her people.

Energetic? Check. Her medical boot hadn't slowed her down even for a second.

Aggressive and confrontational? Check.

Domineering? Check.

Wesley fidgeted in his seat, remembering. A strange sensation hovered in his throat.

("Say it, then," she'd ordered him. "Say you'd love to interview me.") And he had!

A shudder slipped down his spine. It was not unpleasant.

"What's that, Wesley?" Constance asked.

He cleared his throat. "Something's up with the owner of CHATeau Savannah. She witnessed the crash, but she won't tell me what she saw because..." he trailed off.

"Because...?"

"Oh, just that, um..." his voice got quiet. "She thinks I threatened her cat."

Everyone stared at him, appalled.

Constance scooped up Mr. Cinnamon and held him close.

"I didn't! It was a misunderstanding. But she's hiding something. So is Sandworm. Aidan Zachary. Neither of them were affected financially by the trolley—her cafe's thriving, she has customer parking from the hotel, and the real site of Dune Buggies, U.S.A. is nowhere near the trolley's route—so I don't know why they're acting evasively."

"That goes for Cut & Dried, too," said Trevor. "Not about acting evasively but about not being affected financially. I got a haircut Saturday morning, and they were packed."

Sam brandished her notes. "Okay. To recap, Danny Flores at Texican Table blames the trolley for having to reduce staff and cut the restaurant hours by two-thirds; Martin Onder also hates the trolley and got no joy from his chamber of commerce lawsuit—"

"He's afraid he'll have to cut staff, too," Constance said. "He told me that directly, and his cashier looked upset. She wanted to join our class, by the way, but it conflicts with her knitting lessons."

"That's Olivia Flores," Sam said. "Her parents own Texican Table. So not only was *her* job at stake, *her family's* was too. Lastly, we have Ana Whitley, aka Birdbrain, of the Hummingbird Art Gallery, who hated the trolley for environmental reasons and business reasons and made a speech about justice that matches the tone of the letter to the paper."

Wesley couldn't shake the feeling they'd uncovered something in the last ninety minutes, but whatever it was slipped away when he tried to grasp it.

Sam's eyes were bright and determined. "That's three business owners and at least one employee who had a motive for putting the trolley out of commission, right? Class is over, so I'm giving these to the sheriff. Thanks, everyone."

Wesley hated what he was about to do. "Sam, wait..."

She paused at the door.

"Sheriff Pittman already knows all this. He's had my notes since Saturday, and he's been interviewing everyone who was at the city council meeting. You're not giving him anything new."

"What?" Sam whirled around. Tears filled her eyes and dripped down her face. Wesley felt terrible for causing them. "Then what was the point of all this?"

To Wesley's surprise, it was Constance who went to comfort Sam. She handed Sam a tissue and wrapped an arm around her shoulder.

"The good news is, the sheriff *is* looking at those other people, and I'm sure he'll get to the bottom of it. I know this is hard on you. We just have to wait."

WESLEY HAD no intention of waiting. After class, he sped to the newsroom, his windshield wipers working overtime to dispel the rain.

Editor-in-Chief Reilly sat in a tiny swivel stool at the long table, hunting-and-pecking his way through an article. Hunched over a laptop, he looked like a well-fed vulture, too large for the furniture.

"What happened at the press conference?" Wesley demanded, shaking the wet off his shoes and cardigan. "Why didn't Shawna ask questions or use the research I gave her?"

"Hello, Wesley, how are you? Staying dry?" Reilly

asked calmly. "You of all people should know that just because it wasn't in the paper—yet—doesn't mean it's all we have. Shawna said she needed more time to sort through the information she got yesterday, and I'm giving it to her. Friday's issue will be dedicated to the trolley."

Wesley looked at his boss then. Really looked. The older man's oxford shirt was askew—he'd skipped one of the buttonholes, making the whole thing lopsided. Wrinkles covered the garment.

It was one thing for Wesley to dress like a slob to undercut his looks, but Reilly didn't abide sloppiness. During his correspondence days, embedded in the military, Reilly had picked up the habit of ironing his shirts daily.

To indicate he wasn't fighting Reilly anymore, Wesley sat beside him.

Reilly sighed and closed his laptop. "I hadn't planned on saying this today, but based on your reaction, I think I'd better. This was a test."

"For whom?"

"You. I'll be retiring at the end of the year, and I want to hand the reins to you."

Wesley's heart gave a lurch. "It's too soon for that."

"You had to have known when I made you managing editor that I was preparing you to succeed me."

"Eventually, maybe. Not yet."

"Here's my dilemma. I need to know that A) you can delegate, B) you'll be patient and not rush your staff, and C) you'll nurture new talent."

"You're too young to step down."

"I became the editor when I was about your age," Reilly reminded him.

Because you didn't have a choice, Wesley thought. *You inherited it.*

"You've had three years to learn the ropes, and I believe you can do it. But I can't leave the paper in your hands if you think it's better to be fast than accurate."

"I don't! But realistically, it's Wednesday, and by the time Shawna's article runs on Friday, it'll have been almost a week since the explosion. That's too long for our readers to wait for the most basic information, especially when foul play is suspected."

"Would you rather we falsely smear people's names in the meantime?"

"No, but... Hold on. Did the sheriff ask you to wait again? Are you sitting on something explosive? Wrong choice of word, but is that what's going on?"

"What's 'going on' is I'm giving Shawna the time she requested to write the best article she can write."

Since when does the staff have that much sway over deadlines?

"Are you really retiring?" Wesley asked. He bit his thumbnail while he waited for Reilly to answer.

"That's up to you. Because I guess what I'm really asking is, do you even want to be here?"

Taking over the paper meant admitting he was here for good, in Cherry Hill, in his aunt's apartment. That there was no comeback for him, in Seattle or anywhere else.

"I don't know," Wesley said honestly.

20

TREVOR

TREV.

He called me Trev.

Such a small thing, yet Trevor couldn't stop thinking about it.

After class, Trevor had been the first one out the door. He zipped his jacket up tight under his chin in anticipation of the rain outside. At the sound of voices, he'd turned in time to see Chase exit the community room, pushing Zeke's wheelchair and chatting with Constance.

Rain clouds shrouded the library windows in gray, but Chase was the sunshine that obliterated the dreary framework. His blonde hair was swept into a weightless pompadour, and he was exuberant, eager to engage with life.

He embodied everything Trevor could never do or be.

Chase could chat with *anyone.* He was full of curiosity and vigor. Best of all was his smile: generously bestowed, not kept in a box marked Emergencies Only, like Trevor's was.

He also said you were hilarious.

Trevor's stomach dropped.

Other people had called him hilarious. They were the reason he'd come to Cherry Hill.

He stopped by the library holds shelf to pick up a stack of books waiting for him. *What Color is Your Parachute?*; *The Quarter Life Breakthrough: Invent Your Own Path, Find Meaningful Work, and Build a Life That Matters*; and *Do What You Are: Discover the Perfect Career For You Through the Secrets of Personality Type.*

As a visitor, he wasn't allowed to borrow books from the local library, but the Vitality Hotel & Spa had an account for guests to utilize.

Well, they did *now*; that was Trevor's Legacy. He'd convinced the hotel manager on his first day as a guest that it was a perk worth pursuing. The manager agreed and set up a hotel account the next day.

The manager also asked Trevor for a few favors that Trevor deeply regretted, but since Trevor was leaving town soon, he hoped to outrun the consequences.

The Vitality Hotel & Spa wasn't *exactly* rehab. They called it "Recalibration" and offered rehab-style options like group therapy and 24/7 counselors on staff, but the problem was, they expected Trevor to talk. About himself.

It was a nightmare, and a constant reminder of why he'd started abusing drugs and alcohol in the first place: so he could talk to people.

The real reason he'd joined the Enneagram class was as a replacement for group therapy. He'd wanted to be able to tell his mother he was working on himself. She deserved no less for what she was paying the Vitality.

With this fresh stack of books to create a new plan for his life, Trevor could close out his desert convalescence and return to the east coast. He felt bad for leaving Constance in the lurch, quota-wise, but there was nothing he could do about that.

~

FIVE MINUTES LATER, and CHATeau Savannah was Trevor's lighthouse in the rain.

"Hi, Trevor, good to see you," Crystal greeted him. She still wore a bulbous medical boot for her sprained ankle. "There's an umbrella stand by the door. Would you like your usual?"

"Yes, please."

"Of course."

Rain slammed against the floor-to-ceiling windows, and outside, the palm trees swayed in the wind, making the cafe feel like a ship at sea. The place was near empty for the first time since Trevor had become a monthly member.

He sat at the large corner booth by the front window. He'd never gotten such a plum spot, with plenty of room to spread out his library books.

Trevor couldn't understand why rain kept people *away* from the cafe rather than drew them closer. They didn't like the bleak, grey skies and bullet-spatter raindrops, but the contrast between the cold outside world and the tender warmth of the cafe was what gave the warmth *meaning*.

Not that he wanted people around, though. He was drained from the Enneagram class.

The cats never asked more of him than scratches atop their heads where they couldn't reach. He especially liked the plump gray-and-white Ragdoll, Purr-cy, who had a soft, unruly tuft of fur under his chin that Trevor never tired of stroking.

Cleocatra was a sweetheart, too.

He wasn't as enamored of the hybrid cat, the titular Savannah, who didn't trust easily. Gaining its affection required time Trevor didn't have.

Since his previous visit, Crystal had hung up a corkboard for local announcements. Ads with tear-off phone numbers abounded, for tutors, pet-sitters, gardeners, and the like. A flyer for Texican Table read, "Celebrar! Brunch is back, amigos! Come celebrate with us this Sunday as we reinstate our popular Weekend Brunch, followed by the return of Margarita Mondays for lunch and dinner."

Except they'd spelled it *Wekeend Brunch* and *Mragarita Mondays*. The typos hurt to look at, both because of the lack of care used, and the fact that the restaurant was clearly *celebrating* Isaac Caldecot's death. Everything about it made Trevor cringe.

His eyes lost focus. The corkboard was a near-replica of the one at the University of Buffalo School of Law, the one he'd used to search for a Study Group last fall.

He'd found one, alright.

You're hilarious.

Trevor would have preferred to study by himself, but when he studied by himself, he fell down tangential rabbit holes. Sometimes it took days to climb out.

He thought that if he joined a study group, it would keep him on track. And it had. The group's mere presence reminded him to focus, but it also meant he had to find a way to chat with everyone before and after the studying took place.

His mom was so happy to hear he was being "social" that she put extra cash in his account to make sure he didn't use lack of funds as an excuse to miss out on events.

The group invited him to happy hour at a townie bar multiple nights a week. The pitchers of beer tasted awful, but Trevor noticed that after one or two glasses, his anxiety about the group melted away. People liked him; they thought he was funny. They said it over and over: "You're hilarious."

It also resulted in hangovers the next day; the humiliating realization that when people told him he was funny they didn't mean it in a *good* way; and an inability to concentrate in class, so when someone offered him an Adderall, and assured him it was safe, he accepted instead of doing the research he should have done about the risks of off-label use. He was still exhausted when it wore off, maybe even more exhausted than he'd been *before* taking it, but it got him through his immediate problem. And if it was draining the life out of him, well... he could always take another one.

Trevor spent his 26th birthday in the University at Buffalo library, drinking from a water bottle filled with vodka. Once the vodka and research ran out, he knew he'd be left alone to inhabit a world in which he didn't know how to be himself and have that be enough for anyone.

He blacked out right there at the table. He had no memory of the ambulance ride to the hospital.

It struck him for weeks afterward that the person who'd found him was a stranger.

All his efforts to fit in hadn't amounted to anything. He wasn't meant to have relationships. The requirements were too high; they asked too much of him; he'd only disappoint the other person while destroying himself in the process.

He yearned to meet someone special, to connect with someone in a way that didn't require pills or alcohol to sustain. Someone who would understand that his inner battery life, as Constance had put it, was as real as his heartbeat.

Crystal dropped off his half-caf, half-decaf latte. Then, to his horror, she sat down across from him. He'd had enough human interaction today. The cats were supposed to be a break from that.

"This is probably a longshot, but do you recognize this handwriting?" She placed a postcard on the table. "I'm asking all my customers."

It was a whimsical children's book illustration of two dapperly dressed rats rolling a cat into a burrito. Or not a burrito—he had Texican Table on the brain—but a tube of some sort. A pie? Weren't animals always being baked into pies in these old children's stories? Or at least the possibility of it hovered in the background.

"I realize it looks cute, because it's Beatrix Potter, but the rats are going to eat Thom Kitten, and this is a cat cafe! It's meant to scare me."

To illustrate her point, she flipped the card over.

This is your final warning. No one wants you here. Go!

Trevor's blood boiled. What kind of sicko would terrorize a cat cafe, the epitome of everything good in the world? But Crystal didn't want his ire—she wanted answers, so he tried to help.

"It says 'final,'" he pointed out. "Were there others?"

"No, and this one is postmarked two weeks ago. I didn't see it because I didn't check my P.O. Box much over the holidays."

"Have you told the sheriff?"

"I told Deputy Max, because I already have a case opened against that horrible Wesley, the so-called reporter," she spat. "You were there when he threatened Savannah. I might need you to take the stand as a witness if it comes to that."

The last thing he wanted to do was get roped into *that* situation. Wesley might be obnoxious, but he wouldn't harm an animal. Trevor told her as much, while on the inside, he groaned about his loss of alone time.

All his life, thwarted from peace and quiet.

After several one-word replies from him, Crystal sensed his lack of interest. "Okay, well I'll let you get back to Purrcy."

Trevor had barely breathed a sigh of relief when loud voices from another table cut into his quiet time. The voices belonged to a man and a woman. The woman he recognized as Ana Whitley, aka Birdbrain.

Annoyance shifted into hope. Chase loved the trolley mystery. If Trevor paid attention to Ana's discussion, the next time he saw Chase he'd have something specific and interesting to tell him.

Trevor put his earbuds in, but no music.

This Type Five Observer would do what he did best.

Ana berated her companion with hushed vitriol. "You lied to me, Aidan."

Trevor made a mental note that she was arguing with "Aidan," a muscular guy in a suit and tie. That name was familiar, too. What had Wesley called him? Sandworm? Right, from *Dune*. This was Aidan Zachary, of Dune Buggies, U.S.A.

"You told me it was a liberation," Ana hissed. "You better fix it, or I'm telling the sheriff *everything*."

Aidan frowned at her but said nothing. The two were interrupted by Crystal, who seemed oblivious to the tension at their table.

"Before you leave, this is probably a long shot, but do you recognize this handwriting?" Crystal showed them the postcard.

Aidan squinted at it. Trevor watched him carefully. It was subtle, but he caught it: a quick intake of breath, followed by a clamping of his lips.

Ana had no such compunctions about responding. "Are you kidding me right now?" she screeched.

That seemed an oversized reaction, but then again, Ana was an animal-and-nature lover, so it made sense she'd be upset about the cats being threatened with death-by-pastry.

"What is happening to this town?" Ana wailed.

"Why would anyone go after *you*?" Aidan said to Crystal. "Everyone in Cherry Hill should be thanking you for keeping Main Street afloat single-handedly."

Crystal beamed. "Thank you. It's nice to be acknowledged." Her tone shifted back to a serious one. "Do you have any idea who might've sent this, or where it came from?"

"I mean, I recognize the image, because I think my grandma had a set of those books from way back, I think."

Two "thinks" in one sentence did not inspire confidence.

"It's from the *Roly-Poly Pudding*, sometimes known as the *Tale of Samuel Whiskers*," Crystal said.

Aidan worried at his lip and closed his eyes, as though struggling to remember.

Trevor didn't buy it.

"And I might've seen... Never mind."

"Tell me," Crystal demanded.

"I might have seen them at Kaftans 'n' More," Aidan said in a rush. "They have postcards in the dollar bin."

Trevor thought K 'n' M only sold frozen pizza and

dubious hotdogs. Aidan seemed more like a chicken-and-steamed-vegetables kind of guy.

As though he knew what Trevor was thinking, Aidan added, "It's next door to my admin office. It's convenient."

"Right," Crystal said. "But the handwriting doesn't ring a bell?"

"No. I'm sorry this is happening to you. You don't deserve it," Aidan said, and this Trevor believed. Aidan appeared to be genuinely distraught.

"We should get going," Ana said.

Once the duo left, Trevor abandoned his ruse and removed his earbuds. Tomorrow he'd stop by the library, and if Chase happened to be working and happened to notice Trevor and happened to say, "Hey, Trev, what's up?" he'd have something ready.

Maybe.

If he could work up the courage.

No sooner had his earbuds hit the table when Crystal sidled over. Would he never get a moment to himself?

"Refill?" she asked.

"I'm good."

He wracked his brain for something to say that would close out the conversation. "I'm sorry about your ankle." He paused. "Good luck."

She didn't leave. She very much hovered.

"Do you want me to go?" he asked. He was the only customer left. "You could close early."

"No, please stay," Crystal said, and sat down. *Again.* "I'm just giving my ankle a break. I probably should've skipped Savvy's walk the day of the crash, but you know how she is. Rain or shine, she needs her exercise or she's completely cuckoo." It took Trevor a moment to figure out what had led to that comment. Oh, right. Her injured ankle.

She'd sprained it because Savannah had yanked hard on the leash.

Crystal didn't seem to require a response, so he waited.

"I'm glad I don't need crutches. How would I balance the drinks? Which reminds me, I'm looking for another barista-slash-cat-lover, if you know anyone. My host had to quit and it's left me empty-handed."

Savannah trotted over, and Trevor's heart beat wildly. Was today the day Savvy would give him a chance? But the beautiful, otherworldly cat suddenly halted. Her throat undulated, and her neck lurched from side to side.

"Oh, no," said Crystal. "Here we go again."

Savannah leaped onto the closest cat perch, almost falling twice with a clumsy scrabbling motion. Trevor had never seen the elegant cat look so out of sorts.

He backed away in time for the poor creature to vomit in an arc from the highest perch.

"Why does she go up there to do that?" Crystal moaned. "Stay on the ground, Savvy! Poor, poor Savvy."

Despite her medical boot, Crystal thumped rapidly to the cafe counter and grabbed some cleaning supplies to take care of the issue. "She's been ill for days," she told Trevor as she scrubbed. "I feel terrible. The vet said to come back if it keeps happening. With Wesley's threat, and that horrible postcard, and now her illness, I'm worried someone *did* something to her."

"But when?" Trevor asked, confused. "Isn't she always with you?"

Crystal didn't answer.

It seemed to Trevor as though she didn't *want* to answer. She hummed loudly to herself while she cleaned, as though she hadn't heard.

With tongs and a Ziploc, she picked up the evidence of

Savannah's illness. Trevor hoped she would boil the tongs later or throw them out entirely. "I'm going to bag this up. Maybe it'll give us information. There's an animal ER ten minutes away, but I can't just leave during business hours, and—"

"I'll watch the place," Trevor offered. Savannah was the only cat who hadn't warmed to him, so if Savannah wasn't there, and chatty Crystal wasn't there, and no other customers were there... the cat cafe would be his, all his. *Utter heaven.*

"I'll sit and read until you get back, and if anyone comes in, I'll explain how the place works, direct them to the booking system and then ask them, politely of course, to come back another time." He smiled, picturing it. He felt relaxed already.

Crystal shot him a grateful look. "Would you? Are you sure? That would be amazing. Thank you, Trevor."

She managed to coax Savannah into a large cat carrier, but the cat wasn't happy about it. The sounds it made broke Trevor's heart. He hated seeing it in distress.

"I feel like that reporter put a curse on me," Crystal said. "Stupid pretty boy sociopath. And the weirdest thing about it is that Savvy *loves* him. She *cuddled* him, and suckled his neck. She never does that! Wait, why am I telling you? You were there; you saw it. The sheriff says we don't have any proof tying him to the postcard, but I wonder... I might need to make another stop after the vet. Is that okay?"

"Take your time," Trevor said. "I'll be here."

21

PENELOPE

"TELL him Penelope Scott is calling because she solved the trolley crash. Yes, that's right. Yes, I'll hold…"

Penelope hit speaker on her smartphone so Henry could hear both sides of the conversation. Was she seeking a pat on the head from the sheriff? Yes. Did she want to be viewed as Helpful Girl, Solving-the-Crime Girl? Oh, yes. But her main reason for calling was to prove to Henry she hadn't moved him somewhere unsafe. Despite her best efforts to shield him, he'd heard about the trolley explosion at school, and he'd found it hard to sleep ever since.

"Sheriff Pittman speaking."

"Great, hi. Ready to close the case?"

The sheriff did not immediately reply. She assumed he'd gone mute with gratitude.

"So yeah. Henry and I solved it. Henry's my son—you met him when you gave us a ride back from U-Stor-It, remember?"

"I remember," said the sheriff. "Hi, Henry."

"Hi, Mr. Sheriff." Henry waved, even though it was a voice call.

"Anyway, Sheriff, we went back to U-Stor-It because we never did get our winter clothes last time. Thanks for giving us the number for the senior center van. We didn't use it, but it reminded me I have a friend there—Kelly Arden, used to be on *SNL?*—and he was happy to give us a lift." She had hoped the name-drop might earn her credibility, but the sheriff either didn't know who Kelly was or didn't care.

Once Kelly launched his comeback, *everyone* would know him again. If only she had an extra hour in the day to help him.

"Anyway, when Henry and I were digging through our boxes, we heard two employees talking about the trolley. I don't know if this would be admissible in court, but at least *you'll* know, and *I'll* know." *And Henry will know.*

"What did they say?" the sheriff asked.

"The first employee goes, 'So there were never any rats?' and the second employee goes, 'If there were, there aren't anymore. There was only one customer who ever complained. To be safe we called our pest guys, and the sheriff was mad we did it before he could scour the place, but if there was trouble with the trolley's engine, I wasn't going to take the fall for it.' So then *I* said, 'Gross, what's this about rats?' and they panicked. 'Nothing, nothing. No rats. We have a certificate from the pest company proving it if you want to see.' And I was like, 'Hmmm.' Henry wasn't buying it either, were you, Henry?"

"No," said Henry. "Hmmm."

"There you have it, Sheriff. Nobody hurt the trolley on purpose. Nobody meant for the driver to die. They tried to stop you finding out they had a rat problem, because that's bad for business, but it didn't work, thanks to me and Henry being Johnny-on-the-spot."

(The "Johnny" thing was a weird, old-timey phrase

she'd learned from Kelly, who was probably using it ironically, but it was hard to tell with him.)

There was such a long pause, Penelope thought Sheriff Pittman had hung up.

"Are you there? Rats got in the engine, and that's why it crashed. U-Stor-It was worried they'd lose customers if word got around, so they lied to you and hid it. Are you there?"

"I'm grateful for the information, and I'll be sure to make a note of it," he said. "Have a good night now, Miss Scott."

Penelope saw red. She turned off the speakerphone to keep the rest of their conversation private. "Don't you agree that solves it?" she asked tightly. She gave a big fake smile and a thumb's up to Henry, who smiled back, relieved.

"Miss Scott," the sheriff said in a tired voice, "there was no evidence of rats in or around the vehicle. There was no evidence of rats at U-Stor-It. We interviewed all relevant personnel, including the pest company."

"Maybe they paid off the guy, the cedar fog guy, to *say* there were no rats," she said quietly.

"Goodnight, now. Thank you for your... whaddayacallit, diligent citizenry."

Click.

"'You're welcome,'" she sang sarcastically, a la The Rock in *Moana*. Henry didn't pick up on the context and sang along with her for a moment.

"Okay, doodlebug," she said, "Mr. Sheriff agrees it was rats. Case closed. Get ready for your bath, and I'll be there in a minute." She'd warm up some milk for him, too, and hope it would be enough for him to drop off easily tonight.

Twenty minutes later, she'd wrapped Henry in a towel

and sent him to his bedroom to change into PJs when her phone rang.

Assuming it was the sheriff begging forgiveness and telling her she was right, she answered without checking the caller I.D. Too late, she saw she'd accepted a video call, with an alert 60-something woman with gray streaks in her hair looking back at her. It took Penelope a second to place her: the Enneagram teacher, what's-her-name. Constance.

A glance at her own image in the tiny box made Penelope recoil. She was a mess, with smeared mascara and flyaway hairs.

"Hello there," Constance said. "Sorry to call without warning. I had your number on my class list."

First Sam had abused her position as room parent to snag Penelope's number, and now Constance was taking liberties from a one-time class attendance. Penelope might have been flattered if it weren't so annoying.

"I promise I won't keep you," Constance continued. "I wanted to ask about the possibility of your coming back to class. We missed you today."

Penelope very much doubted that. She knew she'd behaved poorly at the first one.

"Thanks. One second. I'll be back."

She set her phone down and darted to her bedroom, where she re-did her makeup, and re-slicked her hair into a bun before returning to the call.

"Sorry to keep you waiting," Penelope said, though she didn't mean it. Looking this good took time, but it was worth the effort, even if they'd only be interacting for a few minutes. "Is this about your quota? You need five of us, right?"

"No. Well, partly. But I also believe the class will be beneficial for you."

"In what way?"

"It might be nice to get a break from being the best at everything," Constance said gently, "and see that it's enough to be yourself."

Penelope's expertly manicured fingernails dug into her palm. "Sorry, I don't have time for it. I barely have time to take care of Henry, run my consulting business, or fend off my ex-husband's lawyers."

"Sam has offered to share her babysitter."

"She told you that?"

"Is there a reason you're reluctant to accept her offer, or am I reading too much into it?"

"She's not my type of mom friend or whatever. She's pushy, you know what I mean?"

"I see. I'm sorry to hear you're having legal issues with your ex-husband."

"He refuses to pay me what I'm owed for co-writing a TV theme song."

Constance's face lit up. "You're having an intellectual property dispute?"

Why does she look excited? "Yeah. It's horrible."

"Would you do me a favor and google 'Hwang v. Warner Brothers'?"

"Why?"

"It'll be clear in a minute."

Hoping this would speed things along to get Constance off the phone, Penelope typed the phrase into her search bar. Results flooded her screen. "Dr. Hwang's tattoo case," she murmured. Why did that ring a bell?

"Fifteen years ago, a talented tattoo artist known as Dr. Hwang—" Constance began.

"—The best in the business," Penelope whispered. She

followed his Instagram account. He was always showing up on rock stars' private jets to ink them with intricate designs while they soared over the Atlantic.

"He is now, but at the time he was new. He tattooed an action star with an original design, and the movie studio opted not to cover the tattoo for the film. I argued in front of the Supreme Court that Dr. Hwang's design entitled him to compensation since it featured in almost every frame of that year's highest-grossing film, not to mention film posters, still shots, and other advertisements, without credit or permission. It became synonymous with the franchise and materially contributed to its success. We got a 20-million-dollar settlement."

Penelope's mouth fell open. "Are you for real?"

"Yes. Assuming you have proof of your claim, I'd be happy to represent you in your dispute. Pro bono."

"It's contingent, right? I come back to class; you send a scary letter?"

"No, I'll help either way. This is not a transaction."

But everything in life was a transaction, Penelope knew. The trick was to make sure it was mutually beneficial.

"Think it over, and let me know." Constance ended the call.

Mind racing, Penelope fed Henry and tucked him in before jumping on her laptop and researching Constance. Apparently, she was a giant in her field, a precedent-setting wunderkind. Electricity soared through Penelope's veins.

She sent Constance a text: "I'll be there Saturday. Looking forward to it."

Then she held her nose, unblocked Sam the SAHM, and sent her a note, too, asking to share the flipping babysitter.

A thumbs-up emoji came back right away.

Dale will be thrilled!!!!!

Penelope took a moment to breathe.

So will Henry. Thanks.

Whatever it took.

22

CONSTANCE

HOW'S THAT FOR UNLIKEABLE? Constance thought.

Would an unlikeable woman have checked up on a student and thrown her hat in the ring of a contentious divorce, with no expectation of said student rejoining the class?

She hoped she had sufficiently conveyed the absence of a quid pro quo to Penelope.

Chase had given her and Mr. Cinnamon / Sassy Pants a lift home after class in his lavender SUV and encouraged her to call Penelope as he drove.

After thanking Chase for the lift, she picked up the mail from the upside-down mailbox and waved at "double-worse" Deputy Max, parked on her street to keep watch.

He stared back, unblinking. Still not a fan, then.

Inside, she removed her wet shoes, set her bag down so Mr. Cinnamon could burst free, and turned on the shower for a well-earned soak. While she waited for the water to heat, she gave Mr. Cinnamon some head scritches.

"I know it can't happen again, but I loved having you in class with me today. You make everything better."

He responded with a loud purr and a slow blink.

For the first time in weeks, Constance was pleased with herself.

She ticked off the current roster of students on her fingers. Sam, Wesley, Penelope, Zeke, and Trevor made five. Chase provided a cushion if one of the regulars was ill on Wednesdays, provided he didn't get bored and quit. As a Type Seven Enthusiast, his impulse was to jump from interest to interest. Arthur had been the same—and not only that, but he'd jumped from woman to woman, too, apparently.

Stop. Take the win, she chastised herself. For today, for this moment, Penelope was back in the fold, and that was a victory. And today's class had been fun! Sam's takeover had infuriated her, of course, but then it became exhilarating, using her knowledge of the Enneagram to theorize about the trolley murder, everyone chatting and laughing and getting to know one another on a deeper level—it was the community she'd been craving.

She tossed her damp clothes in the laundry and tested the temperature of the shower with her wrist before stepping inside. It was perfect. Hot but not boiling. She pulled the curtain closed, shut her eyes, and let the steam envelop her in bliss.

When she opened her eyes, she screamed.

Written in blood on the inside of her shower curtain were the words: "IT SHOULD'VE BEEN YOU."

23

CONSTANCE

HER SCREAM BROUGHT an unlikely white knight to her rescue. Deputy Max Evert banged on her front her door in less than a minute.

"Ma'am? Ms. Kincaid?" Max shouted. He must have leaped over the gate. "Are you hurt?"

Whimpering, she shoved the curtain to the side, wrapped herself in a robe, and fled the bathroom. Maybe she should have stayed where she was and locked herself in, but she couldn't bear to stay near that horrible, bloody message.

Was the perpetrator still in the house, hiding inside a closet, ready to spring out at her with a knife or a gun?

She needed to find Mr. Cinnamon.

"Did you fall? Can you stand?" Deputy Max bellowed from outside.

Constance couldn't decide what was more insulting. The assumption that she'd fallen and couldn't get up, a la those medical alert ads from the 1980s, or the assumption that she was hard of hearing and needed him to shout.

"Scan your body for injuries," Max yelled.

"I'm not injured."

"Roll onto your side. Crawl to a chair. Get into a half-lunge position, use your dominant leg and rise. Riiiiiise."

"Max, I didn't fall."

"Don't be embarrassed. We'll practice getting up, like a fire drill!"

"Please stop shouting. I'm unlocking the door."

She'd never been so relieved to see another human being in all her 67 years.

"Why'd you scream?" he asked. "I thought you shattered your hip. Nobody approached your dwelling; I know because I've been patrolling since you arrived."

"Thank you for that. *This* is why I screamed." She led him to the bathroom and showed him the message written across the inner curtain of her shower. "I think it's blood."

Max recoiled, then touched a red letter with his fingertip and sniffed it.

"Spray paint."

That was less horrifying, but only just.

Someone had entered her home intending to terrorize her while she stood naked and helpless in the shower. She couldn't believe how relaxed she'd been ten minutes ago, congratulating herself on her win.

Beside her, Max held a flashlight to illuminate the crime scene. Eyes wide, he snapped images on his phone. "Who could have done this? And when?"

"It must have been while I was teaching my class at the library." She gasped and started to cry. "Thank goodness Mr. Cinnamon was with me. What if he'd *been here*? What if the criminal had *hurt* him? Oh, poor Mr. Cinnamon..." Tears poured down her cheeks. "I need to find him."

"Little foxy guy, right? The boss man told me about him. I'm sure he's fine. Probably hiding."

She nodded.

"I got here half an hour ago, to relieve Deputy Cole," Max told her, "but there was a five-minute window where no one was parked on your street. I didn't think it was a big deal because *you* weren't here, either—first thing I did when I arrived was knock on your door—but that must have given the perpetrator enough time to strike and get out."

"How did they get in?" She wiped her tears away, but more kept forming.

"Good question. I'm going to check every room for broken windows or locks. Stay here."

It felt like years before he returned. "No one's inside," he assured her. "Not even in the upside-down room, I made sure of that."

"Did you see my cat?"

"Yes, he's on the couch."

"Okay. That's good. Uh, what are you doing?"

Max had knelt on the bathroom floor in front of her, his hands folded over his bent knee.

"I didn't care for you at first," he said, "and that haunts me. You may be a new citizen of this town, but you *are* a citizen of this town, and therefore someone I've sworn to protect. I won't leave your side until your tormenter has been neutralized. I'll shield your life with mine."

"Oh, my goodness, that's—here, get up, can I offer you an espresso?"

"I have the feeling adrenaline will power me through the long night ahead, but thank you, m'lady, I accept with gratitude."

Oh boy. He was really committed to the knight fantasy. She was grateful for his company, though, and his behavior calmed her down. It was hard to be scared when she felt like giggling.

"While you make the coffee, I'll take more photos and remove the curtain for evidence. I'll ask Deputy Cole to bring it to the station." He smacked his thigh. "Darn it! My radio's in the car. I'll be right back. Quick as can be."

And he was.

"Do you have a fold-out couch?" he asked, once he'd downed the espresso and made a grim expression, as though it were rotgut whisky.

"Yes, here in the living room. I'll get the sheets from the hall closet."

When that task was complete, Constance's heart rate returned to a stampede. More tears slipped down her cheeks, and she had the urge to crawl into bed and never come out. She'd cocoon herself for the rest of the winter while Deputy Max, of all people, stood guard.

"Don't worry, Ms. Kincaid. You go on and rest, secure in the knowledge that you're safe," he told her.

Dizzy, she staggered down the hall to her bedroom. Mr. Cinnamon trotted alongside her, which provoked another round of quiet tears. She didn't know what she'd do if she lost Mr. Cinnamon. It was too painful to contemplate.

"And tomorrow," Max called from the den, "I'll be both bodyguard and driver. I'll drive you anywhere you need to go, and stay by your side, alright, m'lady?"

It turned out she didn't need Max to drive her anywhere.

She didn't leave the house for two days.

She became the hermit everyone accused her of being, living an upside-down life in an upside-down house, closed to the public.

24

WESLEY

FRIDAY'S ISSUE of the *Cherry Hill Gazette* was dedicated to the trolley, alright, just as Editor-in-Chief Reilly had promised Wesley.

Remembering 100 Years of the Jolly Trolley! screeched the headline. It was a collector's edition, six-page commemorative glossy with archival photos, an interview with the mayor, and a lengthier obit for Isaac Caldecot—none of which mentioned the manner of his death or subsequent investigation.

The byline was attributed to "*Gazette* staff." Wesley bristled at the implication that he was party to it.

Rounding off the issue was a whimsical, fold-out map of "Tomorrow's Main Street," courtesy of the tourism office, meant to show what Cherry Hill would look like once its tourism came roaring back. In the bottom corner of the map, an excruciating cartoon rendering of the Jolly Trolley gazed at the new city with wonder in its childlike eyes.

"Well, as long as we have your blessing," Wesley howled, before crumpling up the issue. At least, he tried to.

The paper stock was so thick it only resulted in pain and paper cuts.

He facetimed Shawna Neuman, the cub reporter. The time for contacting her was long overdue. He flapped the issue at the camera.

"What even *is* this?"

Shawna frowned. "How should I know? I thought you wrote it."

"This propaganda tripe did not come from me."

"Reilly had me going through archival photos all week, but I didn't know it would be for this bizarre retrospective. He told me not to bother you, that you were taking the lead on the investigation."

"He told me not to bother *you*, because *you* were handling it."

"I attended the press conference and asked a bunch of questions—thanks for your notes, by the way—but he cut it down to three sentences. I figured he didn't like what I turned in."

"Which was...?"

"A timeline of events since the crash, information on the gambling ring at Senior City, a list of persons of interest—including someone I'm calling Envelope Drifter—and a request on behalf of the sheriff's department that anyone with information come forward ASAP. Reilly hated that part the most. He said it was, quote, 'a red flag for imminent democratic collapse.'"

"What on earth...?"

"He said if we printed the sheriff's request, we would be 'encouraging neighbors to inform on each other.'"

"Maybe this sounds strange, but do you think this could be PTSD from his time reporting in war zones?"

He and Shawna spoke back and forth, filling in each

other's gaps from their recent interactions with Reilly. Wesley felt guilty for discussing his previously trustworthy editor behind the man's back. But what choice did they have?

"What happened between Sunday, when you turned in your first article on the trolley, and Monday when he started lying to us both about the other person taking the lead?" Shawna asked.

"Martin from Kaftans 'n' More showed up at the newspaper office early on Monday," Wesley recalled. "He was worried he'd be implicated in the trolley crash because of the chamber of commerce lawsuit. He was furious when Reilly told him he didn't have any information to help him. As far as I know, that's the only person who came by. What else did he say to you about democracy? Was it coherent, or more of a rant?"

"More of a rant. The state of the world, newspapers folding, something about 'when news is suppressed, it's all over.'"

Wesley hated the idea of Reilly losing his grip. The fewer people who knew, the better.

"Let me talk to him again," Wesley said. "In the meantime, can you send me your original write-up of the press conference?"

She agreed, and after they hung up, Wesley sprang into action. He wanted to catch Reilly in person without warning. First, he checked the *Gazette* office, to no avail, and then Reilly's home. He'd only ever been there for the annual holiday party, and he associated the one-story craftsman with twinkling lights and home-made cider. It was strange to see it unadorned in the harsh reality of late January.

The editor-in-chief's wife, Celia, answered the door.

She looked exhausted and said Reilly had been hospitalized for pneumonia.

Wesley offered sympathy and then hesitated, trying to find the right words. "Even before the pneumonia, had he been... different? Agitated, or stressed?"

Celia gave him a look of pity that he didn't understand. "What do you think has been happening this whole time?" she asked.

"That's what I'm trying to... Could you help me out?"

"Ask yourself: Who's been affected by the trolley investigation? Not the *death*, but the *investigation*?" She sounded exasperated. "Why don't you start there?"

"If you could just—"

"Wesley, I'm tired. I'm going to bed. I'm putting my phone on do-not-disturb except for the hospital. I'll tell him you stopped by."

~

AFTER RETURNING to the office and informing the other staffers of Reilly's condition, Wesley tried to make sense of Celia's question. He went to pull up the angry letter from last summer that had sounded like a Type One Perfectionist.

401 File Not Found.

Heart in his throat, he checked the physical archive.

Missing.

He called tech support and learned the server was working. No technical glitches or compromised data.

His only printed copy of the letter had been crumpled up for Constance's cat to chase in the library community room on Wednesday. It had probably been recycled by now.

Who or what was Reilly protecting?

Even if Wesley uncovered the truth—about the trolley, about the newspaper cover-up—he couldn't report on it. Reilly wouldn't let him. He'd made that clear with his underhanded, possibly criminal behavior. Wesley would have to take the information to the *L.A. Times*, or go national, which would bring down his own newspaper in the process. Three generations of Reilly's family, tarnished. Cherry Hill's only local news source, destroyed.

For the first time since moving to Cherry Hill to live in his aunt's apartment, Wesley cared deeply about what happened to the *Gazette*, and what the paper meant for the town.

LAW ENFORCEMENT DIDN'T RETURN Wesley's call until Saturday morning.

He paced outside the library, waiting for it to open at ten, in a last-ditch effort to see if his crumpled-up paper was still on the premises.

When his phone buzzed, he almost dropped it in his haste to answer.

Deputy Cole apologized for the delay in contacting him. They were swamped, but the sheriff had asked her to call him back.

Before Wesley could fire off his first question, she added, "You know, it hurt the sheriff's ego to ask people with information to come forward. We were *extremely surprised* when it didn't appear in the paper."

By "extremely surprised" Deputy Cole clearly meant "livid."

That makes three of us. "Have you recovered anything from Shawna's camera from the day of the protest?"

She sighed. "We're working on it."

"Was there anything suspicious on the security footage from U-Stor-It where the trolley was parked?"

"No."

"Anything pan out with the drifter?" Blaming drifters for crimes was both cliché and lazy, but he had to ask. "The guy with the envelope?" he clarified.

"No. We have yet to I.D. the 'drifter with the envelope.'"

Wesley thanked her and hung up, his pulse bobbing in his throat.

"Hi, Wesley." Constance appeared, followed closely by Deputy Max. When she stopped, Max knocked into her, and her eyes bugged out.

"Sorry, m'lady," Max said.

"You don't need to stand quite so close," Constance told him. Wesley had no idea why the deputy was shadowing her or calling her "m'lady," but he could tell this new development was unwelcome.

In a kinder voice, she told Max, "Why don't you keep watch from the bench?"

"No, no. I'll stay by your side, as promised."

At ten, Chase unlocked the doors and waved at Constance and Wesley.

"Zeke's already in the community room," he said, then reflected on his statement. "I don't actually know how. Huh. Oh well!"

With Deputy Max safely deposited in the computer room, and a dozing Zeke resting in the corner (how *had* he gotten in before the library opened?), Wesley scanned the room in vain for the letter.

"What are you looking for?" Constance asked, so he revealed his tale of woe.

"As you can see," Wesley finished, "I can't stay. I wish I could, but there's too much to do."

"It's fine," she said.

"But without me, you won't have enough students."

"It doesn't matter. I came in person to shut it down for good."

He noticed then how despondent Constance looked. He'd been so consumed by his own troubles he'd failed to see hers.

"Constance, why is Deputy Max guarding you?"

"Because the killer isn't finished, and I'm next on the list."

25

———

SAM

DESPITE HER TUMULTUOUS sleep the night before, filled with nightmares about Will being perp-walked in handcuffs along Main Street while people rode the trolley, jeering at him and hurling tomatoes, Sam dragged herself out of bed to attend the third Enneagram class.

Everyone else was already seated when she and Penelope walked in.

"Welcome, welcome," Constance said. "Looks like we have a quorum, which is ironic, but that's how it goes sometimes. I'm afraid class is canceled."

"What? Why?" asked Sam.

"As most of you know, I was the last person to ride the trolley before it exploded and killed Isaac Caldecot. Then, three days ago, I received a message that said, 'It should have been you.'"

"Oh, my gosh." Sam was shocked. "That's terrible. I'm so sorry."

"Was the message on a postcard?" asked Trevor.

"No, it was spray painted on my shower curtain."

Sam gasped. "I would've had a heart attack. You poor thing."

"I was too busy screaming to have a heart attack, but thank you. Why did you ask if it was a postcard, Trevor?"

"Crystal got a threatening postcard. I thought maybe the two were connected."

Wesley looked alarmed. "*Crystal* got a threatening postcard? What'd it say?"

"Who's Crystal?" asked Penelope.

"She owns the cat cafe," said Constance, while at the same time, Wesley said, "Very pretty Korean American woman?"

He flushed. "I mean, not pretty. Not ugly, either. *Definitely* not ugly, but not—forget I said pretty. But not *not*-pretty. Average. Not in a bad way." He exhaled. "Just—forgettable."

"Clearly." Penelope smirked.

"I was just at CHATeau Savannah," said Constance, "dropping off Mr. Cinnamon so he wouldn't be alone at the house. She was protective when I explained my situation, but she never mentioned her own threat. What did it say?"

"'No one wants you here' with a picture from a Beatrix Potter book of a cat being rolled into a pie. She thinks Wesley sent it," Trevor said. For Penelope's benefit, he added, "Wesley hates cats, but they love him."

"I don't 'hate'—"

"Anyway," Constance said, "I've decided to be proactive. I can't ask you to help, but—"

"We're going to solve it using the personality types after all," Sam cried. She was right to have come.

It was a *little* irksome that Constance had insisted it be theoretical when *Will* was in trouble, yet jumped into action when it was *her* neck on the line... but at least they were getting somewhere now.

"Constance and I are hitting the streets," said Wesley.

"Field trip, field trip," Sam chanted.

Penelope raised her hand. "No need. I already solved it. It wasn't murder. U-Stor-It and Car Park had a vermin problem. Rats got in the engine, did some damage, and kaboom. I already told the sheriff." She clasped her hands on the table, at peace.

Sam felt a strange rage bubble up inside her.

Why was Penelope always so polished, so certain, so unflappable? The more Sam fell apart under stress, the more pristine and untouchable Penelope looked.

When they'd arrived at the library to share the babysitter, Henry and Dale had shrieked with happiness. In contrast, Penelope had offered Sam a stiff "thanks again" but otherwise didn't engage. (And the "thanks again" hadn't sounded sincere.) After all of Sam's hard work to make this playdate happen, she and Penelope had traipsed through the library single file rather than side by side, not bonding over their kids or getting to know one another.

It was infuriating.

"Did rats threaten Constance, too?" Wesley asked, eyes wide with sarcasm. Sam silently cheered him on. "Did they take over the *Gazette* and force Editor-in-Chief Reilly to suppress information? Were they extra-special-smart-rats like in *Mrs. Frisby and the Rats of NIMH*?"

Penelope huffed. "Yeah, no. It wasn't murder. Just negligence."

"'Just negligence?'" Sam repeated. "Negligence can get someone falsely accused."

"Wesley has reason to believe there's a cover-up at the

newspaper, allowing the murderer to walk free," Constance explained. "You weren't here, Penelope, but on Wednesday, Wesley read us a damaging letter about the trolley that was sent to the paper. We determined it had been written by a Type One, the Perfectionist. We think it holds the key to the killer's identify, but it's been wiped from the *Gazette* server as part of the coverup, and we have no physical copies."

"We're in a library," Trevor said.

"What's that? Oh, right. Of course," Constance said.

They summoned Chase to find a copy in the print archives, but five minutes later, he returned empty-handed.

"It's not there," Chase said slowly. His natural exuberance was replaced with confusion. "We have Monday's and Friday's issue from the week you asked for, but not Wednesday's."

"I knew it," Wesley said. "Which means..."

Everyone leaned toward him.

"... Penelope's rats must have shredded the newspaper to throw us off their scent! What do you think, Three?"

She narrowed her eyes at him. "Funny."

"Hi, Chase," Trevor said loudly.

"Oh hi, Trevor, what's new?"

Trevor filled him in on their plan to "hit the streets."

"I want to come. Can I come?" Chase leaned his head out of the community room and yelled, "I'm taking my break, Roberto."

"Shh," Roberto yelled back. "People are trying to read."

Then they came to the wrong library, thought Sam.

Constance cleared her throat. "We don't need the letter. We have me. To paraphrase Chase the other day, 'Who better to catch a Type One than another Type One'?"

"Here's who we need to talk to." Wesley pulled up a slide on his laptop with photos and bios of the Main Streeters, as Sam thought of them.

SUSPECTS:

- Ana Whitley, Hummingbird Art Gallery. Motive: Save the earth, punish the trolley. "Justice"
- Martin Onder, Kaftans 'n' More. Motive: Failed lawsuit, failing business.
- Danny Flores, Texican Table. Motive: Failing business, daughter's employment. (see below)
- Olivia Flores, Kaftans 'n' More. Motive: Fears losing her job, and parents' restaurant closing. (see above)
- Drifter with the Envelope, ???. Motive: ????

Penelope got up and stabbed her finger against the images of Danny Flores, Martin Onder, and Ana Whitley, in turn. "Okay, I'll give you this. I saw this trio of jokers at school pickup, talking about how happy they were about the trolley's crash. Danny wore a knitted hat and scarf at the time, so I didn't know it was him, but I do now."

Sam's heart pounded. New evidence!

"Ana was thrilled," Penelope said. "It was gross. She said it was an act of God, and she 'got what she wanted.' They also talked about a 'planner.' I told the sheriff that, too."

"I heard Ana arguing with Aidan Zachary at the cat cafe," Trevor said. "She told him, 'You lied to me; you said it was a liberation.' She said he better fix it."

"Juicy," said Chase. "Nice work, Trev."

Trevor smiled shyly at him.

"Speaking of Aidan," said Wesley, "we need to talk to him." He clicked to his next slide.

SHADY WITNESSES:

- Aidan Zachary, Dune Buggies, U.S.A. Seems like he's protecting someone??? Who? Crystal? (defended her on the phone with me)
- Crystal Bae, CHATeau Savannah. Directly witnessed the crash, seems nervous when asked for details. Got a postcard threat with a pie-related cat death. "Pie" for "cafe"? "Cat" for "cat"?

"Wow," Penelope deadpanned. "'Cat' for 'cat.' That is some A-plus investigative work, Wesley. No code can stump you."

"Aidan and Crystal didn't seem like they knew each other," Trevor said. "She showed him and Ana the postcard, and he was upset on her behalf, but not in a personal way if you know what I mean. More like he was insulted anyone would target the one business that was doing well."

"Good to know. Thanks, Trevor," said Wesley.

SHADY WITNESSES (Cont'd):

- Kelly Arden, Senior City. Involved in a gambling ring with a dead pool on the trolley. Swallowed his ledger with the winner's name on it.

"What does Kelly Arden have to do with anything?" Penelope looked disturbed.

"You know him?" Sam asked. Kelly Arden was a celebrity, or at least, he used to be.

"Yeah, I bought his house." Penelope tossed her hair. "He's my mentor, actually."

Sam was surprised. His house must've cost a fortune.

"Someone made a lot of money off the crash," Wesley said. "Kelly wouldn't tell me who."

"Martin gambles," Constance said. "He told me he picked the winning Lotto numbers three times at the store but couldn't play since he worked there. What if the dead pool winner was Martin? The store's his life. Even a modest amount of cash could help keep him solvent."

"On it." Penelope facetimed Kelly, who picked up right away.

"Hey, kiddo. You and the squirt need another ride?"

"No thanks, we're good, Kelly. Who won the dead pool on the trolley explosion?"

Even if the question startled him, he didn't hesitate to answer. "It was weird. Not any of the regulars. Didn't give a name. He showed up out of the blue with an envelope of cash, placed his bet, came back later to grab the winnings, and disappeared."

"What did he look like? How old was he?"

"Young, in his twenties, real scruffy looking. Baggy shirt, baggy shorts, unshaved."

"The drifter with the envelope," said Wesley and Constance in unison.

Trevor's arm jolted, and he spilled his bottle of water. Everyone screeched back from the table to avoid the mess. "Sorry, sorry," Trevor said. Sam reached into her bag and handed him a sheaf of napkins.

"Thanks, Kelly. Talk soon." Penelope looked smug. "'You're welcome,'" she sang at Wesley. Sam almost sang along; Dale loved *Moana*.

So did Farren.

Sam's heart spasmed with pain, but she forced herself to concentrate on the here and now. She was taking action to help Will and that's all she could do. With the entire class working together, surely an answer was close at hand.

"If Envelope Drifter sabotaged the trolley to win the dead pool, he's long gone now," said Wesley. "And being a drifter, he obviously didn't write the letter to the paper."

"All the threats might be unrelated," Chase pointed out. "Someone who hates cats, and someone who hates Constance. No offense, Gram."

"None taken. Let's divide and conquer," said Constance. "I'll talk to Martin Onder. He trusted me enough to tell me about the lawsuit. Maybe I can find out if he's had a recent windfall."

"I'll talk to Danny Flores and Ana Whitley," Wesley said. "Who wants to lean on the shady witnesses?"

"I'll talk to Crystal," said Trevor. "She owes me a favor."

"Can I go with you?" Chase asked. "I want to see the cat cafe."

"Sure." Trevor looked both pleased and terrified, Sam noted.

"Can you check on Mr. Cinnamon while you're there?" asked Constance.

"Of course." Chase grabbed Trevor's hand and raised them high. "To the Chase-mobile. Nah, we'll walk. I just wanted to say that."

Inspired, Sam raised Penelope's hand. "We'll talk to Aidan at Dune Buggies, USA."

But instead of cheering, or thanking her, Penelope averted her eyes. "Oh, are we teaming up? I thought I'd go with Con—"

"Go to the actual dune buggies, not the admin office," Wesley told them.

"We'll bring the kids," Sam hollered. She *would* finagle a chance to bond out of this situation, whether Penelope liked it or not. "I have a BOGO coupon."

Assignments doled out, excitement and determination in the air, the group scattered.

Well, except for Zeke.

26

PENELOPE

PENELOPE COULDN'T UNDERSTAND why the first order of business was getting Constance out of the building without Deputy Max noticing.

"Quick, we need to slip past him. I don't want him coming with us," Constance murmured outside the computer room. Deputy Max sat by himself, playing Minesweeper.

"But he's an officer of the law."

"… To an extent."

"Wouldn't he be helpful?"

"You might think so," Constance said. "But—oh, no."

Deputy Max leaped out of his seat. "Finished? I thought your class was two hours."

"Only a bathroom break," Penelope lied smoothly. "You know us girls—we always go in groups."

She nudged Constance, and they scurried toward the ladies' room. "That's right. We have much to discuss on the toilet," Constance said.

"I'll get my hairspray from the car," Sam added loudly.

"The one I was telling you about." She darted for the exit. "Be right back."

"I'll be right here, m'lady." Deputy Max bowed.

Unlike in the movies, the window in the women's bathroom did not open wide enough for a 67-year-old and a 27-year-old to squeeze through in a bid for freedom.

"I'm not willing to risk Winnie-the-Pooh-ing myself," Constance said.

"Me neither," said Penelope. "New plan. We'll leave separately using the bookshelves as cover. If he sees me, I'll distract him while you get out. And once you're out, send Henry in for me. Deputy Max won't think anything's unusual if I go outside to help my kid." She smirked. "He only has eyes for you, m'lady."

"Hush your mouth."

They both laughed.

Luckily, the lure of Minesweeper combined with the bathroom ruse proved an effective cover. Max didn't look up again as they crept past and found Sam in the parking lot.

Constance headed off on foot to question Martin Onder.

Penelope mournfully watched her go. If only she'd been quicker, she could've paired up with Constance and wouldn't have to endure another death-defying ride in Sam's minivan.

WHILE SAM and the boys rode the dune buggies, Penelope approached Aidan's office, her heart pounding.

Among the magical props in Sam's cluttered minivan, they'd found a thin wallet with a plastic I.D. slot and a cardboard backing from a deck of cards. The moms performed a quick arts and crafts project using scissors and glue from Dale's backpack and the remarkably accurate-looking "Riverside County"-embossed deputy sticker Sheriff Pittman had given Henry. Abracadabra, a badge-in-wallet to flash at Aidan.

It was a crackpot idea, but Penelope had been "faking it till she made it" her whole life.

She took a deep, centering breath and knocked on Aidan's office door.

"Aidan Zachary? Hi, I'm Deputy Angelina Evans. May I have a moment of your time?"

He stood. "I thought I knew everyone from the sheriff's department."

"I'm on loan from L.A. County while Deputy Max tends to other matters. They just have me going over witness statements again regarding the trolley accident. I'm sure you're busy, so I'll make it quick."

"Oh. Okay, sure," said Aidan.

Penelope was surprised to see that Aidan didn't look the way she imagined a dune-buggy operator would look. He wasn't a hairy, beer-bellied, overly tattooed man with a safety goggle-shaped sunburn on his face. (Penelope had a cute fox tattoo on her biceps, but she disliked when people did a full sleeve.) Rather, Aidan stood tall and fit, with a pleasant, clean-shaven face and a natural-looking tan. He wore a suit and tie, and shined Ferragamo shoes. He understood the importance of appearance, and Penelope found herself glancing around his tidy office for proof of a significant other.

Darn, there it was: an office-appropriate selfie of a woman kissing his cheek. Beside it hung his diploma from the School of Management at Claremont Graduate University.

"You want me to repeat my previous statements?" Aidan asked.

"That's right." Sam had briefed her on the drive over. "Last time, fingers crossed. Tell me about the city council meeting and the protest. No detail is too small."

"There was practically a brawl at the city council meeting. I hate to say it, but the old man was stubborn about the trolley. He never took anyone's advice."

Penelope took note of his annoyance. "About...?"

"About working with the other businesses to everyone's benefit. He refused to consider rerouting the trolley or making any other changes. When the protestors asked to use my office as a meeting point, I said sure. I thought if we showed solidarity in a peaceful way, our concerns might be taken seriously. Emphasis on peaceful, but we all know how that turned out." He sighed. "I know it wasn't my fault; it was Ana Whitley's and—" he stopped, his face pink.

"Ana Whitley's and...?"

"Just Ana Whitley," he covered quickly. "For breaking the reporter's camera."

"And whoever threw the rock, of course."

"Right." Aidan swallowed.

He was living up to his reputation as a shady witness. But why?

Penelope pointed to a tote bag from U-Stor-It & Car Park hanging on a hook. "I use them, too. Do you store your buggies there?"

"The overflow inventory, yeah." He leaned in. "Well, I used to. Until I saw a rat in the garage." He shuddered. "I called it in, but I don't think they did anything about it."

"You're the one who called?"

"Yeah, why?"

"Well, they eventually did something. Apparently, pest control didn't find any rats and chalked it up to a one-off."

"Does that seem likely to you?" Aidan asked. "A single rat? Don't they run in packs?"

His eyes were dreamy. And unlike *some people*, he wouldn't mock her "rats got in the engine" theory.

"They seemed to think you were the only person who saw one," Penelope told him.

"Sure, a phantom rat. Except I have 20/20 vision." He rolled his eyes so hard his 20/20 vision got a glimpse of his forehead. "I warned Mr. Caldecot, too. Should've known he wouldn't heed my words and park elsewhere." Aidan looked everywhere except at Penelope. "I wish I'd pushed harder, and I wish he hadn't been so stubborn."

Penelope waited until his gaze met hers. "If you want peace of mind, you could tell me what you left out earlier. Ana Whitley and *who else* was violent at the protest?"

Aidan took a deep breath and closed his eyes for a second.

Penelope felt the rush of conquest. *Here we go.*

"Danny Flores threw the rock," Aidan mumbled. "I was hoping when the reporter's camera got fixed, she might've captured it on film and I wouldn't have to be the one to tell you."

She patted his hand. His warm, strong hand. "You did the right thing."

"After he threw the rock, I saw him run off and double back to the front of the trolley and crouch down. I can't say what he was doing. Probably hiding. I'm sorry I didn't say anything before. I hate what's happening to Cherry Hill."

"Me too." Penelope thanked him and promised to keep his name out of the papers.

"Everything in the past week has me rattled. I know it's

not my fault CHATeau Savannah was threatened, either, but it's upsetting, you know?" Before she could ask what made him bring up the cat cafe, his eyes narrowed. "Wait, if you're here from L.A. County, why do you use U-Stor-It & Car Park?"

Penelope's guts twisted, but she was saved from answering because Sam and the boys appeared in the doorway, covered in dirt, worn-out but happy, and Aidan focused on them.

Sam's hair was a bird's nest in a tornado, but what killed Penelope was that Sam pulled out her phone and used the camera to re-do her lipstick. Like it would make a difference!

"Did you guys have fun?" Aidan asked the boys. They cheered. "You both earned yourselves certificates."

He opened a drawer and extracted two "Expert Driver" certificates for them to sign.

Five minutes later, to Penelope's horror, Sam pulled her minivan into a McDonald's parking lot. Mercifully, it was a bare-bones McDonald's, minus a PlayPlace. At least they could avoid the germ paradise of tunnels, slides, and shoe cubbies.

"What did you think of Aidan?" Sam asked once the boys had their Happy Meals and were seated at a different table.

"He was gorgeous," Penelope said. "Tailored suit and tie, Ferragamo shoes, crisp haircut, muscular but not scary-muscular, tall, good with kids... Everything I've been looking for."

Sam looked impatient. "Did he believe you were a deputy? What did he tell you?"

"Yes. Okay. He was annoyed with Isaac and called him stubborn, but he felt bad about his death. Apparently, he warned Isaac about the rats at U-Stor-It. But the biggest takeaway is that Danny Flores from Texican Table threw the rock."

"That's huge. He just told you that?"

"I kept the pressure on until he cracked. He feels guilty about what happened at the protest even if it wasn't his fault. He also said it wasn't his fault the cat cafe was threatened."

"Why would *that* be his fault?"

"Beats me. Maybe he's one of those people who can't stand conflict."

"Oh, maybe he's a Type Nine, the Peacemaker," said Sam. "Their core desire is internal and external harmony."

"Now we know *who* he was protecting, but not *why*."

Henry darted over. "Dale's sneaking. I can't find him."

"Not this again," Sam groaned. The moms moved from table to table, searching. It turned out Dale was squeezed into a (thankfully empty) garbage can.

"When we get home, we're doing a super scrub," Sam told her son, guiding him by the collar back to the kids' table. "No more sneaking."

Back at the grown-ups' table, Sam continued where they'd left off. "Any idea who the woman in the photo was?"

"I clocked the photo, but I didn't recognize her."

"Good thing I took a photo of the photo, then, isn't it?" crowed Sam.

Penelope frowned. "When?"

"Did you think I was checking my lipstick? After this?" Sam gestured to her crazed hair and dust-covered face.

Both women started laughing, especially when Penelope noticed a crayon embedded in Sam's hair. She reached across the table and plucked it out. "How did that even get in there?"

They laughed harder, until Sam's laughter turned to tears—agonized ones.

Penelope fought the urge to flee. She hated making a scene. "Are you okay?" she whispered tensely.

"It's been—so—stressful," Sam heaved. "It's my fault my husband is a suspect. He was only riding the trolley that day because I made him stop traveling for work, so he could spend more time with Dale, but the ride he and Dale took together was the last straw for my daughter Farren, who went 'no contact' with me and Will afterward."

Penelope was lost. "Wait, slow down. You have a daughter?"

Sam fisted some napkins and dabbed at her eyes. "An adult one, the same age as you. I thought if you and I became friends, you could help me fix things with her."

That's why Sam is obsessed with me?

"Why did she go 'no contact'?"

"Her childhood was unsettled. We moved so much for Will's work, but when Dale was born, we kept to one place, one house, one school. She thinks we love Dale more because we gave him the stability she never had. She was beside herself over the holidays. The trolley ride sent her over the edge. 'He *never* did those things with me. You didn't mind his traveling every holiday when *I* was a kid. Now all of a sudden, it's important for him to be home? Are you kidding me?' She said she needed time and not to call her. Meanwhile, Will's business is failing, and despite what Farren thinks, he's not actually spending more time with us. The one time he *did*, ended in accusations of murder. I've ruined my relationship with my daughter and my husband, and for what?"

Several pieces of Sam's odd behavior fit together to form a picture in Penelope's mind. The ancient minivan, from an earlier child. The things she'd said last week during the drive to U-Stor-It. "One kid at home, and one in the field." The free clothes that wouldn't have fit Sam but would have fit Penelope.

"Her name's Farren, and she's twenty-seven." Sam paused and looked Penelope in the eye. "I'm forty-six," she added.

"You had her when you were nineteen," Penelope said quietly. "Just like me and Henry."

"Now imagine *Henry* is nineteen, enrolled in college. Fully launched. And you find out you're pregnant, and you start all over again. That was me."

"I thought you were the type of later-in-life mom who couldn't understand what it was like to have a kid so young. I thought you'd judge me for not being able to join the P.T.A." Penelope laughed ruefully. "Sounds so stupid when I say it out loud, but I've been avoiding you so I wouldn't feel more judged than I already do."

"Oh, I understand all about that. The looks you get, the unsolicited advice."

Penelope's respect for Sam had skyrocketed. But she still needed to set boundaries for both their sakes.

"You came on pretty strong, Sam."

Sam hung her head. "I know. I'm sorry."

Penelope appreciated that Sam didn't make excuses or try to explain further. As far as Penelope was concerned, that was enough to wipe the slate clean.

"I'm sorry, too. You were being generous, and I didn't give you a chance. Tell me more about the Magic Mirror. Why is it failing?"

"Whether it's the concept, the economy, or the location, I don't know. He's so talented. He's so good. But it's a money pit."

"Until now."

"What do you mean?" Sam looked ill. "Because he'll be arrested?"

"No, that's not what I'm—"

"He didn't do it!"

"I know he didn't. Neither of you is that interesting. Also, pro tip: you would not make a good spy. All I said was, 'Are you okay?' and you told me *everything*."

They laughed together again. It felt right, and Penelope found she didn't care if anyone saw.

Once their laughter died down, Penelope told her, "I'm a branding and marketing expert. I'll have a plan for you by tomorrow."

Sam opened her mouth, excited. Then she looked down. "We can't afford to pay you."

"You don't have to."

Constance had taken her on pro bono.

Penelope would do the same for Sam.

27

TREVOR

"WHAT BROUGHT YOU TO CHERRY HILL?" Chase asked.

"The short version or the long version?"

Chase grinned. "The scandalous version."

Trevor and Chase strode toward CHATeau Savannah from the library. Trevor consciously averted his eyes at staggered intervals, so he didn't stare too long at Chase, who was as luminous as ever.

"I'm on leave from law school, after partying a little too hard."

"That is, sadly, relatable."

"Actually, that's the lie version." Trevor slowed his pace. "I'm not on leave. I dropped out. No job, no degree." That was more than enough honesty. No need to confess how he'd started drinking long before that, to socialize.

Chase's sunny demeanor shifted, and Trevor discovered that Serious Chase and Sunny Chase were equally fascinating to him. "That sounds rough."

"Thanks. I have no idea what to do next. That's what I'm trying to figure out."

"You probably went from high school to undergrad to law school without any time off in-between, right? How would anyone know what they wanted if they've never had a chance to look at what's out there? We all do it—we get on the hamster wheel, but you broke free."

"I'm pretty sure I broke my *future*. Squeak, squeak."

"We can be free-range hamsters together."

Trevor ducked his head to smile.

"But seriously," said Chase, "What if this is what you're meant to be doing?"

"Not knowing? Lowkey panicking all the time?"

"No, being *okay* with not knowing. What if you stopped trying to force an epiphany and waited for one to show up?"

"How would I make money?"

"Oh, you can get a job, but as part of the journey, not the endgame," Chase said. He made it sound so easy. Nothing was that simple, though. "It doesn't mean you've decided your whole life. Maybe that could help bring you back to yourself."

They arrived at CHATeau Savannah, where a "Help Wanted" sign hung in the window. Trevor recalled Crystal mentioning she needed a barista.

Ha. If only. But he flew home in two days, and he'd never see any of these people again. Not Purr-cy, not Crystal, not Chase. (That one hurt.) Not Constance, who not only didn't judge him for his study habits and love of libraries but *embraced* them. In fact, everyone in the class accepted him for who he was.

It was a stark contrast to the classmates he'd tried so futilely to impress at law school, by drinking until he became someone else. Someone he didn't even like.

"How does the cafe work?" Chase asked. "We can't just go in, right?"

"Right. But I have a monthly membership, so I'm welcome anytime, and you can be my plus-one. How long do you have? Won't Roberto get mad if you're gone too long?"

"Please," said Chase. "I told that old man I was investigating a lead on the trolley murder, and he practically shoved me out the door."

"You told him the truth?"

"I mayyyyy have implied it was for his mystery book club. They're also investigating."

Trevor blinked.

"Don't fret, I'm loyal to Gram," said Chase. "He'll get nothing from me. Even if he pulls out my fingernails."

~

"HI, CRYSTAL, I'M HERE TO—"

"Apply for the position? I knew it," Crystal interrupted. "I put that thought out into the universe last night, that you, specifically, would apply. And here you are."

As further enticement, she deposited warm, sleepy Purr-cy in Trevor's lap while they spoke, sitting across from each other at the window table. "Imagine: you'd see this sweetie-pie all day. Better than healthcare, right? As an aside, this job does not come with healthcare."

He was about to correct her assumption, but the ruse of interviewing for the job would give him carte blanche to ask questions.

"Would I need to walk Savannah as part of my duties? I don't want to twist my ankle the way you did," Trevor said, hoping to segue into trolley talk.

"I got her a new harness," Crystal replied. "She won't be able to slip free again."

His heart raced. "'Again'? Has she slipped free before?"

Crystal's eyes darted. "Only once. The day of the crash." She said it off-handedly but Trevor's spine tingled.

"What happened that day?"

She leaned in. "I'll tell you, but keep it between us, okay? As potential colleagues."

"Absolutely."

He felt bad for misleading her, but his time in Cherry Hill was always going to be temporary.

"So there we were, walking in the rain, when we heard an awful sound. We went over to see what was going on, and once we came in view of the trolley, all crumpled and smoking, Savvy took off after a squirrel. As you know, she jerked so crazily I sprained my ankle trying to contain her. My glasses flew off and broke, and she—she was *gone*. I was screaming because A) it hurt like crazy, and B) the fire! I didn't want her near the fire! Luckily her— interest..."

Prey, Trevor thought. *Crystal avoided saying prey.*

"Went in the other direction. I was on the ground in pain, and by the time I hobbled to my car and got checked out at the urgent care, she'd—she'd been missing for over two hours." The memory haunted Crystal, if her shaking hands were any indication. She lifted her cup of tea to her lips with trembling fingers. "No one knows. I didn't even tell the sheriff. I can't have it getting out that I can't control my serval mix, you know? It could ruin me. She's not wild, but people might be scared of her. Which is ridiculous! That *reporter* kept calling her feral. Can you imagine the headline if he found out? 'Feral Cat Loose on Main Street.'"

"Where was she?"

"Oh my gosh, it took ages. Especially with my ankle boot, and with no one else to help me. Law enforcement and the fire department—normally helpful to cats in trees, if

I know my comics—were too busy with the trolley, and again, I didn't want misinformation to spread. I eventually found her in the playground next to the elementary school. Luckily, not the one *in* the school, or I couldn't have gotten to her."

"I'm so glad she was okay."

"But *was* she? I can't shake the feeling that someone *did* something to her. You saw how sick she was the other day. And look, she's been sleeping so much more."

They both observed Savannah, flopped on a banquette, eyes closed, tail twitching. The tuxedo kitten, Oreo, was snuggled against her. Trevor yearned to take a photo of the domestic scene. Something to remember this place by, and the peace it had given him.

"After the vet checked her out," Crystal continued, "I brought the... sample... to the sheriff and asked him to test it for poison."

"What did he say?"

She sighed. "He said it would be, like, five thousand dollars, and there's no money in the budget for something like that. Deputy Cole, the nice woman, called me later and said if I funded it myself, she'd do her best to make it happen in conjunction with the ASPCA, but I can't afford it, because my uncle, who I live with, needs every penny we've got for his medical tests, and meanwhile..." Her eyes hardened. "Savvy's still not herself."

Trevor didn't hesitate. "I'll pay for it."

"Plot twist," said Chase, who'd been perambulating around the cafe.

Crystal gaped at Trevor. "Are you serious? How? Why?"

"Christmas bonus from my previous job," he lied. "And I want to. I insist."

Crystal tilted her head. "Is this a bribe so you'll get the job? Because I accept! Not because of the money. You were a rock star the other day when I needed to run to the vet. You're a natural with the cats, and I know I can trust you. Can you start tomorrow? It'll be salaried, plus 50/50 profit sharing until I pay you back for the loan. After that, we'll figure out your other benefits. I'll get you healthcare some way, somehow, I promise."

"I wish I could, but I don't even have a place to live right now."

He figured he could bow out gracefully with that statement, but it only electrified her. "I forgot the best part. The job comes with housing."

"Uh... where?" He pictured living in the house she shared with her uncle, and shuddered. No space to himself, no way to be alone.

She pointed up. "There's a studio apartment on the second floor. It's part of my lease, but I don't use it because, as I mentioned, I help my uncle. I had it refurbished and repainted. What do you say? Best commute ever."

"Can I let you know early next week?" he stammered, sweat gathering at his temples.

"The sooner the better, but for *you*, yes." She smiled, and his stomach clenched.

"Why is there a dartboard back here with my future husband's face on it?" Chase called from the back, and now Trevor's *heart* clenched. *Future husband?*

Chase held a print-out of Wesley's face from the *Cherry Hill Gazette*'s staff page. It had holes in it from darts, but you could still tell who it was. For now.

"Did you take that from my office?" Crystal asked. "That's off-limits to customers."

"Whoops, my bad," Chase said. "I was looking for Sassy Pants."

"Sassy Pants?"

"Mr. Cinnamon," Trevor corrected. "Our friend Constance asked us to check on him."

"Mr. Cinnamon is having quiet reflection time," said Crystal.

"He's in a cage," Chase translated. "Was he a bad kitty?"

"*No kitties are bad.* He's in a private suite because he peed in the merch box. Not every cat enjoys communal living."

"Cool, cool," Chase said, and continued swooning over Wesley. "Speaking of bad cats, Wesley is like if every guy on the WB, the CW, and Fox-from-the-'90s merged into the ultimate tortured bad boy with perfect hair." He pointed at Crystal. "You don't get him, straight girl."

"I don't want him! He's horrible! He asked me flat-out what I would do when Savannah *dies*. Who says that? I play darts with his face every morning to stave him off."

"She thinks Wesley might have sent her the nasty post-card or done something to Savannah when she was on the loose last weekend," Trevor added.

Chase looked stricken. "No..."

"I don't *really* think he'd hurt her," Crystal admitted. "Savvy's a good judge of character, and she adores him. You can see how it's weirdly confusing for me. Anyway, the Cat Ladies are on the case. My Monday customers. They're kind of like the Red Hat Society."

"My Nana was part of them," Chase said fondly.

Trevor must have looked lost—he couldn't stand it when he didn't understand a reference—so Chase told him, "It's for women over fifty who dress in purple and red to make growing old a happy, playful thing instead of all sad."

"Right," said Crystal. "I mean, it's a little more than that, but the Cat Ladies wear cats on their clothes, and they meet here for coffee and cats. When they heard about Savvy's troubles, they decided to investigate."

How many amateur sleuths can one town hold?

"They'll be thrilled to hear I can afford the toxicology test and get to the bottom of this. So will Savvy." Crystal nodded to herself, pleased.

"Can I see the postcard again?" Trevor asked.

"They're both with the sheriff, but I have them memorized."

"'Both'?"

"I got a second one. The first was more gross, with Tom Kitten being rolled up in dough, and the second was more juvenile."

"What did it say?" asked Chase.

"'Democracy dies in kitty litter.' Mad about the newsstand closing, so you can see why your 'future husband' is the most obvious candidate," she told Chase.

"Was it the same handwriting?" Trevor asked.

"It was a Sharpie marker both times, but the second one was more slanted."

Two different senders. But who? And why? Does it tie in with Constance's threat?

The trio chatted for a few more minutes, and then Trevor and Chase exited the cafe, only to run smack into Wesley and Constance.

They did not look happy.

"What was in the envelope, Trevor? The one you gave to Isaac Caldecot?" Constance demanded.

28

CONSTANCE

THIRTY MINUTES EARLIER

AT KAFTANS 'N' More, Constance was surprised to see kaftans in stock. Despite the store's name, kaftans were rarely available. Martin Onder was pinning them up for a window display.

Martin hummed as he worked, in tune with his stereo playing Turkish electronica music. The volume was low, so Constance sensed the pulsing beat more than she heard it, but what she did hear was catchy.

She pretended to examine the fabric. It would be a cold day in... well, Cherry Hill before she'd buy a kaftan, but it gave her cover for the conversation.

"All new stock? Business already looking up?" she asked after they exchanged hellos. *Perhaps from a windfall?*

"Not new, just liberated from storage." He looked pleased.

Liberated. That word again. Trevor said Ana used it, too.

Did everyone on Main Street feel liberated with the trolley gone?

"Do you use U-Stor-It?"

"No, no, in my home. Why pay for storage when I have extra room in my garage?"

"I assume you dropped the lawsuit?"

"Yes. And once the sheriff stops this silly witch hunt, all will be well," he said.

"Did he call you in for questioning?"

"Not me, *all* of us," Martin corrected her. "All of us on the chamber of commerce, all of us at the protest, all of us at the city council meeting. But no arrests, you see? Nothing to prove anyone did anything. The trolley was old, and now it is gone. This will blow over."

"It must be a relief." She wanted to see if Martin would display black-and-white, right-or-wrong thinking, a hallmark of unhealthy Type Ones. "All your problems are solved."

Martin frowned. "I am sad for the mayor. I am even sad for Isaac. I am not sad for his lawyers, but..."

Constance nodded and left him to his task. She pretended to peruse the aisles, picking up a packet of instant mashed potatoes and putting it back while she considered what to ask next.

Angry voices erupted at the checkout. Olivia Flores, of the purple striped hair, was raging at her father, Danny.

"Could you be more obvious?"

He raised his hands defensively. "It was a coincidence, Livvy."

"It says 'celebration!' on the flyer!"

"Because we're returning to full hours and full menu, not because—"

"You don't think people will notice you re-instated brunch the day of his funeral?"

"Come back to the restaurant. Come back to work," Danny pleaded. To Martin, he called out, "I'm stealing your most valuable employee."

Martin had heard this before, it seemed. He waved off Mr. Flores and didn't get involved.

"I have asked you over and over to stop joking about that," Olivia said. "I don't want to work at the Table. You're just like my boyfriend. You both think you know what I should do. You want to decide for me."

"Everything's different now. We have the hours. You can work part time and still make more with us than you do here," Danny told her.

Olivia whipped her face toward Constance. "Hi," she said sharply. "Can I help you find anything?"

Embarrassed, Constance brought the instant mashed potato packet to the checkout.

To purchase.

And eat.

Investigating was not without sacrifices.

"What's this about brunch?" Constance asked faux-brightly, opening her purse.

Olivia and Danny stared at her.

Danny cleared his throat. "Texican Table is re-opening for brunch tomorrow. I should get back."

Danny leaned over to kiss his daughter on the cheek, which she allowed, and left.

"It's not that I don't love my family," Olivia said, refusing to pretend that Constance hadn't heard their argument. "It's that everyone in my life wants to control what I do. If I'd been let go from here, I would have survived. I've been meaning to get my nursing degree. Maybe that would've been the push I needed."

"What schools are you looking at?"

"I heard good things about OHSU in Portland."

"You'd leave California?"

Olivia looked troubled. "Maybe not, I don't know."

Olivia rang up Constance's purchase, and Constance figured she couldn't justify further lingering, so she left K 'n' M and reconvened with Wesley on Main Street. He stood in front of the Hummingbird Art Gallery, hands in his pockets.

"Any luck?" she asked.

"It's closed, but I saw movement in the window. The lights went off, and the blinds flickered. I think Birdbrain's watching me to see if I leave."

"Think she's feeling guilty about something?"

"Maybe. Should we try to wait her out?"

They sat on the covered bench where the trolley used to pick up Constance.

"I miss it," she said, surprising herself. "Or at least, I miss the *idea* of it. It's a shame the town couldn't figure out a way to make it work."

"No one was willing to compromise. Mostly Isaac, let's be honest, but still."

"It's certainly quieter on Main Street," Constance noted. No music, no tourism spiel, no horns honking, no trolley wheels trundling along at 15 mph as the world spun around it.

"But it feels emptier, too," Wesley said, and Constance had to agree. "It'll take time for the businesses to bounce back," he continued. "And there's still not much parking, unless they use the hotel. Did you get anything good from Martin?"

"I don't think he's our Type One Perfectionist. He displayed nuanced rather than all-or-nothing thinking. Olivia said some interesting things, though. She considers her dad and her boyfriend to be 'controlling,' which is a hallmark of unhealthy Type Ones."

"Who's her boyfriend?"

"No clue. Miss Marple would know. She'd have a mental chart of every entanglement in the village, going back three generations."

"At least you spoke to people. I struck out." Wesley's sigh managed to convey years of disappointment. "Danny Flores wasn't at Texican Table, and his wife and cousins couldn't talk because they were busy preparing for tomorrow's big re-opening."

"Danny wasn't there because he was at K 'n' M, arguing with Olivia."

"About?"

"He wants her to work at the restaurant again, and she was furious they were celebrating the return of brunch on the day of his funeral."

"Furious how? Concerned that it looked bad? Drew attention to them?"

"Maybe. There was a lot that *wasn't* said, if you know what I mean."

"I've been treating them like separate suspects, but what if that was naïve?" asked Wesley. "What if they were in on it together? They have twice the motive."

"About that... Olivia told me if Martin had let her go, she would take it as a sign to enroll in nursing school."

"Man, if I could have Texican Table for every meal I'd be ecstatic, but the woman who gets to eat it whenever she wants is jaded about it."

"Perspective is everything. That's why I love the Enneagram. It reminds us that the same event can be perceived nine different ways. Did I tell you Olivia wanted to take my class?"

He gave her a sympathetic look. "I'm sure a lot of people—"

"No, no, listen. It conflicted with her *knitting class*."

Wesley's eyes widened. "Sewing scissors were used to cut the wires."

"It's circumstantial, but worth noting."

"We keep forgetting that you have a unique perspective," he pointed out.

"As a Type One?"

"You were the only person who saw Envelope Drifter."

She started to speak, but he stopped her. "Take a moment. Close your eyes, go back to last Saturday, and picture it in your mind."

She settled onto the bench and let her mind return to the weekend prior.

"Let's start with your vantage point," said Wesley. "Where did you sit that morning?"

"In the back, by the window."

"At what point on the route did Envelope Drifter get on the trolley?"

"After we passed the elementary school and the public pool, and we were heading around the back of the Vitality Hotel. I was surprised because he flagged down the trolley instead of catching it at a stop, which normally Isaac would have ignored."

"So the trolley stopped in the middle of the street, and Envelope Drifter got on. Was the envelope fat or thin?"

"Not bulging, but certainly full."

"What did Isaac do with it? Did he pocket it? Look inside it?"

"No, he shook his head, and gave it back, unopened."

"Could you hear what they said? Any words at all?"

"No, I was too far away."

"How old was he? You said young, but what does that mean?"

"Twenties, I think. Even though it was cold out, he wore shorts, which was strange. He had sunglasses on, and a beard, and sloppy hair that needed a cut..." Her eyes flew open.

"What?" said Wesley.

Constance gripped his arm. "It was Trevor."

"What are you talking about?"

"He wore shorts in class that first day, but I never put two-and-two together because by the time he showed up in class, he wore rimless glasses instead of sunglasses, and he was clean shaven with a buzz cut. Which he must have gotten done between the time I saw him on the trolley and the time class started."

"He went to Cut & Dried that day! He said it was crowded, remember? A buzz cut doesn't take long. You set the electric trimmer and go."

"Envelope Drifter was never a drifter," said Constance. "I've been staring at him all week."

Two minutes later, they confronted Trevor outside the cat cafe.

"Well?" Wesley said, echoing Constance's demand. "What was in the envelope?"

Trevor looked wildly at Chase, who stepped away from him as though fearful of contagion.

"Nothing bad," Trevor insisted. "I—I—I'm between jobs—"

"That's true," Chase said. "We talked about that."

"I'm—I've been using the spa at the Vitality." Trevor

gestured across the street. "The manager offered to pay me to run some errands around town. His assistant was out with the flu, and he needed me to make a few deliveries."

"Of cash, by chance?" Constance asked, eyebrows lifted.

"Y—yes."

"Did you keep some of it for yourself?" Wesley asked.

"No, I didn't touch it. He was already paying me; I wouldn't skim off the top."

"I believe you," said Constance after a moment.

Wesley cast her a sidelong glance. "I don't, but go on, Trevor."

"Um..." Trevor looked uncertain about what to say next. He pressed a finger down the bridge of his nose, squinted, and adjusted his rimless glasses. "So, one of the people they asked me to pay was the trolley driver."

Wesley's eyes were hard. "Why?"

"Because the hotel was funding his defense," Constance realized. "Isaac kept referring to a 'benefactor' with deep pockets."

Trevor nodded. "From what I understand, the hotel *wanted* Main Street parking to be a logjam, so businesses would be forced to pay the hotel for parking spots. Crystal has a deal with them, but everyone else refused, and the hotel manager was trying to keep the pressure on. They raised the price every week, and they protected the trolley by paying off his parking tickets and funding his lawyers to drag things out."

"So it wasn't Trudy," Wesley said. He dragged a hand through his luxuriant hair. Chase's eyes locked onto Wesley's movement. "I was worried the mayor was funneling money from her campaign fund."

"That's what Martin Onder thought, too," said Constance.

"She's family to me, so this is a load off my mind. Thanks."

"You're so welcome," Chase gushed.

"About the mayor..." Trevor started, but Wesley was already talking over him.

"Constance said Isaac refused the envelope. Why?"

"That's where it gets crazy," said Trevor. "Isaac handed back the money and gave me an errand of his own, to place a bet at the senior center on when the trolley would 'die.'"

"*Isaac* placed a bet?" Wesley asked.

"Not a 'bet' at all," said Constance. "A sure thing. He knew the exact moment the trolley would run out of steam, because he was the one deciding. Might as well make money off his naysayers, right?"

"He wasn't allowed to participate for that exact reason, so he used me as his proxy," said Trevor.

"Why would he want the trolley 'dead'?" Wesley asked. "He said he would never retire."

"'You have no idea what's coming,'" Constance quoted. "'And soon, too.' That's what he told the protesters. He even sang and danced a jig." She smiled at the bittersweet memory.

"The mayor told me something similar," Wesley conceded. "How in recent days Isaac was boasting about big changes. That 'something was coming.'"

"Do you know what it was, Trev?" asked Chase.

"No. All I know was that he had me place a bet that the trolley would die the next day, Sunday."

"Sunday," Wesley repeated. "Not Saturday?"

"That's right. He said when he won, I could keep fifteen percent as thanks. But then, well, you know what happened." Trevor swallowed. "His bet was the closest to the actual day, so he *did* win, but... all the money came to me."

"How much?" Wesley asked.

"He put 200 in and got 10k out."

Chase's jaw dropped. "You laundered it through Crystal."

"No! I—well, sort of." Trevor was beet red. "I didn't know what else to do with it. I was going to give it to my mom to help pay her back for my... spa visits but then she would wonder where I got it, and I felt so weird about the whole thing, I thought if I could do something good with the money, it would be like it never happened."

"You're a criminal mastermind," Chase whispered.

"No, I'm really not."

"A *nice* criminal mastermind. Although you should probably tell Crystal it's ill-gotten," Chase told Trevor.

"Why did you give it to Crystal?" Wesley asked.

"So she can run a forensic test on her cat's barf," Trevor said.

Wesley rubbed his eyes. "Why did I ask?"

"Let's go back to the library," said Constance. "We still have twenty minutes left of class, and I need to be in position when it ends, so Deputy Max doesn't know I snuck out."

"Question," said Trevor, as they fell into step with one another. "Why does everyone call Deputy Max 'Deputy Max,' using his first name, but we call Deputy Cole, 'Deputy Cole,' which is her last name?"

"An indicator of competence?" Constance said, then clapped a hand over her mouth. "I'm sorry, that was mean. He's been nothing but gallant lately."

"I think you're right, though," said Wesley. "It's sort of

like Max is playing dress-up and Regina Cole is the real thing."

The group reflected on that and found it sound.

Back at the library, Chase directed a series of evasive maneuvers meant to hide Constance's return. It was impossible to know from her vantage point, but if Deputy Max had looked up from his screen in the computer room, he would have seen Chase pushing a large re-shelving cart, Wesley and Trevor sideways shimmying to further block her, and Constance crouch-walking behind the cart, keeping pace as best she could.

"What did you find out?" Roberto boomed.

Constance clutched her chest. "Shhh."

"Everything," Chase replied. He escorted Constance, et. al to the community room. "I'll make something up," he whispered to the Enneagram students, his eyes mischievous.

Constance was about to protest—even if she didn't care for Roberto, it wasn't fair to send Book 'Em on a wild goose hunt—but she decided that was up to Chase. Roberto could fend for himself.

Trevor blushed and smiled, watching Chase go; he couldn't be more enamored of Chase's mischief, Constance noticed. Too bad Chase only had heart-eyes for Wesley, who seemed preoccupied with "forgettable, not-pretty" Crystal.

"You need to tell the sheriff everything you told us," Wesley lectured Trevor, who nodded vaguely.

"I can accompany you if you're nervous," Constance offered, and then, to take the spotlight off him, she face-timed Penelope to check in.

The two moms were at McDonald's, their children flailing in the background. Sam looked like she'd been dusting crops. Hair askew, makeup in places it shouldn't be, eyes filmy. But she also looked the happiest she had in days.

"What did you get?" Wesley asked, trying to be heard above the din.

"If you ask me, Aidan is Cherry Hill's most eligible bachelor—" Penelope started.

"Well, not exactly eligible," Sam cut in.

"No ring."

"But clearly a girlfriend, as you well know."

"Who's his girlfriend?" asked Wesley. "Is it Crystal?"

"Who?" Penelope asked.

He frowned. "Crystal."

"Who?" She looked amused.

"Crystal."

"Oh, is this you remembering her? I thought she was so forgettable."

Wesley narrowed his eyes. "Funny."

"No, this is the girlfriend." Sam showed them a photo she'd taken on her phone of a photo hanging in Aidan's office, viewed via Penelope's phone, and transmitted onto Constance's.

Constance marveled at the times they lived in.

The photo showed a brunette from the side, hair partially obscuring her face as she gave Aidan a peck on the cheek.

"I didn't recognize her at first," said Sam. "But then..." Sam produced a purple crayon.

The women grinned at each other, and Constance felt warm inside. Her class had brought them together.

Sam held the purple crayon up to the image on her phone. "Look. The photo was taken before Olivia got the purple stripe in her hair, but if you make your eyes go fuzzy, you can picture how it is now. Olivia's his girlfriend."

"How is this relevant?" Wesley asked impatiently.

"I'm getting to that," Penelope replied. "Aidan was acting shady because he knew who threw the rock at the protest: Danny Flores. Danny also lingered by the trolley's engine afterward. Aidan didn't want to tell anyone because that's his girlfriend's *dad*." She flicked imaginary dust off her shoulder. "But we connected. He was disturbed by the threats and violence around town and kept saying it wasn't his fault. Including the cat cafe postcard."

"Why would *that* be his fault?" asked Constance.

"That's what I said," Sam agreed.

"We have a theory he's a Type Nine Peacemaker and other people's conflicts upset him," said Penelope. "Unrelated, but Constance, which Types would you say Nines are typrically attracted to?"

"Seriously?" said Wesley.

"Perhaps we'll discuss that in our next class," Constance joked. "You'll have to find out."

"Anyway, Aidan's the one who saw the rats at U-Stor-It and called it in," Penelope said. "Proving once again, for the people in the back: IT WAS RATS." She sang the next part. "I don't know howwww or whyyyy, but it was raaaaaats."

"No," said Wesley. "It was pinking shears. A word I never thought I'd have to say, let alone so frequently."

Next, Wesley filled in the moms regarding Trevor's identity (Trevor apologized multiple times), and then Trevor explained why Crystal had been acting shady: she hadn't wanted it known that her cat had run amok, and been discovered at the playground hours later.

"We can check off the shady witnesses," Wesley said. "As for suspects, I'll remove Envelope Drifter" (Trevor apologized again) "and Martin Onder, who didn't benefit from the dead pool and displayed empathy for those affected by Isaac's death. I'm keeping Ana Whitley, who remains the most likely Type One Perfectionist, and both Floreses on the list."

"Let's sleep on it and reconvene tomorrow at Isaac's funeral," Constance said. "We'll observe the Floreses especially, and plan to speak with Ana Whitley. Sound good?"

Everyone agreed.

It wasn't until Constance, Wesley and Trevor had exited the community room that it occurred to Constance the room had been empty when they'd arrived a few minutes ago.

No Zeke.

29

———

WESLEY

AT ISAAC'S funeral on Sunday morning, the young pastor at Cherry Hill United Methodist Church relied on the *Gazette*'s glossy tribute issue to inform his remarks.

As a result, Wesley would be forced to quote Friday's issue to feed Monday's. Why write an article at all when you could reprint the tribute, add a photo of the pastor, and call it a day?

For all he knew, that was Reilly's plan, and wasn't that a depressing thought.

Next to him in the pew, Constance seemed equally troubled. Maybe this was her first funeral since her husband's. Why *was* she pretending she had never been married?

On the other side of Constance, Penelope wore a little black dress and a trendy crocheted bucket hat. Apparently, she strove to be "best dressed" at the funeral. Of course, Wesley had no right to judge. He was jealous of the corpse.

Isaac didn't have to *worry* about anything anymore. He'd lived a long, good life, and now he got to be done. He got to be *done*.

A rustling around him, and a collective swiveling of heads, pulled Wesley from his ruminations. Olivia Flores was saying a few words at the podium. Or at least, she had been, but now she was sobbing, her words a strangled mess of pain over the microphone.

"He was my fr—friend, he always rooted for me, he ne— never tried to make me into someone I'm not. None of you cared about him. You all hated him. Didn't you, Martin? I quit, by the way. I'm gone."

Wesley blinked back tears of his own. Was the cashier at Kaftans 'n' More the only authentic mourner at the funeral?

Olivia's father Danny stood, as if to approach her, but Olivia stomped out his impulse.

"Don't. You hated him too, Dad. You can say all you want about raising a glass to Isaac's memory at that disgusting brunch you're having, but we both know you're happy he's gone. Nobody's here to pay their respects. They're here to gloat. I can't stand it. I really can't stand it!"

Olivia gave another anguished cry and covered her face with her hands. She wasn't near the mic anymore, but her sobs filled the church all the same. Gasping, heaving.

Wesley thought about going up to offer support, so that Olivia wouldn't be alone, but Mayor Trudy beat him to it.

The mayor rose from her seat in the front row, passed a few assorted relations, and pulled Olivia into a tight hug. They cried together, and a collective sense of relief rippled through the crowd. Someone was managing the outburst.

Wesley thought of Aunt Nora, and the heartache he and Trudy still harbored over her loss. The hugs Trudy had given him in his time of need had been anchoring and vital.

Trudy offered Olivia a tissue and spoke to her in quiet

tones, then motioned to another figure in the front row. That person extracted some papers from a briefcase, which Trudy showed to Olivia. They hunched over it, reading together, and Olivia nodded and wiped her eyes.

She and Trudy strode toward the exit together, without making eye contact with anyone else.

"Good for them," Constance murmured. "Good for them."

MOST OF THE Enneagram students gathered in the church parking lot. Bulky, fibrous palm fronds lay scattered on the concrete, ripped from trees during the recent storm. Wesley stepped over and around them to meet with the others.

Sam and her husband remained in the church, looking for Sam and Penelope's boys, who were apparently playing hide-and-seek.

Constance had managed to escape Deputy Max, who stood by the sheriff's patrol car, talking to his colleagues.

"I think we can take Olivia off the list," Chase said. "No way was she faking those tears. All those in favor, say 'aye.'"

"Aye," replied the group.

Ana "Birdbrain" Whitley flounced out of the church and said to her companion, "My goodness, I never. To be accused of not caring! What was that child going on about?"

Wesley watched, fascinated, as Penelope reared up like a viper.

"Are you serious? She was talking about *you*," Penelope hissed. In her impeccable outfit, impeccable makeup, and impeccable heels, she looked like an heiress overturning a birthday cake on a yacht. "I heard you outside the school. You said you got what you wanted when he died. You called it an act of God."

Ana Whitley turned pale. She shoved her handbag at her companion and gathered strength for her response.

"I was talking about the tamarisk tree, not Isaac. It was an evil tree! I've been trying to get that invasive horror-show removed for years."

Penelope frowned, a pouty heiress now instead of an enraged one.

"I said as much at the city council meeting," Ana insisted. "Wesley heard me; he was there. Everyone was going on about the trolley, and I agreed with some of their points, especially the gas guzzling, but *I* was there to defend the very ecology of our town. So yes, I got what I wanted: no more tamarisk. But I hope Isaac rests in peace, and that's the truth."

Penelope slunk backwards, her cheeks pink. "Is that true?" Penelope asked Wesley. "Did she talk about the tree at the city council meeting?"

"Her mic malfunctioned at first, so yeah, it's possible."

"My focus has always been that unnatural tree," Anna snapped. "Good riddance to it. 'Let justice roll on like a river...'"

"'Righteousness like a never-failing stream,'" Wesley finished. "Funny story, Ana, most palm trees in California are non-native—"

"Don't." Constance held a finger up.

Ana glared at Wesley. "Now if you'll *excuse me...*?"

"I think we can take her off the list, too," said Trevor after Ana exited in a snit.

"Seconded," said Chase. "What do you think, Gram?"

"Ana sees God's hand in everything, whereas an unhealthy Type One thinks he or she *is* godlike, capable of reshaping reality according to what's 'fair' in their view," said Constance. "In that sense, I can see how she's not the Type One after all."

"She chose her quote for the nature aspect, not the justice," Wesley agreed.

Sheriff Pittman ambled over, looking tired. "I didn't want to believe it, but now I've seen it with my own eyes."

"Hello, Sheriff. Seen what with your own eyes?" Constance adjusted her shoulder bag and looked ill at ease.

"I have it on good authority that you are interfering in my investigation. Worse, you seem to have gotten your students to do your bidding."

"I told you it was a cult," Deputy Max said, joining in. Then he whispered, "Sorry, Constance. We good?"

"Does she seem charismatic enough to have formed a cult?" Penelope said, which Wesley thought was rude. "Constance is seriously bomb, but she's not handing out Kool-Aid and making us choose a flavor."

Sheriff Pittman turned his focus to Penelope. "I don't understand what you said, but I don't like hearing the word 'bomb' near a church, Ms. Scott."

"'Bomb' means she 'slays,'" Chase said. "Wait, that's bad too."

"Stop talking, both of you," Sheriff Pittman said. "I can't hear myself think."

As usual, Penelope would not be deterred. "It was a field trip to see the Enneagram in action. It's not her fault we got better results than you."

Wesley winced. *Way to antagonize law enforcement, Three, while also making everything about <u>you</u>.*

"Are you mad because I didn't agree with you about the rats at U-Stor-It?" Sheriff Pittman asked helplessly.

Roberto Guerrero, head librarian, entered the arena and glared at Constance. "I knew you were Marpling. What are you all talking about? Do you have an 'in' with the sheriff? That puts Book 'Em at an unfair disadvantage."

The sheriff didn't know where to look or whom to address, and his dilemma only grew when Crystal, leading Savannah on a military-grade harness and leash, wandered over and chimed in, "My customers, the Cat Ladies, are avenging Savvy and investigating as well."

"What qualifications do they have?" Wesley cried.

"What qualifications do *we* have?" Penelope asked.

"I'm a journalist, at least, and Constance knows about human nature. You're on the winning team, Three. Don't worry," he added sarcastically.

"Stop calling me Three, *Four*," she replied.

"Five, six, seven, eight," said Trevor, like a countdown to a rock song.

Chase guffawed, and Trevor smiled shyly at him. Wesley envied the ease of their interaction. What would make *Crystal* laugh? (And why did he care?) Wanting to say something to her, but uncertain what it should be, he fell back on reporter-mode.

"What are you doing here?" he asked. "Did you know Isaac?"

"No, but this is my church, and it's Sunday, so I was here for the fellowship," Crystal said. Savannah the Savannah wound herself through Wesley's legs, gliding in figure-eights, and rubbed her face against his shin.

"She wants you to acknowledge her," Crystal told him.

"What happens if I don't?" Wesley asked dryly. He couldn't help noticing how adorable Crystal looked in her tan duffel coat with toggle buttons. Like a radiant Paddington Bear.

Crystal crouched to address Savannah. "Why do you love him?" she begged. "Why?"

"Enough chit-chat," Sheriff Pittman roared. "Constance, do I need to bring you and your students to the station for a reprimand, or can we finish right here and move on with our day?"

"Here is fine," Constance replied stiffly.

"Everyone else, go." The sheriff waved his arms to disperse them, and Deputy Max copied the gesture.

"You heard the man."

"If we're in trouble, Book 'Em should be, too," Chase said, pointing at his boss. "And the Cat Ladies." To Crystal he whispered, "Sorry. We good?"

"We haven't acted or interfered," Roberto explained to Sheriff Pittman. "We've only analyzed, assessed, and speculated. From within the library walls."

"And the Cat Ladies are only looking at things that affect CHATeau Savannah," Crystal said. "The stuff *you* wouldn't investigate."

"Such as a cat spew toxicology report?" Sheriff Pittman asked. He sounded exhausted. "Does no one trust me to get to the bottom of Isaac's death? We're throwing every resource we have at it."

"Well, you can't be everywhere at once," Constance said. "Who knows, maybe we'll bring you something helpful."

"No. This ends now." He addressed Crystal and Roberto. "Continue your thought experiments and... what-have-you, but keep it to yourselves. Now please be on your way."

Crystal shrugged and led Savannah away. Roberto

frowned at being excluded and walked slowly to his car, turning back every few feet to look at them.

"Bye, Crystal," called Wesley, stupidly. Crystal ignored him.

"'Bye, Crystal,'" Penelope mimicked.

Alone with the Enneagram students, Sheriff Pittman took a breath and addressed Constance. "According to my source, yesterday you divided into factions based on your numerology numbers and spread out to, quote, interview shady witnesses and suspects. You ordered your students to participate."

"That's not—I didn't order my students to do anything. And it's not numerology. I don't even know what numerology is," Constance replied.

Sam arrived, with her family and Penelope's son in tow. "It wasn't Constance's fault. I started the whole thing to exonerate Will."

"I'm glad you're both here," said the sheriff. "I finally heard from Isaac's mechanic. He gave the trolley a clean bill of health *after* Will opened the engine. Will is no longer a person of interest."

The group cheered. Wesley felt his heart lighten. *Absolved.* He knew he'd only been doing his job by piecing together the trolley's breakdowns for his article, but Sam's deterioration and Will's ordeal because of it had unnerved him.

"Did you hear that, honey? Our nightmare is over," Sam called to her husband, who'd been keeping the kids occupied with a magic trick. He strode over and swooped Sam into a big hug and kiss.

"Who betrayed us to you?" Penelope asked the sheriff.

Wesley wondered that, too. Everyone had been happy to help, or so it seemed. All five of them.

Oh.

"Zeke," he groaned.

It seemed to have hit Constance at the same time. She went limp, eyes half-closed.

"Zeke," she confirmed.

30

CONSTANCE

"HE'S MY BROTHER-IN-LAW," Sheriff Pittman explained. "He didn't like what he was hearing, and he came to me the moment you-all scattered, because he feared you were up to no good. And it sounds like he was right."

"He was awake?" Constance lamented. They'd talked about him while he was sitting there! Wesley had placed sunglasses on him.

"Sometimes yes, sometimes no. Your first class, he was asleep, and surprised to wake up in the community room."

"Gram needed the headcount, and I won't apologize," said Chase, arms crossed.

"After that, I sent him in on purpose, undercover, to make sure you weren't, in fact, a cult," the sheriff said.

There had been hints, Constance realized. "Sleeping with his eyes open" and the fact that he'd made an involuntary noise when Constance mentioned the sheriff's wife (Zeke's sister).

"Zeke was in an accident a few years back. He spends most days in the library because it's safe for him if he nods off," the sheriff explained.

"How did he get inside the library when I hadn't opened it yet?" Chase asked.

"As part of his undercover work, I provided him with a master key. It opens every building in the civic center block."

Chase looked briefly disturbed. "Does anyone else have a master key?"

"The visitor center, for upkeep on certain tourism attractions."

It occurred to Constance that everyone in Cherry Hill had deeper connections than were visible at the surface. Wesley was a surrogate nephew to the mayor, the sheriff was related by marriage to Zeke, Olivia's parents were two storefronts down from her, and that was only scratching the surface.

"Wait, does that mean Zeke will never come to class again?" she asked.

"That's up to him."

Her hands clenched, and her insides shrank.

It was never enough. All the scraping and bowing she'd done, allowing Sam to blackmail her, taking on Penelope's divorce case, letting Zeke sleep during her lessons, watching Trevor watch the clock the whole time, all for a quota that still, *still* slipped away from her.

Why did the people of Cherry Hill make it so hard for her to teach them? Why didn't they want to be better than they were? People should've been lined up around the block for her class and the knowledge she was willing to share. She offered them so much, but they refused to take it.

"I believe in second chances," the sheriff told her, "but from this moment on, you are not investigating anyone. Neither will you ask your students to investigate anyone.

Deputy Max will ensure it, won't you, Max? You'll stay on her."

"He already is," Constance said, confused. "He's attached himself to me like a barnacle. Any headway on my shower curtain threat, by the way?"

"What threat? And Deputy Max has been on leave, taking care of his mother."

"No, he—"

Before she could finish, an unmistakably familiar song sounded in the distance, growing louder.

Was she hallucinating? It would make sense, today of all days. A funeral, one year after Arthur's. Not to mention the stress of the past week: trying to uphold that stupid quota, re-living the trolley explosion every night in her nightmares, becoming a target...

Against her will, Constance swayed to the beat.

Because it was back, that infernal, triumphant jingle:

> Cherry Hill, Cherry Hill
> A place to get your fill
> Cherry Hill, Cherry Hill
> Where time stands still

Sam and Wesley swayed as well.

"I'm not the only one who hears it?" Constance asked.

The Jolly Trolley careened into view from the east. *Beep, beep.*

Except it wasn't *exactly* the Jolly Trolley. It was better. Same colors, same shape, same writing on the sides, but gleaming, shiny, and new, with solar panels and Olivia Flores at the helm. She wore a conductor's hat and waved from the window of the driver's seat. Happy and free, she leaned on the horn again. *Beep, beep.*

The mayor waved from a passenger seat, as though on parade. She was the sole passenger, but not for long, no doubt.

Sheriff Pittman removed his starred hat and held it to his chest in astonishment.

"How long have there been two trolleys?" he asked.

"All aboard," Olivia called once the song finished. "Who wants a ride to Texican Table?"

PART 3

31

CONSTANCE

"IT LIVES," Olivia cheered.

After driving everyone from the church parking lot to her family's restaurant, Olivia fielded questions on the small stage typically used for live music.

Sheriff Pittman had allowed Constance and her Enneagram students to attend the impromptu Q & A, but he sat at their table to keep an eye on them, as did Deputy Max and Deputy Cole.

It had been lovely riding the trolley with a crowd for once, every seat filled, the sound of laughter and conversation surrounding her.

She was reminded of the article she'd read last year about how to write an obituary. *Since obituaries are typically only published once, it's important to get the facts straight.* Ha! Wesley had his work cut out for him. *The trolley is dead; long live the trolley.*

And in fact, Wesley was the first to ask what everyone was thinking: "Where did the new trolley come from?"

"Apparently, Isaac purchased a new one last month with all sorts of upgrades, but kept it hidden in a separate storage facility to U-Stor-It. He planned to retire the trolley on Sunday of last week, break it down into parts and offer it to the tourism center as an exhibit of the town's history. He was going to unveil this one and surprise everyone. In his will, he bequeathed it to me, along with his job, if I want it." She grinned. "And I do." Olivia shook her head in wonder. The skin under her eyes was puffy from the crying she'd done at the church, but now her eyes sparkled.

Constance's own eyes stung. If only Isaac had unveiled it a month, a week, a day earlier. If only he'd "killed" it earlier, and been driving the new one last Saturday, he might still be alive.

She scanned faces in the crowded restaurant, seeking out the business owners of Main Street. Martin, the Floreses, and Ana Whitley were there, looking surprised by the trolleys' resurrection. Crystal and Aidan were not in attendance, as far as she could see.

"Before you all freak out—because I know what you're thinking—I'm making changes," Olivia declared. "I didn't always agree with Isaac. Like I said at his funeral, we were friends, and I miss him. Like, a lot." She shook her head out and gave a shaky, embarrassed laugh. "Don't worry, I won't start crying again. Or yelling at you all."

"If you need to cry, you go ahead and cry," Wesley said vehemently.

Olivia looked around, uncertain of who'd advised her. "Anyway, the main reason he didn't want to do all the things you guys suggested was because you went about it all wrong. Maybe if you'd *asked* him instead of *told* him, he would've listened." She looked at her parents. She looked at Martin.

"I know, because I know how that feels," Olivia said. "When people try to steamroll you instead of working together to figure things out. None of you approached him with respect. You treated him like a child, or an idiot. His family is a huge part of Cherry Hill's history, but you made him feel like a useless relic instead of the town's lifeblood." She sniffled. "I want the trolley to last. I'm going to adapt it to the town's needs. I'm going to implement every suggestion from the town hall meeting. Starting with Plan A) A new route to exclude Main Street during business hours. The new route will include the Magic Mirror because, unlike a lot of our tourist attractions right now, it's open for business as we speak, and it needs support."

Now Sam had tears in her eyes. "Thank you," she mouthed. She whipped out her phone and began texting, presumably to let her husband know the good news. He was watching the boys at home.

"B)," Olivia continued. "Replace the diesel engine with solar panels. Done. C) Provide the tourist recording and music strictly via headphones for passengers, so it doesn't cause noise pollution. And Plan D, Speed up. Oh, you know I will." She laughed.

It was as though she knew the letter by heart.

"How did Isaac afford a new trolley?" Deputy Cole asked.

"I don't know," Olivia replied.

"I do." It was Mayor Trudy, who joined Olivia on stage. "May I?" she took the mic. "The Vitality Hotel was bankrolling him. They *wanted* the trolley to cause traffic problems, so everyone on Main Street would be forced to purchase parking at the hotel."

Constance nodded. They'd already learned that from Trevor.

"I have something to confess," Mayor Trudy added.

Wesley froze.

Trevor looked anxious as well.

"The Vitality tried to pay me off to ignore their price gouging." Mayor Trudy removed a fat envelope from her purse and brandished it like a white flag.

Trevor must have delivered that one as well. He had tried to tell them that yesterday, but Wesley had cut him off.

"I never used the money." She handed the envelope to the sheriff and returned to the stage. "I was tempted, though. Why? They said if I helped them change certain bylaws in their favor, they'd convert ten percent of their suites into affordable hospice rooms for anyone who needed it. We're desperate for more and better housing for our oldest and most vulnerable citizens, and I thought the good of that might outweigh the bad of their business practices. It was foolish. My only defense is that, as some of you know..." She took a deep breath. "My best friend Nora had a tough battle with cancer, and it was with her in mind that I thought, if better hospice care were available, her final weeks would have been more comfortable. A little easier. Not only for her, but everyone who loved her."

The mayor wiped her eyes, and this time it was Olivia's turn to comfort her, with a hand on her shoulder. Trudy patted Olivia's hand and cleared her throat.

"I'm sorry for my lapse in judgment. I will put the full power of my office behind stopping the Vitality's aggressive business tactics so everyone on Main Street can have affordable parking and thrive." She was about to cede the floor when her political instincts kicked in and she added rapidly, "I can only hope to earn back your trust by the next election."

Constance hadn't noticed him leave the table, but Wesley escorted Trudy off the stage and moved her to a private corner, where she buried her head in his chest.

"If Isaac kept the new trolley out of U-Stor-It and Car Park, maybe he *did* listen to Aidan's rat warning," Penelope said. "Someone should tell him. Is he here?"

"He's recovering from food poisoning," Deputy Cole said. "My daughter and I were at Dune Buggies last night for a sunset ride, and he took off, green in the gills." She lowered her voice. "It was the instant mashed potatoes from K 'n' M, but you didn't hear that from me."

For the next few minutes, the group enjoyed their brunch—Constance had never had such exquisite chilaquiles—until Sheriff Pittman turned to her and asked, "Now, what's this about Max clinging to you like a barnacle?"

"It wasn't in the budget for her to have 24/7 protection," Max interjected before Constance got a word out. He sounded tense. "I did it because it was the right thing to do."

"But why did you lie to me and ask for time off, Max?" Sheriff Pittman asked. "And why didn't you tell me about the threat she got?"

"Because my mom wrote it," Max hollered.

"Jenna? From the visitor center?" Constance asked, confused. "Why? I thought she liked me. She gave me shelter after the protest."

Max gave Constance an incredulous look. "She hates you for not opening the Upside-Down House. She has that *California's Gold* episode running all day, reminding her of your selfishness." He narrowed his eyes at her, and just like that, she and Deputy Max were antagonists again. "She figured she could scare you into leaving, and someone else could buy the house and open it for tourists."

"That is *extreme*," Constance said, her voice shaking. "I've been terrified for days."

"I know, and I'm sorry, but she wouldn't physically hurt anyone."

"Why did you insist on guarding me then?"

"Because if one person felt that way, other people probably did, too. I meant it when I said I'd protect your life with mine."

Constance believed him, but that did nothing to smother the embers of rage in her gut. What was *wrong* with him? What was wrong with *Jenna*? The fear Constance had suffered the past week—for herself, for Mr. Cinnamon—had been debilitating. Exhausting. *Criminal.*

If they wanted the house opened so badly, *they* could've bought it. Except nobody in Cherry Hill could afford it. It would have lain dormant if Constance hadn't swooped in. But instead of thanking her, they attacked her!

Then there was the fact that Max had *lived with her* for *days*, yet the town's local yokel of a sheriff had had no clue what his underling was up to. Pittman was so out of his depth he'd called on the populace to solve it for him, yet when enterprising people such as Constance and her students strove to do so, he dressed them down publicly outside the church. She, Penelope, Sam, Trevor, and Wesley had gotten far more information out of the suspects and witnesses than Sheriff Pittman had, but he wouldn't even listen to what they'd discovered.

Constance bit her lip and practiced deep breathing out her nose. She needed to rein in her anger lest it consume her, and everyone around her, like wildfire.

Not anger, she corrected herself. *Surprise. Frustration. As anyone would feel in my position.*

"I'm disappointed in you, Max," said the sheriff. "Tell me how this came about."

"Yes, Max, tell us," Constance said through clenched teeth. She could barely speak.

"After I showed up at the Upside-down House to relieve Deputy Cole…"

Deputy Cole's eyes flashed, as if to say, "Leave me out of this."

"I saw my mom outside with a can of spray paint. She told me she only *thought* about doing something but hadn't gone through with it." He turned to Constance. "When you screamed, I really did think you fell, and I was as shocked as you by the message."

I doubt that, she thought. "How did she get in?" Constance asked.

"She has a master key to the tourism attractions as part of her job. The visitor center helps with upkeep. Can we please forget about this? Ever since her stroke, she hasn't been the same."

"Well, no, Max, we can't forget about it," said the sheriff slowly. "I need to interview her. And you're going to be suspended for concealing evidence. I'm also going to have the locks changed at no cost to Constance so Jenna can never stroll right in again."

Deputy Cole's radio crackled. "We've got a ten-sixty-two at the pet store on Clifton Lane."

"A break-in." Max stood, but a sharp look from the sheriff sent him back to his chair, miserable.

"On it," Deputy Cole said, and headed out.

Constance had lost her appetite. Her stomach sat like a stone in her belly, and she pushed her plate of food away. No one around her seemed to notice. They snarfled at their food like pigs at the trough, Wesley in particular, uncaring that Constance had gone through hell the last several days.

Wesley came up for air and addressed the sheriff. "I

know you wanted to put a message in the paper asking anyone with information to come forward and that Reilly prevented that." He wiped his mouth with a napkin. "Consider this a response to that call. We have information, and we're coming forward."

The group nodded.

A sweet-faced woman in a wheelchair, who'd been hovering behind the sheriff, took that moment to lean forward and whisper in Sheriff Pittman's ear. He looked at her, and his tense features smoothed out. "Alright, Alice," he said.

As the woman wheeled past Deputy Max, the two exchanged a discreet high-five.

"I may not agree with your-all's interference, but my wife Alice says I need to be flexible in my thinking and as usual, she's right. It's too important not to consider all the angles, ill-gotten though they may be. Why don't we get some to-go bags and meet at the station in fifteen minutes?" Sheriff Pittman asked.

EVERYONE EXCEPT PENELOPE took the sheriff up on his offer and sat or stood in the largest of the interrogation rooms.

Constance didn't know why Penelope hadn't joined them; maybe she had to check on her son, what's-his-name, Henry. That's how she would remember his name, in a rhyme: Pen and Hen. Like chickens she'd corralled back into her class, at great personal effort, only to have the quota *still* at risk.

She knew her mind was wandering to deflect from the fact that she didn't like being back in the station; it reminded her too much of the humiliating interview when she'd had to listen to her 911 recording.

Wesley had brought multiple takeout containers with him, one of which he was lustily eating straight from his bag.

The sheriff steepled his fingers. "Who wants to start?"

Wesley waved his fork around. "Trevor has something to say first."

"Yes." Trevor explained his role in the gambling ring and trolley dead pool.

"And you didn't think to come forward before now?" Sheriff Pittman cried.

"Half the money's already been spent," Chase said. "You'll never take Trevor alive!"

"Uh, that's not... I don't..." Trevor started. "Are you going to charge me with anything?"

The sheriff looked agonized. "I have no idea."

"If it helps," said Trevor, "I figured out the postcard threats."

Everyone turned to him. This was new. Constance found herself swept up in the mystery again, her personal troubles pushed aside.

"'No one wants you here' and 'this is your final warning' never made sense for the cat cafe, because it wasn't meant for her. It was meant for the trolley."

"But 'Democracy dies in kitty litter' is very much meant for the cafe," Wesley said.

"According to Crystal, the handwriting was different. That one was sent to make it seem as though the first one *hadn't* been a mistake," Trevor told him.

"And to frame me," Wesley muttered. "Thanks, whoever you are."

"Who knew about Crystal's first postcard besides us at this table?" the sheriff asked.

"Everyone," Trevor replied. "She told all her customers about it. Anyway, I looked it up, and the cat cafe and the Jolly Trolley both use P.O. boxes for business purposes. Box 102 versus box 201. Every other part of the address is identical. The numbers got inverted." He retrieved a flyer from his backpack. "Just like some of the letters on the flyer for the brunch. At first, I chalked these up as typos from lackadaisical proofreading, but what if the person couldn't tell the difference? What if it was the same dyslexia that caused the postcard to go to the wrong person? That's another point against Danny Flores."

"But the first postcard had a cat on it," Sam reminded Trevor.

"Caldecot is an old Scottish surname derived from Calico," said Trevor. "It's kind of obscure, but there *is* a link."

Constance slapped the table. "It's on the trolley's commemorative map. The Caldecot / Calico family crest."

"Mayor Trudy Caldecot always wears a calico cat necklace," Wesley added. "It's a known link. Great job, Trevor."

Sam stuffed her Texican Table bag in the trash. "I can't eat food prepared by a murderer."

Wesley stopped mid-chew. Mouth full, he said, "I'm sorry. It's so good." He swallowed. "You don't understand; I had to watch Reilly eat chilaquiles for breakfast last week and..." he trailed off, his eyes far away.

"How? Until today, they weren't open for breakfast or lunch," Chase pointed out.

"They're old friends. I was so fixated on Martin's outburst I didn't think about the fact that Reilly *had to have seen Danny* that morning if he had fresh takeout from the restaurant. Up until then, we were covering the story normally. But after seeing Danny before work that day, Reilly changed. He told Shawna I was investigating and told me Shawna was—and not to communicate with her. Not only did Danny threaten, or try to threaten, the Jolly Trolley with the postcard, he must have written the letter to the paper. Why else would Reilly have erased it from the servers? That's who he's been protecting, same as Aidan."

"That's why Olivia was so familiar with the letter's contents, if her dad wrote it," said Constance. "And did you hear the way Olivia described her dad at the service? 'Telling, not asking. Treating Isaac like a child.' That's Type One Perfectionism."

"The Type One stuff doesn't mean anything to me," Sheriff Pittman cautioned her.

"But it's relevant," Constance argued.

"You're right," Wesley said quickly. "But he hasn't had the benefit of attending your class, so we'll dumb it down for him."

She barked out a laugh, mollified.

"No need for insults," the sheriff said.

"Here's someone desperate to save his family business..." Constance began.

"Who's so all-in with it that he changed his last name from Smith to Flores in support of it," added Wesley.

"... who likely wrote a threatening letter to the paper, followed by a threatening postcard, albeit one that didn't reach its target because he swapped the P.O. box numbers. Penelope overheard him having a suspicious conversation about a 'planner,' and Wesley's editor appears to be protecting him from scrutiny. Lastly, Aidan Zachary saw him throw the rock and crouch down by the engine on the day of the protest," Constance summarized.

"Even if you're right, and you may be, none of this is

proof," Sheriff Pittman said, and the mood plummeted. "It's conjecture. And Aidan might, whaddayacallit, wiffle if he's pressured to swear to what he witnessed, considering Olivia's stake in it. Same with your boss at the newspaper, Wesley. For what it's worth, I think you're onto something, but we need evidence. Forensics swears at least two wires were missing from the engine—torn out, or cut—removed, in any event. We have a motive for Danny, to save his restaurant and his daughter's job, but we're only guessing at method or means."

"I thought we agreed he may have used Olivia's sewing scissors," Constance said. "Without her knowledge, considering her friendship with Isaac."

"And again, you might be right. But how do we *prove* it?"

"I know how." Penelope stood silhouetted in the doorway, hands on her hips in a superhero pose. How long had she been there listening? "I know exactly how."

32

———————

PENELOPE

"READY TO HAVE YOUR MINDS BLOWN?" Penelope asked. Her hair was down today, instead of her usual bun, and she couldn't resist a dramatic hair toss.

There were few things more satisfying than helping other people achieve their full potential. The only way to "add more hours to the day" was to combine objectives:

1. Save the Magic Mirror
2. Help Kelly Arden stage a comeback
3. Force Danny Flores to confess to the trolley murder

Penelope would solve all three problems in one fell swoop. It would be her finest hour. Until whatever she got up to next week, of course.

"I was already multi-tasking to help the magic theatre grow its audience, and this ties in," Penelope explained. "My mentor, Kelly Arden, has agreed to do a comedy set and introduce Will onstage tomorrow night. Kelly's fans will go nuts for a chance to see him live, which will explode ticket sales and increase buzz for both the theatre and Kelly."

"What if his fans leave after he's done?" asked Chase.

"We'll lock the doors," Sam said, not joking.

"And during his show, Sam's husband, a professional magician and mind reader—"

"He prefers the term mentalist," Sam piped up. "Don't you, honey? I've got Will on FaceTime, everyone. The boys are watching a movie, so hopefully they won't interrupt. Go ahead, Penelope."

Did Sam have to ruin the flow of her big reveal?

Penelope tossed her hair again, this time in annoyance. "He'll act as though he knows Danny is guilty and force a confession out of him."

"What does a mentalist do?" asked Sheriff Pittman.

Will chimed in from Sam's screen. "I use magic and psychology to create the illusion of mind reading. I'll need time to build credibility with the audience first, including Danny, for this to be effective. And even then, no guarantees."

Penelope was allergic to doubt. She shared her screen, open to Instagram, where she'd posted a stunning graphic (if she did say so herself). "*Monday Magic Mayhem! One Night Only! Guaranteed to Sell Out! Must-See Comedy & Magic, with an intro by Kelly Arden, Live in Front of a VIP Audience!*" It included an old headshot of Kelly, along with a stage photo of Will looking dapper and performing his mentalism act. Sam had given her access to Will's account, and when she'd reposted the graphic on her own, it got a 4,000% boost. "Basically, you'll bring up the Main Streeters as volunteers, do your mentalism thing and say, 'Amongst you walks a criminal with a dark heart' or whatever."

"That's not really my stage persona," Will began.

"He's the mentalist next door," Sam explained.

"I said 'or whatever,'" Penelope sniffed.

Sam's face softened. "You know what? You're amazing, and I think we need to take a moment to say thank you, Penelope. Thank you so, so much. We'll make the most of this opportunity, won't we, Will?"

"Absolutely. Thank you."

Penelope smiled. "You're welcome." It felt good to say the words and mean them, instead of singing them sarcastically.

"How do we know the Main Streeters, specifically Danny Flores, will attend?" Wesley asked.

"Already handled," Penelope said. "After you guys left the restaurant, I did a song-and-dance about how if everyone there supports the Magic Mirror, you'll support them. Shop Local, blah blah blah. The chamber of commerce committed its members—including Danny—and Olivia will turn the trolley into a party bus to get everyone to the theatre and to celebrate her new route."

The sheriff took a moment to consider his options, then said loudly, "I am going to *exit*, and whatever happens *now*, I will not be *aware* of. If I *come* to the magic show tomorrow night, it will *only* be because my *wife* enjoys live entertainment." He cleared his throat and added quietly, "Max, you can redeem yourself by coordinating with them and setting up the sting, but if it goes south, I'll deny any knowledge of your actions and give you a, whaddayacallit, public reprimand for both screw-ups."

Max saluted. "Double or nothing, yessir."

Sheriff Pittman, looking dazed, left the room.

On Sam's phone, Will marveled at Penelope's efforts. "We're going to sell out. On a Monday. We're not even open on Mondays. This is... this is incredible."

"I DM'd you Kelly's contact info," said Penelope. "He's expecting to hear from you, so you can coordinate rehearsal."

Will looked overwhelmed suddenly. "How am I going to reveal the killer? Exactly?"

"Wesley will write you a script," Penelope said.

"Will he?" Wesley said.

Penelope rolled her eyes. This would've gone so much better without the constant interruptions from everyone.

"Yeah, just put down everything you pieced together in your little chart, describing the most likely sequence of events," Penelope said. "Don't name names, Will, but act like you already know everything, exude total conviction, and go hard until he freaks out. Worst-case scenario, the audience has a great time with you and Kelly, and good publicity ensues. Best-case scenario, we catch a killer. Boom."

33

CONSTANCE

"I BETTER GET STARTED. See you tomorrow night, everyone," said Will. "Sam, can you get everyone's names, and I'll put them on the box office list?"

He hung up, and Deputy Max handed Constance a piece of paper to pass around before leaving the room for whatever it was Deputy Max was allowed to do during his suspension. Use the bathroom?

Without Max as her knight-in-tarnished armor anymore, Constance would need to ask Chase for a ride home. If he couldn't, maybe Wesley could help her.

Anyone but Sam.

She scrawled her name on the sheet and passed it to Trevor, who hesitated. Maybe he disliked crowded theatres?

"I'm not going," Trevor blurted out.

"Why not?" asked Sam.

"My flight's tomorrow."

Constance tilted her head. "Your flight?" A buzzing sound hovered in her mind. "Where are you headed?" More importantly, would he be back in time for Wednesday's class?

"Home to Buffalo." He blinked rapidly. "I don't... I don't live here."

The buzzing sound nearly deafened her. "What do you mean you don't live here?"

"I was staying at the Vitality to 'recalibrate,' which is, um, their version of rest and relaxation. And now I'm going home."

"How did this never come up?" Constance asked. Her words sounded distorted, and far away. "We did several 'getting to know you' segments in class."

"I did say I was staying at the hotel..."

"Only after we caught you," Wesley muttered.

"... which implies I'm not local," Trevor finished in his blandest, most expressionless voice.

"No, you said you were spending time at the spa," Constance corrected him, "which could just as easily mean you *were* local, taking a day or two to relax."

"What's the difference?" asked Sam nervously. "The point is, he—"

"Did the rest of you know he doesn't live here?" Constance interrupted. "Show of hands."

Chase bit his lip and slowly raised his hand. "I knew. Without knowing, if you know what I mean." He sped through the next part. "Also, I'm super sorry about the timing, Gram, but I can't make Wednesday's class either. Roberto changed my schedule—not out of spite, but because the banned book club needed to change days, and I'm in charge of that, so it's not actually Roberto's fault, otherwise I would've stood up to him, you know that, Gram."

"I am not your gram," she gritted out.

Chase averted his eyes. He looked shattered.

Of course he did. Because just like Arthur, the possibility of shame—or any other negative emotion—was unbearable to him. Any second now, he'd rally and present a positive re-frame of the situation.

"It'll work out," he began. "Maybe even for the better—"

"How will it work out for the better, Chase?" she asked in bright, harsh tones. "How? Without the two of you, my class is over. We don't have enough people. Because don't forget, z-z-z-Zeke was never a student; he was a dirty spy when he wasn't snoring over my lectures, so we're down by half at this point."

"I'd be mad too, Constance," said Penelope, sycophantically. "I'll try to stir up interest for you, but it'll have to be backburnered until I catch up on my real work."

Constance didn't hear anything past the word "mad."

"I'm. Not. Mad. All I'm *asking* is for people to take *responsibility* for their *actions*." She whipped her face toward Trevor. "You lied to me, Trevor. Every time you showed up to class and *didn't* tell me you were a temporary student, that was a lie. It led me to believe I could count on you."

"You should probably stop accusing people of lying, Constance, considering how much lying you've done the past two weeks," Wesley said.

Constance laughed. "*I'm* a liar? *You're* a liar. You told me you would publish your article on the class—which was your idea, *I* didn't request it, *you* came to *me*—on *Monday*. If you'd kept your word, more people would have known about it, and I wouldn't be in this situation." She shook her head and chuckled. "You're bad at a job you don't even want."

Wesley's face reddened. "You're not a spinster," he retorted. "You were married for decades to Arthur Kincaid, of Kincaid & Kincaid law firm. That's a huge chunk of your life to lie about. You expected us to open a vein and spill our hopes and fears and vulnerabilities in class while you lied about the most basic, researchable fact of your life."

"I... that's not..." Her heart pounded so intensely she worried she might black out. "That's none of your business," she gasped.

"Leave her alone," snapped Penelope.

"Yeah," echoed Sam.

"You don't have to explain, Constance," Penelope told her, as though Constance were a doddering old nana, incapable of making her own decisions.

"Stop sucking up to me! You don't care about the class either. You're using me to get free legal help, and once I've provided that, you'll quit the next day." She couldn't stop, even if she wanted to. "Chase bailing makes sense to me. He got what he wanted—a new experience. He even got to solve a murder. I can really deliver, huh? But now it might get *boring*, so he's on to the next thing. And then we have Sam-the-*SHAM*. 'Look at me, I'm so helpful, until I stab you in the back and take over your class by threatening to leave if you don't do what I say.' With students like these, who needs enemies?"

Sam gaped at her like a fish.

"We get it," said Wesley, ice-cold. "You think you're above us. Literally. On top of your hill. The symbolism is..." he made a chef's kiss motion.

"Gram, Wesley, please stop," Chase begged.

"For the last time, my name is not Gram. And my cat is not called Sassy Pants; he is called Mr. Cinnamon. You can't just re-name someone's cat!" she roared.

After that, nobody spoke.

The only sound in the room was Sam, sniffling back tears.

Wesley broke first. "Being part of a community doesn't

mean showing up once and expecting people to give you everything you want," he said. "It means showing up for them, too, and regularly. You refused to open a tourism destination that this town desperately needs. What did you think was going to happen when it came time for *you* to need something?"

"I don't 'need' the class," she sputtered. "I was *giving* it, for the benefit of *others*. But everyone in Cherry Hill is too oblivious and small-minded to see that. They think it's a cult."

"If you'd opened the Upside-Down House six months ago, your class would've overflowed," Chase told her. "People would have gotten to know you, seen what you were about, and wanted to support you."

"Can't you admit you made a mistake?" Sam said, tears falling down her cheeks.

"My only mistake was trusting any of you."

She should have known. She'd been so stupid. If *Arthur* could be treacherous, anyone could be treacherous.

Her entire body ached. Deep down, a scream was forming. She refused to let it build. She had to keep it down. Her life depended on it.

Luckily, this wasn't anger. She'd simply been stating facts. Ugly truths that nobody wanted to hear, but that wasn't *her* fault.

The end of her class was a relief, actually.

Waiting for the axe to fall had been humiliating. Wondering, each time she entered the community room, whether there'd be enough people to justify the class's existence (and all her hard work).

She stood and wiped her hands of the whole mess.

She walked out the door and out of their lives.

~

CONSTANCE SPENT the next twenty-four hours in bed.

It had nothing to do with her emotional state. The slog up the hill had sapped her of strength. (That's what she told herself.)

Monday afternoon, Mr. Cinnamon tried his best to engage her, pouncing on her legs above the comforter, and "rao"-ing in her ear but other than feeding him and giving him a pat she remained prone.

Her cat caused mischief, as though hoping to lure her out of her bed and out of her funk. First, he leaped onto her dresser and scattered her perfume bottles to the floor. Then, using his agile paws, he pulled all the books off her shelves.

He darted from wall to wall like a pinball, chasing an imaginary foe.

A tear slipped down her cheek.

She didn't hate Cherry Hill. She didn't hate her students.

She didn't even hate Deputy Max. She missed him.

Well, missed was a strong word, but she'd grown accustomed to his inane chatter from the couch.

Would it be the worst thing in the world to let laughter and joy fill her house? To open her doors to the public and invite the world in? Let them take goofy photos of themselves in that upside-down room to show their friends and family?

Why had she been so stubborn about keeping the Upside-Down House to herself?

Because she hadn't wanted people to know she had purchased an upside-down house without *realizing* it. That she'd ignored her realtor's attempts to tell her. That she'd picked Cherry Hill on a tipsy whim, half-blind without her bifocals, in a desperate bid to escape the pain of Arthur's infidelity and death.

It had been safer to dig in her heels and keep all of that to herself.

To balance the scales, she'd help Cherry Hill in a different way. She'd teach a free class on the Enneagram. Why hadn't it worked?

Because no one asked for that. What they did ask me for —begged me for—I ignored, because I thought I knew better than them. I thought I could decide for them what was best for them and for the town.

(But really, for me.)

She'd been so arrogant. So high-minded and cruel.

Wesley was right: she thought she was too good for Cherry Hill. What had she told herself every single time she rode the trolley? *It's not my fault the town is suffering. It's not my fault tourism is down.*

If she'd truly cared about teaching the Enneagram to others, she wouldn't have fixated on the quota. She would have focused on giving however many students she *did* have, for however long she was lucky enough to have them, a good session. Why hadn't she moved the location of the class? Even one student would have been worth the world. But she'd wanted to beat Roberto. She'd wanted to "prove" her class was worthwhile instead of making *certain* it was.

And yesterday, she'd abused her knowledge of the Types to lash out at people. It was unconscionable. She could never forgive herself.

Mr. Cinnamon hopped onto the bed. "Rao?"

He nuzzled her cheek, his fluffy fox tail raised high. She snuggled him to her and buried her face in his gorgeous albeit tangled fur. His deep purrs rumbled against her cheek. She reached for his grooming brush on the bedside table and focused on detangling his fur. He wiggled and gave her a playful nip before settling in briefly.

For the past year, she'd taken to sleeping on Arthur's side of the bed. It was better than occupying her usual spot and seeing Arthur's side empty, night after night.

But in the process, she'd disappeared.

Not even half-brushed, Mr. Cinnamon burst free, exited the room, and returned with a much-loved, ragged toy in his mouth. She halfheartedly threw it for him, and he returned with it, like a puppy. Somali cats and their Abyssinian cousins enjoyed learning tricks. They were extremely intelligent and energetic cats. Normally she provided Mr. C with all the exercise and interaction he desired, but today she just couldn't.

Add it to her list of failures.

It was early evening when hunger compelled her out of bed, to make the easiest meal imaginable: instant mashed potatoes from a packet.

While eating, she composed a text to the Enneagram group chat, apologizing for her abhorrent behavior. She stopped short of sending it. The entrapment magic show was starting soon; it wasn't right for her to insert herself into the stress of the evening—to make it about her. She'd send it tomorrow. Assuming they hadn't blocked her.

Oh, no, she realized after scraping the bowl clean.

She'd just gobbled up the food that had given Aidan Zachary food poisoning. She could have screamed at her stupidity.

She was in for a rough night. A sweating, aching, purge. It seemed a fitting punishment, and she braced herself for hours of discomfort.

But something strange happened. She felt fine.

Another hour passed. Still fine.

A thought sliced through her mind. *Perhaps Aidan hadn't had food poisoning either.*

Perhaps he'd faked it, in front of a deputy, which provided him an alibi, so he could get out of attending Isaac's funeral the next day. But why?

She cackled. She was losing it.

So he could break into that pet store, her subconscious replied, which made even less sense. The mashed potatoes may not have affected her body, but they sure had affected her mind.

She was starving suddenly. She grabbed a string cheese from the fridge and peeled it into strips. The act of tearing it calmed her. She chewed as she contemplated. When the string was down to a final strip, Mr. Cinnamon launched himself from his scratching post onto her shoulder.

"Ahh!" She dropped the strip of cheese, and he dove after it.

"No, Mr. Cinnamon, drop it," Constance called. "It's not good for you. You don't have the right enzymes."

It dangled from his mouth, and he treated it like a prize, running from her and proudly shaking it back and forth. It was a hostage situation. She coaxed Mr. Cinnamon out from beneath the table by proposing a negotiation: drop the cheese and gain a crunchie. He made a last bid for both, pouncing on the crunchie while maintaining his grip on the cheese string.

The cheese string that, come to think of it, resembled a rat's tail.

The childish words she'd said to herself every time she rode the trolley returned to haunt her. *"It's not my fault. It's not my fault."*

They had the wrong man.

34

───────

CONSTANCE

AS THE TROLLEY rounded the corner of its usual route before peeling off toward the highway, Constance saw something outside her window that led to another epiphany.

Heart racing, she added it to her notecard in a wild scribble.

Olivia had already delivered the chamber of commerce members to the Magic Mirror for a pre-show cocktail. Constance was among the last passengers of the night.

She was so focused on getting the words down on her notecards for Will that she didn't look up until the trolley pulled into the theatre parking lot. The theatre occupied a corner spot in a strip mall that included a Chinese restaurant, a podiatrist, an orthodontist, and a bakery. It stood out with its bright white logo: the word MAGIC twice, one on top of the other, with the second version of the word written upside down, as though reflected in a mirror.

According to Sam, the Magic Mirror was in dire financial straits, but tonight it looked and sounded like a rousing success. The lot was full, and as Constance and the other passengers walked inside the building, laughter poured out from within the theatre. The comedian from *Saturday Night Live*, Kelly Arden, was warming up the audience.

A mixture of groans and laughter greeted his punchline. "Oh, relax, I did not. If you take longer than a five-minute shower at Senior City, they do a wellness check to make sure you're not dead."

Olivia caught up with Constance. "I already checked in, so I'm going to use the bathroom. Enjoy the show."

Constance nodded and got in line behind three other guests at the ticket booth. She was relieved that Sam hadn't removed her name from the list.

After snagging her ticket, Constance realized the person she most needed to warn was getting away. Carefully gripping the banister, she sped down the stairs.

"Olivia," Constance called into the empty hallway. "Wait up, I need to tell you something about Aidan."

Constance searched the hallway for the bathrooms. She passed rooms marked "props," "sound equipment," and "lights," but had no luck. Olivia was nowhere to be found.

"He's not safe," she called desperately.

"No, he's not," an angry voice agreed.

That's when the wall flew sideways to smash her in the face, and everything went black.

35

PENELOPE

I CREATED THIS, Penelope thought, gazing around the packed theatre. The air crackled with excitement. *This exists because I made it exist.*

And she was pleased.

The evening had surpassed her expectations. She'd thrown together the perfect mix of comedy and magic; engineered a triumph of nostalgia for, and renewed interest in, Kelly Arden; and saved the Magic Mirror, at least for one night.

Legendary.

She wore a chic burnt sienna dress, the precise color of the fox tattoo on her biceps, giving her a red glow that brought all eyes to her in any crowd. Well, all eyes except those belonging to Cherry Hill's most eligible bachelor.

Aidan Zachary held hands with Olivia, looking antsy as a June bug (as Penelope's mom would say). He appeared so lost in thought he hadn't even noticed the goddess Penelope touch down on Earth to survey her work.

Forget him, she thought, and she did. Because... *Hellooooo, nurse. Who is this absolute snack with thick, rumpled hair, in a painted-on tux showcasing a tall body and a hot—oh.*

The snack of the century had turned to face her, and it was Wesley. *Ew.*

He waved and approached.

"Looking foxy, Three," he said with a dorky eyebrow waggle.

She narrowed her eyes distrustfully.

"Your tattoo," he said. "It's a fox."

"Yes," was all she could say. They awkwardly faced one another, at a loss for words. She told herself it was the shock of seeing him in formal wear when he normally wore thrifted, ill-fitting garbage.

Crystal came over and pointed between them. "Are you two here together?"

"Ugh, no," Penelope said.

It was equally strange seeing Crystal without her jungle cat on a leash. She wore cat's eyes glasses, a leopard print top, and a black skirt that could've used a good lint remover session. She was on-brand, at least.

Was that a piece of old, dried cat food stuck to her medical boot?

36

WESLEY

WESLEY WAS ENRAPTURED.

Besotted.

Mesmerized.

With her medical boot on one foot and a high heel on the other, Crystal made a lopsided figure, but she didn't care. She didn't care about the cat hair clinging to her black skirt, the hot-pink glasses that clashed with her leopard print blouse, or the possible litter box grit clinging to her footwear.

She was passionate, authentic, and unabashedly herself.

Oh, no.

Crystal was his dream girl.

"Meet my boyfriend," Crystal said, tugging on the arm of a man standing a few feet away. She introduced him, but Wesley didn't hear a word.

"Wesley. Wesley!" Crystal snapped her fingers at him, the way she did at Savvy. He thought of the cat as Savvy now.

He was doomed.

"Yes, Crystal?" he asked.

Smitten.

Lovesick.

Screwed.

"Did you hear me? This is Philip, my boyfriend. He's the health inspector here in town."

Wesley felt his legs sink into the floor. He saw himself making the phone call last week, trying to outdraw Crystal. "Yes, hello, I'd like to report a public health violation..."

"He gave me an A+," Crystal said, eyes gleaming.

Wesley spoke to her as if from a distant planet. "They don't..."

"What?"

"They don't give out pluses," he finished lamely.

"I would have if I could have," said Philip. "CHATeau Savannah is pristine."

Crystal leaned into Philip's embrace, but her focus remained on Wesley. "We never would have met if you hadn't sic'd him on me." Her smile was lethal. "I'm with him because of you."

37

TREVOR

TREVOR ROLLED HIS SMALL, battered suitcase out of the Vitality Hotel lobby and into the trunk of the waiting taxi. Aware that public transportation—other than the Jolly Trolley, of course—was scarce in Cherry Hill, he'd booked the ride for his return flight when he arrived a month ago.

What was he going to tell his mom? She'd hoped so badly that the retreat would fix him.

Yet here he was, three weeks older but none the wiser, and no closer to deciding his future.

He wasn't the same person he'd been before he arrived, though.

The people he'd met here had changed him. Before her unkind words yesterday (and he couldn't entirely blame her), Constance had understood and valued him. She'd empathized with his most basic daily struggle—preserving his energy—and delighted in his study habits, which in turn helped Trevor view himself in a new, positive light.

Crystal had trusted him with her cafe. Purr-cy had loved him, too. (Cats counted double.)

Sam enjoyed chatting with him and had invited him to

Sunday dinner at her house. Wesley took him seriously and clapped him on the back for his contributions to the mystery. No one in class had mocked him for being who he was, and when Chase told him he was funny, Chase meant it as a compliment. Chase had even chosen him as a sleuthing partner, however fleetingly. Raised their hands up together, a team.

Maybe it didn't matter what you were doing, but who you did it *with*.

A text chimed on his phone, from Constance, to the Enneagram group text.

> I've decided to move back to New York. I don't belong here, and it's time I headed home. Please don't contact me.

It was a knife to his gut.

"Can you give me a moment?" Trevor asked the taxi driver. He leaned against the car, and felt the heat of it rumbling against his back. He took a deep breath and typed.

> I'll stay if you stay.

CONSTANCE

WHEN CONSTANCE OPENED HER EYES, her head throbbed, her neck and back ached, and she felt dried blood on her nose.

Aidan had locked her inside a storage closet, twenty by twenty feet. She'd come to once or twice while being dragged, only to plunge back into darkness. She slapped at her cheeks now to keep herself conscious.

The room hadn't been used for ages. Dust coated every shelf, and the boxes crammed atop them looked tattered and moldy.

Her phone and purse were gone.

Oddly, her fanny pack with the colorful notecards inside remained secure under her coat. Did Aidan think her body was composed of misshapen lumps? Had he patted her down for weapons or tools while she was out cold and thought, "Nope, nothing strange or squishy here that wouldn't be out of place on a woman of her age"?

She'd be insulted if she weren't so angry.

Yes, angry.

Angry as a nest of threatened hornets. Angry as a feral

tiger protecting a cub. Angry as a woman who's been pushing down her rage for months. No, years.

For the first time since Arthur's death, Constance let out a primal scream. A real throat-scraper.

She was trapped like an animal, waiting for a killer to return and finish her off.

Why?

Because the man who'd sworn to love her till death did they part had checked out early after tossing her aside. She'd never be able to confront him. She'd never be able to reconcile what he'd *done* with who he *was*.

It all went back to Arthur. The reckoning she'd avoided, the anger she'd suppressed because she had wanted to be the perfect lawyer and the perfect wife.

She didn't express anger when Arthur acted evasively or traveled on his own more often. She didn't express anger about anything, only for him to cheat on her and lose his life as a result, which also had the effect of revealing her abject imperfection to the entire world; after all, a perfect wife wouldn't have given her husband cause to stray, would she?

Desperate to escape, she'd burned down her old life, moved to Cherry Hill, and become a recluse. For good reason; the moment she re-entered society, she'd become embroiled in a murder investigation, and now she was about to lose her life altogether.

All because of Arthur.

"Help!" she cried. It sounded feeble. But if she allowed herself to be fueled by other moments in her life, she'd blow the roof off the place.

Adrenaline, anger, and purpose merged.

She screamed at her parents for not letting her dance when she was a child.

She screamed at her law school professors for favoring the male students.

She screamed at her law firm for advancing her male colleagues faster because "men won't take time off for kids."

She screamed at Arthur.

She screamed her throat raw.

She flung herself at the door, and twisted the locked doorknob repeatedly, hurting her palms. She pulled at it, slammed her hands against the door, and howled. She scattered items off the shelves, in a cacophony of chaos.

Dust plumed in the air, making her cough. Forcing her to slow down. The bump on her forehead throbbed. She knew adrenaline was protecting her from feeling the worst of the aches and pains from Aidan knocking her out. Tomorrow she'd be a mass of pain.

Tomorrow. Right. Assuming she lived to see it.

She checked her watch. In sixty minutes, give or take, the performance would be over, Will would have made a fool of himself accusing the wrong man, and Constance would be at Aidan's mercy again. No one knew she was here. No one could hear her.

She took stock of her surroundings. What could she do? What could she use?

At the very least, she could arm herself with something, try to catch him off guard.

There was a ladder in the corner, but what good would that—aha. On the ceiling, a vent. If she screamed through that, perhaps her voice would carry more effectively.

Her anger wasn't done with her yet. It fueled her movements, and she was grateful for it. The clarity. The knife-point intensity. The STRENGTH it gave her. She raged, and it was beautiful.

Because this anger was *justified*. It wasn't the selfish

anger she'd unleashed on her students yesterday. *This* anger was righteous.

She positioned the ladder and climbed it, then wrenched and wrenched and wrenched at the grated vent with all her might, fingers bleeding. It hurt. It hurt so badly. But not as much as suppressing her anger had hurt.

She dug her fingers into the slits. She grunted and yelled, "HELP! HELP! AAAARRRRRGGGGGH!" until she ripped the grate off the ceiling.

A moment passed, and then a little voice from above said, "Hi. Who are you?"

OF ALL THE *moments for Dale and Henry to sneak off, this was the worst one,* Sam thought.

After school drop-off that morning, she had assisted Will in preparing for tonight's whizbang, sell-out show. One thought kept circling in her brain: What if Danny Flores reacted not with a confession, but with violence? If he had tampered with the engine after throwing the rock at the protest, he could be capable of anything. Especially if Will exposed his actions to a room full of people. She couldn't risk Will's safety.

And yet, the publicity that would ensue could save the theatre and transform their lives.

She went back-and-forth for hours. She'd seen Will ruminate this way, unable to decide on a course of action, but tonight it was her turn to fixate on What Ifs.

"Don't bring the Main Street volunteers up on stage," she made Will promise. "They can stand at their seats but don't invite them up. Don't let them near you."

Having that *SNL* actor kick things off was a brilliant idea, and a tiny part of her had worried Will couldn't live up to his glowing introduction, but then Will had exceeded her wildest hopes. The audience adored him. They'd come for the comic, but stayed for Will, as Penelope had predicted. The moment the spotlight hit his face, Will exhibited total control of the audience.

He had read minds, helped volunteers read *other* volunteers' minds, made outrageous yet true predictions, and told various audience members about childhood memories, relationships, and trips he couldn't possibly have known about.

He'd proven what Sam already knew: he was worthy of sellout crowds.

Now it was intermission, and she couldn't find Dale or Henry, who'd begged Penelope to let him hang out backstage with Dale during the show.

40

CONSTANCE

"I'M DALE," said the voice in the ceiling. "I'm sneaking."

Dale, Dale, who was Dale?

"Are you...?" Constance struggled to think of an identifying question. "Are you someone's child?" *Of course he's someone's child. Everyone is someone's child.*

"My daddy is the magician, and my mommy is my mommy."

Sam the SAHM's boy!

"Henry didn't think I could fit in the tunnel, but I did."

"Could you get a message to your mommy or daddy? Right away, fast as you can? A very important message?"

"Okay."

"Fantastic. My name is Constance. Please tell them I'm locked inside a storage closet beneath the stage. Tell your mom first and then give this to your dad. Okay?"

Constance stepped off the ladder, rustled through her fanny pack for the notecards,

and scrambled back up. "Give these to your parents." Her life, entrusted to that small hand. "Quick, quick as a fox now."

She thought of foxy Mr. Cinnamon, whose antics with the string cheese combined with her own Type One Perfectionism had helped her solve Isaac's murder, and sent up a prayer: *Please get me out of here alive. I need to see Mr. Cinnamon.*

"You were mad before," Dale said.

"I was. And look how it helped me. I wouldn't have been able to pull off the grate and see you if I hadn't been. Sometimes anger is a gift."

"Bye!"

41

PENELOPE

PENELOPE WATCHED with heightened interest as Will continued his second act. Trust had been established; time to work his mentalism on Danny Flores.

Dale and Henry had gone missing during intermission, but both boys were now secured—her own beside her in his seat—and Dale had performed in a skit with his dad when Act II began.

Penelope could've sworn Dale had slipped Will a colorful notecard when he walked onstage. He did it discreetly, but because his hands were so small, a corner was visible to Penelope when he transferred the card to his father. It nudged a memory in the back of her mind.

She glanced around the theatre and was relieved to find Deputy Cole by the back exit. Deputy Max was also visible from Penelope's vantage point, in the wings of the stage.

"Did you have fun tonight?" Will asked the crowd, which rewarded him with whoops and cheers.

"Me too. Which is why I feel terrible that I've got to cut the program short." Will's affable, kind face morphed into one of dismay. "I've tried to ignore it all evening, but I can't anymore. Nine days ago, someone in Cherry Hill was murdered. The killer remains at large. In fact, he's here tonight in this theatre."

Someone screamed.

Will stopped pacing. "As I said, it's been bothering me all night: a heavy, regretful feeling in the air. Maybe regret is the wrong word—more like resentment. Anger and resentment, and abject failure."

Will shook his head sadly. "I'm going to talk directly to the killer now.

"It should've been simple. *Justice* should *always* be simple. How many *perfect solutions* could one person be expected to come up with? How many *warnings*? The letter to the paper. The postcard of a cat being eaten by rats. Isaac Caldecot, with the Calico family crest, bested by rats. You clearly warned Isaac what would happen if he didn't change course.

"Plan A, Plan B, Plan C... and finally, amongst a secret cadre of Main Street business owners, Plan R," Will said. "Rats."

Penelope gasped. She thought she'd heard Martin say "planner." But he'd said "Plan R."

"But the warning never reached him, because you sent it to the wrong address, didn't you? It defies logic how anyone could be that *sloppy*.

"You paid the stockboy at Kaftans 'n' More to throw a rock at the trolley and halt it in its tracks. Under the guise of helping an older resident exit, you boarded the trolley in plain sight and dropped the rats inside.

"They were only supposed to wreak havoc—teach Isaac a lesson: a rat for a rat. They weren't supposed to kill him, just get the trolley shut down for a while, so everyone would see how great life was without it. Everyone would know you were right.

"You didn't count on the rats crawling inside the engine and chewing the wires. You didn't count on the rats causing so much damage that death was the result.

"There's a term for people like you: Too Sloppy to Live—"

"I wasn't sloppy!" Aidan stood, incensed. "Danny was sloppy! He's the reason Isaac died! If Isaac had gotten his warning, I wouldn't have had to make good on my threat!"

Penelope was shocked—Aidan had transformed from a crush-able hunk into a rage monster.

Silence filled the theatre, thick with confusion and distress as the audience stared at Aidan. He blinked, as if coming back into his body and realizing what he'd admitted to.

He turned and fled, shoving past the people in his row, toward the exit at the back.

"No," Olivia Flores screamed, and dropped to her knees in the aisle. Her father crouched beside her and wrapped an arm around her shoulder. Her scream seemed to shake the rest of the audience out of their stupor. People stood and craned their necks to see what was happening.

Even with his speed and strength, Aidan didn't make it past Deputy Cole.

"One last thing," Will said.

The theatre went quiet.

"This message is for Sheriff Pittman. 'You'll find the proof you seek in a land of play. Where human children gather but can never go, a place where cats can leap, and feast, and hide. You'll find the proof in the robot slide.'"

"Where's Constance?" Penelope yelled. The "older resident" Aidan had helped exit the trolley could only be one person, and the color-coded index cards Penelope had glimpsed in Dale's handoff to Will were familiar because Constance used those in class.

"I'm alright, I'm okay," Constance replied, limping toward the stage with Chase, Sam, and Sheriff Pittman surrounding her and holding her up.

Constance had a wicked bruise on her forehead, and dried blood stuck to her nose and chin. Penelope's heart clenched, seeing her in such dire condition.

But the relief in Constance's eyes was palpable. "It's over."

42

CONSTANCE

AFTER A CHECK-UP AT THE HOSPITAL, Constance was released with a concussion and pain meds at one a.m. The pills felt like a soft layer of cotton between her and the outside world.

Sheriff Pittman drove her home and conferred with her about Aidan's arrest, answering her questions and asking some of his own. He drove slowly so as not to bump her around. It reminded her of riding the trolley, especially when they worked their way up the hill at 15 mph.

To her astonishment, Chase, Sam, Wesley, and Penelope waited for her outside the Upside-Down house and insisted on spending the night.

"No ifs, ands, or buts, Gra—I mean, Ms.—I mean, *Mrs.*—you know who you are," said Chase. "You're stuck with us. Someone needs to wake you every hour, and we're taking it in shifts. We can play Uno."

It seemed pointless to argue. "Okay." She waved goodbye to Sheriff Pittman, and yawned.

"I choose not to be insulted that you yawned in the face

of Uno." Chase looked at the others. "Did anyone bring Uno?"

"You said *you* were bringing it," Sam replied.

Constance unlocked her gate and led everyone inside the house. It felt strange, and wonderful, to have guests.

According to Sam, Will's social media had blown up in the hours since he'd unveiled a killer, with his show sold out for the next two months. He'd taken Henry and Dale home for a sleepover while the moms stayed with Constance.

Tucked in for sleep, pillows fluffed and adjusted, Constance found herself lying in the middle of the mattress, instead of the Arthur-less side.

Maybe in another year she'd migrate from the middle to her old side again.

Mr. Cinnamon nestled against her and tucked his paws beneath his body like a bread loaf. His purr vibrated against her side, calming her. She gave him a slow blink, and he responded in kind before closing his eyes.

"Sass—*Mr. C* is the cutest, and I think he knows it," Chase said from the chaise lounge beside her bed. Sam, Penelope, and Wesley had pulled in chairs from the living room so they could gather at Constance's bedside.

"He absolutely does. He's the reason I rediscovered my love of the Enneagram. And tonight he helped me catch a killer."

Constance couldn't understand why everyone was being so lovely to her. She kept trying to apologize, but they insisted on learning how she'd solved the mystery instead.

"When I saw Mr. Cinnamon with a piece of string cheese dangling from his mouth, it made me think of a rat tail and a *different* cat, who happened to disappear for two hours after a close encounter with the trolley crash. Penelope was convinced it was rats, and Wesley was convinced it was foul play. And I realized, why couldn't it be both?

"When I spoke with the sheriff just now, he confirmed there were rust holes in the engine. The rats crawled in there to keep warm and chewed through the wires, which started the fire. Forensics attributed the jagged edges to fabric scissors, but it was rats."

"Can we take a beat to acknowledge I was right?" Penelope said with a grin.

"Yes, Penelope, it was rats," Constance said with all the gravitas of "Yes, Virginia, there is a Santa Claus."

"When the trolley crashed," Constance continued, "the rats leaped free before the fire engulfed them, only to be pounced on by an unexpected predator."

"Savvy ate the rats," Wesley said slowly.

Penelope and Sam covered their mouths and gave each other wide-eyed looks of horror.

"Including the wires the rats had ingested. That's why she got so sick, and that's why there was no evidence at the scene," said Constance. "After her feast, Savannah made a nest in the robot slide, where she... had the worst day of her life, I'm guessing. Let's just say the meal and wires came back up."

Sam slapped at Penelope's arm. "The slide smelled bad, remember? Henry and Dale told us that." Penelope nodded mutely, still green around the gills.

"How did you figure out Aidan paid the stockboy to throw the rock?" Wesley asked.

"I can't believe he lied to me about Danny," Penelope huffed.

"This just in: murderer is also liar," Wesley said sarcastically. Then he softened. "Don't feel bad, Three, he lied to everyone. Even U-Stor-It about the rats, to deflect from his own activity."

"He felt justified framing Danny, since in his view, it *was* Danny's fault Isaac died, for bungling the postcard warning," Constance explained. "When I saw the stockboy, he claimed he'd been on a smoke break, but I didn't smell smoke on him. He threw the rock, fled, waited for the coast to clear, then ran back to work and entered the store through the back. The sheriff confirmed it."

"*Why* did Aidan want him to throw the rock?" asked Penelope.

"To force the trolley to stop, so he could board it under the guise of checking on Isaac and place the rats inside. He didn't think anyone—me—would be riding the trolley, and I'd like to think he was genuinely distraught that I could've gotten hurt—but maybe I'm giving him too much credit as a fellow Type One. I believe he let the rats loose from his bag or his pocket when he went to retrieve my cane. What I thought was a cut on Aidan's hand, from shattered glass on the ground when he picked up Shawna's camera, was a bite from one of the rats."

"I hate thinking of you trapped in the storage room during Will's performance," Sam said. "Do you think Aidan would have come back and...?"

Constance considered lying to spare everyone but changed her mind. "I do. That, or left me there to rot."

"A long time ago it was a practice room, and they sound-proofed it," Sam explained.

"That's so creepy," said Chase, and shuddered.

"Aidan recognized deep down that he *was* to blame for Isaac's death, but so long as no one *else* knew, he could keep the cognitive dissonance at bay. Letting me live would destroy the illusion, pardon the expression, Sam.

"Trust me," Constance added, "Aidan was angriest with himself. That's why he kept emphasizing that nothing was his fault." She cleared her throat. "Just like I knew, deep down, that I should open the Upside-down House, but I convinced myself I was blameless; that I didn't owe anyone; and that none of it was my fault. Once I recognized Aidan and I were using the same Perfectionist coping strategy, things fell into place."

"What was his motive?" Wesley asked. "It wasn't hurting his business."

"I believe his need for justice was real. I believe he felt resentment and anger toward the trolley for causing *other* businesses to fail, as we saw with his letter to the paper. At the same time, it was personal. He wanted to make sure his girlfriend wouldn't lose her job, because then she might leave him for nursing school in Oregon. He wanted to control an outcome that wasn't his to control, namely Olivia's future, based on what *he* wanted and thought was best for her. Another hallmark of unhealthy Type Ones.

"I hoped that accusing him of being sloppy—a One's worst nightmare—would infuriate him into responding."

"It was a big risk," said Penelope. She gave Constance a sly smile. "Go big or go home, right? I love when those work out."

"The stress over Isaac's death, the guilt eating away at him day after day, Olivia's sadness, the resurrection of the trolley, and the fear of getting caught... He was ready to burst. Will's taunting was the last straw. He had to set the record straight that it 'wasn't his fault,' and also that he wasn't incompetent."

"Where does Ana Whitley come in?" Chase asked. "Remember, Trevor heard her arguing with Aidan at the cat cafe?"

Constance inhaled sharply. Of all the people she'd berated yesterday, she regretted Trevor perhaps the most. It wasn't in his nature to blab about his personal life. How could she have offered him acceptance and then ripped it away like that? And now she'd never see him again.

"Sorry. Right. You might want to brace yourselves. According to the sheriff, the local pet store sells two types of rats: fancy rats (which are pets) and feeder rats, which are... well, snake food. Ana found this grotesque and planned to 'liberate' the feeder rats because Aidan told her he'd found a home for them. She was captured on tape purchasing them, and when she realized Aidan had used them against the trolley, and that she was now implicated, she threatened to turn him in unless he fixed it. He broke into the pet store on Sunday to destroy the camera footage."

"Why did he outsource so many things?" asked Penelope. "I'm just saying, if you want something done right..."

"Plausible deniability, I'm guessing. Having Danny send the postcard threat, having Ana purchase the rats, having the stockboy throw the rock—all of these helped Aidan maintain a fiction that *he* wasn't doing those things. And he kept his co-conspirators in the dark as to the true purpose of their activities.

"Danny thought Plan R was a joke threat to let off steam, not a real plan," Penelope reminded the group.

"I'm guessing Danny believed it started and ended with the postcard," Constance agreed.

"And after all that, the trolley came back to life, driven by the girlfriend Aidan was so desperate to protect," said Wesley. "I almost feel sorry for the guy."

"Not protect, control," Constance reminded him. "Big difference." She cleared her throat. "May I come clean about something?"

"Go for it," said Sam.

"I wanted to control how you all viewed me, which is why I lied about being a spinster. When I moved here, my heart was broken. My late husband of forty years had been cheating on me, and I discovered it in the most painful way possible. That's why I pretended he didn't exist. I thought if you saw how imperfect I was, you'd never want me for a teacher.

"But I've come to see that his infidelity was because *he* was imperfect, not a reflection of *my* imperfection. And why was he imperfect? Because everyone is. Including me. Above all, Type One Perfectionists are... embarrassed to be human."

It was the most vulnerable she'd been since moving to Cherry Hill. Wesley, Sam, and Penelope offered her sympathetic looks. Sam scooted her chair closer and held Constance's hand.

"I'm so sorry for how I treated all of you on Sunday," Constance said vehemently. "I wanted community so badly, but I was unwilling to examine what that *meant*."

She took time to address each of her students—her friends?—in turn.

"Chase, you've been extraordinarily kind from the moment I met you. If it weren't for you, Roberto would have quashed my class before it started. It's an honor to know you, and there's no one whose 'gram' I'd rather be."

Chase exhaled. "Thank God because I've been trying so hard not to say it but 'Constance' just does not roll off the tongue."

"Sam, you love fiercely, and I cherish your laughter and empathy. If I'd been in your place, I'd have done the same thing you did, to clear Will's name. He's a lucky man.

"Penelope, no one else could have enacted a triple-play

tonight at the theatre with such style and aplomb. I can't wait to see what you do next.

"Wesley, our conversation in the library was the first real conversation I'd had in months. It meant so much to me. You're an immensely talented journalist, and it was hurtful and ridiculous of me to suggest otherwise—"

"It's okay. Really. You were under enormous stress," said Wesley. The others nodded. "I mean, come on, you were roommates with Deputy Max. Anyone would crack."

She chuckled. "He's not so bad, you know. He was trying to protect his mom, and he did ferry me around town for several days. But thank you." Constance swallowed, her eyes wet. "I won't squander your forgiveness, and I hope to live up to it.

"To prove I've changed, I'll be opening the Upside-down House one weekend per month to ticketed visitors. Half the proceeds will go to Cherry Hill's Rebuild Main Street fund, and the other half will go toward booking CHATeau Savannah, where my Enneagram class will meet from now on. No quotas, and feel free to drop in anytime your schedule allows. I'll be there either way." Her chest felt tight. It was difficult to breathe.

"So will we," said Sam tearfully. She and Penelope took turns giving Constance a gentle hug, considering her injuries.

Constance felt the tension leave her body.

The last thing she heard before sleep embraced her was Chase saying, "See you in an hour."

43

CONSTANCE

"YOU'RE SAYING you figured it out because you didn't get sick from a packet of instant mashed potatoes?" Roberto demanded.

The head librarian was desperate to understand how Constance's group had prevailed over his.

"If you interrupt me again, I *will* start over," Constance said.

It was Wednesday midday, and all three groups of amateur sleuths—including the Cat Ladies and Book 'Em— had been summoned to CHATeau Savannah by Sheriff Pittman. They wouldn't have fit inside his office, and he wanted Crystal present, so Crystal had rescheduled some customers and reserved the sheriff's guest list for an hour of cat-time on the house.

To Constance's surprise, Trevor had decided to stay in Cherry Hill and work at the cafe, as well as occupy the loft apartment above it. The Enneagram students surrounded him and cheered when they saw him serving drinks and wearing a Savannah-themed apron.

"I'm so glad you're staying," Constance told him warmly.

"You too," said Trevor, his eyes bright behind his rimless glasses. "I wish I'd been upfront with you that I was a visitor."

"That's okay," Constance replied quickly. "I'm delighted it's no longer true."

When Aidan stole her phone, he'd sent a text to the Enneagram group chat claiming to be leaving town so that no one would look for her. Trevor had offered to stay if she did.

"It upset me when you didn't respond to my message, but then I realized I had to make the choice for myself. And right now, this is where I want to be." Trevor grinned and ducked his head. "With all of you. And the cats, of course."

"How's the loft?" Chase asked.

"I need to buy kitchenware and at least one lamp. And maybe replace the blinds."

This was downright chatty for Trevor. His new job agreed with him.

"Since I didn't spend the five grand, you can have it back and go on a shopping spree," added Crystal, passing by.

Trevor cringed and looked at the sheriff, who sipped his juice, deep in thought. Constance had offered to buy Sheriff Pittman a latte, but he'd held firm to his no-caffeine rule.

"Gambling in the state of California becomes a crime when it is run for profit by a 'bank' or 'house' that collects funds or takes a 'rake,'" the sheriff said at last. "Ergo..."

"Ergo?" Trevor begged.

"Ergo, yours seems to have been a, whaddayacallit, private social game played with friends or family."

"You got off easy this time," Constance translated.

Trevor exhaled. "I'll donate the money to the tourism board for its memorial to Isaac."

Trevor got back to work, but Constance could see he was listening in on the meeting, too. The information he'd gleaned from Crystal had been pivotal to the case.

"May I continue?" Constance asked the Sheriff. "I think Roberto needs closure on his inability to solve the case."

Book 'Em consisted of three middle-aged people (or at least, three middle-aged people who'd been willing to show their faces at the meeting).

"You had an advantage," Roberto griped. "If *I* were to go around asking questions, I'd come off too strong. But you Marpled all about, fluttering and dithering."

"I've never fluttered or dithered in my life."

"Finish your explanation, Ms. Kincaid," said the sheriff. "And when you're done, that will conclude your involvement in this or any other case." He made eye contact with the various busybodies clustered around him. "That goes for all of you."

There was movement at the cafe entrance, and Sheriff Pittman's wife Alice entered in her wheelchair. Constance smiled at her, and Alice smiled back.

The sheriff took his hat off. "Alice? What are you doing here?"

"I'm part of the Cat Ladies. Sorry I'm late." She joined her friends, who made space for her.

"We need to have a talk later," the sheriff muttered.

Alice stared straight ahead, smiling.

"Aidan was bumbling and reactionary when you get right down to it," Roberto said. "When he discovered Danny had messed up the postcard's address, he panicked and sent a second one to Crystal, to throw us off the scent."

"'Us'?" Constance chided.

Roberto forged ahead pompously. "The only reason you solved it was because your group exhibited the precise level of bumbling-ness as the criminal. Book 'Em was simply too smart."

"Yes." Constance made herself drip condescension. It wasn't exactly difficult. "That must be it."

To be fair, some of the groups' hunches had overlapped. Book 'Em had studied the *Gazette* letter as well, hence the missing newspaper at the library.

She still didn't know why Roberto disliked her, but she found she no longer cared.

"By the way, Roberto, my students and I will be meeting here at CHATeau Savannah from now on. Your quota has lost all power over me."

"Bye, bye, now," Sam said sweetly. She burned Roberto with her eyes until he and the members of Book 'Em exited, tails between their legs. Chase left too, for a shift at the library, but his exit was a happy, drawn-out dance routine that lingered near Wesley, who didn't notice.

Come to think of it, Wesley had been silent and gloomy the entire meeting.

Crystal perched on the armrest of the couch.

"I'm sorry I didn't tell you Savvy went missing, Sheriff." She glared at Wesley. "I didn't want anyone thinking I couldn't control my 'wildcat.'"

Wesley sat like a chastened schoolboy, hands in his lap.

The Cat Ladies exited as well; they'd lost interest, and they'd already had their own meeting on Monday.

Sheriff Pittman escorted his wife to the door. Before they left, he turned back. "I owe you my thanks, Ms. Kincaid, and a reminder: I will not tolerate your interference in my investigations again."

She nodded and then turned to Wesley. "Are you okay? You haven't said much."

"I'm still in shock," Wesley replied. "Shawna and I met with Editor-in-Chief Reilly yesterday. He admitted to censoring us, but not for the reason I expected."

"Oh?"

"As you know, Martin Onder from Kaftans 'n' More came to his office and yelled at him. I witnessed the aftermath, but Reilly didn't tell me the real reason for the visit. Martin said if Reilly named a single chamber of commerce member in the paper in connection with the crime, every member would pull their ads, and never place another one. Reilly wasn't trying to protect Danny *or* Martin. He..." Wesley's voice broke. "He was trying to protect *me*, and Shawna, and the rest of the *Gazette* staff, from the paper shutting down.

"With the newsstand gone, and subscriptions dwindling, ads are the only reliable revenue source we have left. To save costs, Reilly took on more jobs than he could handle, including sales, and our staff has been hanging on by a thread. He even took out a second mortgage to pay our salaries. He thought if he could stall me and Shawna for a week, the sheriff would have time to solve the murder and Martin's threat could be neutralized. When the tourism board offered to fund a glossy issue last week dedicated to the trolley's history and the renovation of the tourism industry, he jumped at the chance for an influx of cash.

"He's exhausted and ashamed, and his immune system is shot, hence the bedrest with pneumonia." Wesley cleared his throat. "He said he could no longer be trusted to run the paper and that it was time for someone outside his family to be in charge. He offered me the position, and this morning, I accepted. I'm the new editor-in-chief."

The group offered him congratulations, though it was clear he felt conflicted about it.

Savannah the Savannah climbed his body and flung herself across his chest in a hug.

"Uh, hello, Cat." Wesley shifted in his seat, attempting to see the group around Savannah. "I'm going to make big changes at the paper. I won't stop until I've made the *Gazette* so vital that businesses will beg me to take their money for ads." He addressed his feline admirer. "Savvy, you want to see a preview of Friday's issue? You're the star."

"What's this now?" Crystal extracted Savannah and placed her on the floor. Savannah meowed and jumped onto the couch, settling between Wesley and Constance. Outside of nature documentaries, Constance had never seen such a wild-looking cat. She stroked the cat's head and thought of Mr. Cinnamon. Would he smell Savvy on her? Maybe that would be good—he could get used to the scents of the cafe. After all, Constance would be spending a lot of time here.

Wesley pulled a mock-up of Friday's front page from his shoulder bag.

INSANE WILD CAT AIDS AND ABETS MURDER, ACCESSORY AFTER THE FACT, screamed the headline.

Crystal's face went pale. She took a deep breath, filling her lungs with air so she could berate Wesley.

"It's a joke," he said quickly. "I thought it would make you laugh—I can see I was wrong—it's not the real headline —oh, come on."

"Clever," Crystal said flatly.

"Could we reschedule your interview?" he asked sheepishly.

"No."

His face fell.

"But. I was wrong about you sending the postcard. Also, for reasons known only to herself, Savvy continues to enjoy your presence, so I've decided to purchase twenty subscriptions to the paper to have on hand at the cafe. Newspapers are so twee and old-fashioned they add to the cozy atmosphere I'm cultivating. And the ones that aren't taken by my customers I can shred and use as pellets for the litter box."

"Nice. Thank you." Then he seemed to realize what she'd said about the cats' litter and looked put out.

"I'll set up the account," Trevor offered.

"Great. Here's today's issue to get you started."

Wesley held it up for all to see. The front page posed the question: **LOCAL MENTALIST SOLVES MURDER?**

"We already have it framed and displayed at the Magic Mirror," said Sam.

Constance skimmed the opening paragraph: "On Monday night, magician and mentalist Will Orlaith appeared to have used his skills for more than entertainment, correctly deducing the identity of trolley driver Isaac Caldecot's killer."

Will had offered to give Constance all the credit, but she'd demurred. It satisfied her to see his business reap the benefits of good publicity.

"What should we call the class now that we have a new location?" she asked her students. "'Nine Lives, Nine Types'?"

"Purrs and Personality Types," Penelope said, which won the vote. She was the marketing expert, after all.

Savannah approved as well; squished between Wesley and Constance on the couch, she gave a rumbling purr.

For the first time since Arthur's death, Constance

looked toward the future with something like optimism. "Which brings me to your homework assignment."

Everyone groaned.

"Don't worry, it's easy. I already told Chase about it because I have the feeling he'll excel at it. Even if he can't always attend." Constance cleared her throat. "I want a list from each of you of your favorite things to do in Cherry Hill. I want to try them all! I'm also going to learn how to drive.

"In the Enneagram," Constance finished, "the spectrum of self-awareness goes as follows: No clue what I'm doing or why. Then, noticing a default pattern but not knowing how to change it. And finally, noticing the default pattern, taking a pause, and *choosing* how to behave. Consider this an invitation. I hope you'll join me. As we move from objective knowledge to self-awareness to choosing how we respond."

"While solving crimes," Sam said.

Constance shuddered. "Hopefully not."

THE END

Thank you so much for reading!

To be notified when book two, IT TAKES TWO TO MURDER, comes out, join my email list.

You can find it here: https://subscribepage.io/Lt85jx
or on my website: https://purrsandpersonalitytypes.com

You'll also receive a free short story, THE MYSTERIOUS

MR. CINNAMON, all about the fateful day Constance met Mr. Cinnamon. *A not-so-grieving widow. A rescue cat full of secrets. Where did Mr. Cinnamon come from, and can you solve the mystery before Constance does?*

I hope you enjoyed ONE IS THE DEADLIEST NUMBER. If you can, please leave a review. It would mean the world to me, and will help other readers discover the book.

See you soon, and thanks again!
~ Hadley

ACKNOWLEDGMENTS

Enormous hugs of gratitude to my sister, Rachel Murphy, who not only helped inspire this series, but read this manuscript multiple times and offered amazing feedback. Lynne Kadish also read more than one draft and gave such helpful, detailed, supportive reactions. Thank you!

Kathy Foley helped me pare it down and shape the story and characters for better pacing, and I'm so grateful. Thanks also to the lovely, brilliant, and encouraging Leslie O'Sullivan, Lizzy Gayle, Ed Klau, J.J. Cross, and the Drummies for their cheerleading and thoughtful notes throughout the process. Pub Club and BP Mamas group chats and get-togethers kept me sane(ish). You ladies rock.

Thank you to my parents, Earl and Ros Hoover, for their unending support. Thank you to Richard and Lydia Skilton for the warm fingerless mittens all those years ago that allow me to type at all!

To my darling husband, Joe, thank you for giving me the courage to self-publish and the ability to take that risk. You inspire me *every single day*. Thanks for being my tech support and mentalism expert, too. I love you and Elliot with my whole heart.

Mariah Sinclair created the cover art, and I couldn't be more thrilled with it. I want posters of it in every room.

This novel was written by a flawed human. ProWritingAid helped me catch typos and grammatical errors. At times, its suggestions were unhinged. All mistakes are my own.

The following podcasts aided in my writing and research: The Creative Penn with Joanna Penn; Fiction Writing Made Easy with Savannah Gilbo; The Enneagram Journey with Suzanne Stabile; Enneagram 2.0 Podcast with Beatrice Chestnut and Uranio Paes; and Typology with Ian Morgan Cron.

Don Richard Riso and Russ Hudson's classic text *Personality Types: Using the Enneagram for Self-Discovery* was a terrific guide as well.

Reclaim Your Author Career: Using the Enneagram to build your strategy, unlock deeper purpose, and celebrate your career, by Claire Taylor helped me with the mindset shift I needed, exactly when I needed it. Thank you!

The Enneagram symbol seen on Constance's flyer is attributed to Twisp - Own work, Public Domain from wikipedia.

Constance learned how to write an obit by paraphrasing from the following website: https://beyondthedash.com/blog/obituary-writing/listing-family-members-in-an-obituary/7222

Lastly, the works of Dame Agatha Christie remain a source of delight and inspiration to me and millions of readers around the world.

Cat cafes are real and they're glorious. Check out the Resources pages on my website (www.purrsandpersonality types.com) to find a cat cafe near you.

Although I have studied the Enneagram for several years, I am not an Enneagram teacher or coach. Nothing from this story is intended as a substitute for learning the tools of the Enneagram. But if I've sparked your curiosity, or you found something in here that resonated for you, there are lots of places to learn more.

The best way to discover your Type is to read all the descriptions in a book. Here are some titles to get you started:

Personality Types: Using the Enneagram for Self-Discovery, by Don Richard Riso with Russ Hudson (Houghton Mifflin Company, 1996)

The Journey Toward Wholeness: Enneagram Wisdom for Stress, Balance, and Transformation, by Suzanne Stabile (InterVarsity Press, 2021)

The Modern Enneagram: Discover Who You Are & Who

You Can Be, by Kacie Berghoef & Melanie Bell (Althea Press, 2017)

The Wisdom of the Enneagram: The Complete Guide to Psychological and Spiritual Growth for the Nine Personality Types, by Don Richard Riso and Russ Hudson (Bantam Books, 1999)

Online tests are not always reliable for discovering your Type, but they can be fun. I have not personally taken these (I decided to read the books and grow increasingly alarmed when my Type was described to a T) but they're highly regarded. All cost money ($10 - 15).

- https://www.enneagraminstitute.com/
- https://www.narrativeenneagram.org/enneagram-test/
- https://www.wepss.com/

ABOUT THE AUTHOR

Hadley Hartwell is the pen name of Sarah Skilton, whose traditionally published novels have been published in seven territories and translated into six languages. She was a 2019 Edgar Awards judge in the best juvenile mystery category. Her love of *Murder, She Wrote*, cozy cat mysteries, and the Enneagram led her to create the *Purrs and Personality Types Mysteries*, a series straight from her Type Four heart. She lives in a suburb of Los Angeles with her magician husband and teenage son. When she's not writing or parenting, Hadley volunteers at a cat cafe.

Books and updates:
www.purrsandpersonalitytypes.com

instagram.com/purrsandpersonalitytypes